The Other Exodus

by

J Stewart-Kearns

ISBN 978-1511992084

Cover design and artwork by thecovercollection.com

To my husband for his love and support

CHAPTER 1

"Good to meet you and welcome to Number 5."

Taft's handshake emanated confidence, authority and energetic engagement with his environment as he swept Bailey over to the conference suite through open double doors. Bailey checked his nondescript tie in the mirrored cabinets before sitting opposite the Commander at the large cherry wood table. He unbuttoned his jacket letting out a small sigh of relief, thinking that he really must hit the gym before this jacket needed replacing with a bigger one.

The Commander cleared his throat, opened a buff coloured file whilst simultaneously passing a duplicate over to Bailey. Commander Taft tapped the table in a staccato type rhythm; his immaculate black uniform lending an air of gravitas that Bailey was beginning to find unnerving.

Bailey looked directly at Taft's well-proportioned features and beyond to the cloudless skyline elegantly punctuated with new, postmodern glass and concrete office blocks.

Through the tinted window behind the Commander's chair he noted that despite the bustle of weekday city life outside, nothing could be heard in the conference room save for occasional quiet movements in the outer office where the Commander's PA resided. Bailey began to relax and decided to get straight to the point, meeting the serious gaze of the Commander head on.

"The Archbishop hasn't told me very much, Commander, except that I'm expected to gather information pertaining to missing artefacts. His Grace thinks I could do a bit of cultural immersion, low level stuff as I understand it, under the guise of researching for a book on the island. I'm to be seconded to Number 5 for the next six weeks … maybe longer. I'm to liaise at all times with your office. That's all I've been told, sir."

Commander Taft relaxed his stern gaze and nodded at the folders sitting unopened on the cherry wood table.

"Let's have a look at what we have here," he half smiled. "I think you'll find this assignment more than a little interesting, feeding as it does into your speciality. Celtic History isn't it?"

"Yes, sir," Bailey responded, visibly brightening at this revelation.

Commander Taft explained. "You're right, it's low level intelligence gathering for the moment. We can't forward the investigation until this aspect is thoroughly covered and we simply don't have the staff with the right sort of academic background to be able to meet this particular challenge. Essentially, that's why you've been roped in Robert. Archbishop Odo reckons you can aid our enquiries considerably. Enquiries, I might add, that concern both temporal and spiritual. We provide the temporal, you and the good Archbishop provide the spiritual."

Robert Bailey gave a brief nod. He understood the logistics. What he needed to understand was the brief, the remit.

Commander Taft unbuttoned his pristine jacket, placing it on the back of the stiffly padded bronze leather chair. His gleaming white shirt contrasted sharply with Bailey's rather faded blue cotton that, on closer examination, looked in need of a good iron and the replacement of a button or two. Commander Taft didn't blink.

He prided himself on his good manners. Bailey reminded him a little of himself twenty-five years ago: all brain and no sartorial sense. To get to his position you needed both. Twenty-five years in military intelligence had created a steep learning curve.

He opened the buff-coloured folder, indicating, with an amused look on his handsome, regular features, that Bailey should do the same.

CHAPTER 2

Bailey decided to take the scenic route.

The A55 was more direct, he conceded, and, according to the satnav, he could be there in four to five hours depending on the traffic. Yet the A5, ancient highway that the Romans had marched upon almost two thousand years ago would, he thought, feed his nostalgia for the world of Celtic legends, passing as it did through the ancient heartlands of Owen Glendower: silent, awesome Snowdonia, the epic landscape of the Berwyn Mountains. It was the old road. The ancient time-travelled route to Ynys Mon – Anglesey, Tudor heartland, Druids.

His Mercedes A Class was reliably discreet, solid yet not flash, classy yet affordable and Bailey felt confident that dressed in his faded Gap jeans, sporting a well-loved Musto sweater and Nike trainers that had seen better days, he would pass for any average *saesneg* heading to the island seeking peace, tranquillity and inspiration.

Commander Taft had told him to stop off at The Bridge Hotel at some point, insisting that there would be someone there who could help with the task at hand. Bailey was unconvinced, slightly reluctant even, but orders were orders, he grumbled to himself. He felt confident that he could manage alone. Hadn't he always managed alone? A background in foster homes followed by an unexpected scholarship to Westbury Park where he'd excelled academically had led to a magical five years at Cambridge. Somehow, after an interview for a job he had no recollection of applying for, he'd been recruited into the office of the Archbishop upon graduation. And there he'd stayed. He was used to being alone.

Self-sufficient, agreeable, still smarting years on from the love of his life leaving him for the prospect of a glittering career via the Met 'fast track', as she called it. Bailey determined not to leave himself open to any more rejection in his life. He had his books. He had his work. He had his daily routines that kept him grounded. Apart from the Archbishop and a handful of colleagues at the ancient cathedral library, he trusted no one. No one. And that suited him just fine.

Bailey saw the sign for The Bridge Hotel just as the satnav indicated a right turn coming up. It was quiet; there was little sound except for the distant twittering of small birds calling out to each other. A gentle tinkling and bubbling announced the tumbling of water in a narrow stream across which a small link bridge was set, precariously swinging in the summer breeze. He was energised.

Drinking in the glorious sweep of verdant hills surrounding the hotel, he noted a narrow track stretching upwards toward the distant mound, seat of an ancient stronghold that once dominated the landscape as far as the eye could see. A solitary bird flew overhead, tracking his movements, circling overhead then hovering over the car as he negotiated the small car park attached to the hotel, before shooting up, high in the sky, in the direction of the ancient stronghold a mile or two in the distance.

The evening stretched ahead with the promise of dinner, a shower, a good night's sleep and a walk tomorrow, early morning, to this ancient site he'd wanted to visit since his Cambridge days: The Castle of Dinas Bran. He'd read everything there was on the castle and its history. How it was shrouded in legends and named for the son of Llyr, Shakespeare's Lear no less.

Lear had fathered several sons and daughters but the greatest of all his offspring was the mighty warrior Bran: Warrior King, Arch Druid, and poet. Husband, so legend had it, of the daughter of Joseph of Arimathea.

There was another legend, said to have proof of veracity in a manuscript held at Windsor, that after the death of Anna, Joseph of Arimathea's daughter, when Bran was in his fifties he had remarried a young woman linked to the decimated Iceni tribe, wiped out in the genocide inflicted by the Romans in the first century. That manuscript was impossible to locate he'd been told, though he continued to search in his archives for any reference to it.

Known as Bran the Blessed, the same legend asserted that the great warrior eventually became an initiated Arch Druid. It was the legendary Bran who, according to old stories, ancient lore, kept Britannia safe. He was buried on the White Hill where, subsequently, the White Tower, the Tower of London, was built.

The name Bran was Brythonic, Welsh for Raven or Crow. Legend also said that Bran, in the form of the ravens and crows, guarded these islands. Whilst they remained, whilst Bran remained, the kingdom would be safe.

The windswept Castle Dinas Bran, known as Crow or Raven Castle to the locals, was now in ruins. Named for the mighty Bran who had seamlessly welded together both druid legacy and early Christianity in what eventually became the Celtic Church in the first century.

Bailey was intrigued by the stories of the first century AD.

In the past ten years, more and more fragments of court-lists, manuscripts, archaeological finds, and genealogical scrolls had surfaced from ancient abbeys on the continent. He had heard that there were scrolls yet to be curated that had been taken from Glastonbury to Windsor during the Reformation. A reference to one of these documents had surfaced while he was at Cambridge, yet despite his best efforts, not even the Archbishop of Canterbury could gain access to it. It was a matter that continued to haunt his thoughts in quiet moments.

He was reminded of a private collection auctioned off for death duties in recent times that had delivered some intriguing new information awaiting corroboration on the exodus from Glastonbury to Anglesey by early Celts. He was convinced there was a link. He was convinced that if he could just find the missing pieces of the puzzle, he could re-write early Celtic History and document the melding of the Druid heritage with the early Celtic Church.

He knew that there were other stories, other legends, linking Bran with strange, other worldly powers, but he shrugged those ideas to one side as he entered the welcoming reception area of The Bridge Hotel.

A large lounge bar area took up almost half of the ground level. Grey, worn flagstones, smooth with the patina of age, covered the floor. A magnificent inglenook took up the length of one wall while above his head old oak beams criss-crossed the cream painted ceiling. The place appeared to be empty apart from a huge, bald-headed man who looked to be in his late 50's, shouting to someone out of Bailey's line of sight.

"The coach party has been delayed. Bloody traffic!"

The sound of a cockney accent this deep in the heart of Wales came as a surprise to Bailey and he couldn't contain his amazement as he blurted out in his brusque, well-modulated voice, "I've a reservation. Robert Bailey. I've travelled down from Canterbury."

The landlord palmed his cell phone while wiping his huge hands on the striped cloth thrown casually, like a miniature Roman toga, over his right shoulder.

"Afternoon, sir, and welcome to Wales. Oh and yes, Commander's been in touch and I've been told to brief you on developments."

Bailey dropped his overnight bag on the stone floor and stood bemused, his face a picture of incomprehension.

"The Commander's been in touch with me, Robert. Or shall I call you Rob?"

Steve Waterman, 57, six foot three, square, muscular, lopsidedly grinning from ear to ear, shook Bailey's hand, warmly adding, "It's a beautiful spot, though not without its own challenges. One of which is lack of customers in the winter months. We get by … just." He added, with a wry frown, "Come, sit." Waterman shooed Bailey onto a handy bar stool.

"Commander Taft's been in touch?" Bailey repeated.

Steve Waterman straightened his broad shoulders. "You've received the general briefing I take it?"

Bailey nodded, eyeing up the frothy amber liquid Waterman pumped into a clear sparkling pint glass. "Yes, as clear as mud quite frankly. Seems I'm to dig around and find out as much as I can about the missing artefact recovered from Lake Gwynfor. My Archbishop reckons it's on its way back to the island – but you know all this, don't you?" Bailey sighed. He took a grateful mouthful of the beer and raised his eyebrows questioningly.

"Old Dog." Waterman pointed a pudgy finger at the brass nameplate on the bar pump. "One of our heritage beers. Very popular too," he grinned. "I expect you'll want something to eat," Waterman enquired solicitously, making no move to organise a menu but cheerfully rattling on about his previous life, impervious to Bailey's stunned silence.

Bailey decided to go with the flow. This Waterman character was interesting, in an odd sort of way, Bailey thought. There was something about him that could be trusted. He was warm, that was the word, Bailey realised. The guy had warmth and decency bred into his very bones. Bailey relaxed. He had no plans until the morning so he settled himself comfortably onto the black leather-covered bar stool, its brass nails gleaming in the reflected light from a small log fire in the stone inglenook opposite.

"So, you were in the Met?" Bailey asked, wondering if he should mention Ceris. Wasn't she now flying high in the London office? He was tempted to just ask but, cautious as ever, he held his tongue.

"25 years, man and boy," Waterman grinned, setting up another two pints of Old Dog from the polished brass beer pump gleaming on the glossy bar. "I was in Special Services for the last ten years," he explained, taking a frothy sip. "Ended up on assignment at Number 5 for the majority of that time. Which is where I got to know Commander Taft. Did you know he was ex military?"

Bailey didn't. Yet he wasn't surprised. There was something all knowing about the Commander, just as there was something all knowing about the Archbishop. Each, in their different ways, masters of their game. Bailey was intrigued.

"So, what led you from London to here?" he asked bluntly.

Waterman shrugged his vast shoulders. "Let's just say I'd outstayed my welcome down south. Commander Taft offered me a place on his new team at Number 5. Started off with surveillance operations then went deep cover for a big enquiry into missing paintings. National Trust properties were being targeted throughout the North West, works of art stolen to order and the monies raised used to fund dissident groups. There were cells all over the region, head-quartered in a tiny hamlet in the Berwyn hills.

"The whole shooting match, we discovered, was being run by a minor royal very upset with his bit of the Privy Purse being reduced year on year. Reckoned he was entitled. It all got hushed up.

"Replicas of the stolen art works were commissioned and if you visit any of the properties in the region that is what you will see. The originals, I'm afraid, are long gone."

Bailey shook his head in disbelief. "So you're telling me he, they, got away with stealing valuable works of art?"

"Well, yes and no." Waterman rubbed his grizzly chin thoughtfully. "Yes, in that the main perpetrator was never convicted, and yes, in that the art works were never recovered. But no, in that our minor royal is currently persona non grata. He's also under surveillance. We're working on a link between himself, a Cabinet member and a cabal that's been masterminding thefts of ancient artefacts for the last few years. Targeted stuff. 1st to 19th Century being the most popular time frame they now appear to be interested in. Very eclectic! There's more to it, Bailey."

Waterman narrowed his small grey-flecked eyes as he glanced above Bailey's head to a framed print hanging on the panelled wall behind him. It was an old sepia reproduction of the ancient hill towering over the Bridge Hotel. The hill on which the original stronghold and subsequent castle of Dinas Bran had sat for almost two thousand years.

Bailey glanced behind, noting the dark oak original panelling framing the A5 sized print. "Castle Dinas Bran!" he exclaimed. "Plan a hike up there in the morning. Been longing to see it in the flesh and can't pass up on the chance now I'm here."

Waterman did one of his lop-sided grins, mentally noting that the coach party was due in an hour and he needed to chivvy on the kitchen staff in readiness. "It's a bracing climb to the top," he commented. "But well worth the effort. Do you know much about the monument? We've a couple of leaflets just in if you're interested. Written by the CADW people who did a site survey up there fairly recently."

Bailey shook his head. "Thanks, but I downloaded them before travelling and there's not really much new information uncovered so far. I'm more interested in the deeper stuff. Academic stuff, if you like." Bailey shrugged his shoulders and waited for Waterman's sarcastic response.

He was used to people puzzling then dismissing him for his fascination with Celtic History. He supposed he must come over as obsessive, single-minded, boring even. Not that he was particularly bothered by that, yet it was always an expectation of sorts.

He expected, when outside the confines of the cloisters, away from his tucked-away office in the vast, mighty cathedral, that others would see him as somehow apart, somehow different. And so he'd built an armoured shell of protection that he liked to call indifference. Waterman surprised him.

"It's OK," he said simply. "These hills can talk and these valleys are born of the ancient stories that wove this place into existence. It is only when we can fully know, fully understand what those stories mean, that this land, this people, will fulfil its destiny. And so it is written."

"Who...?" Bailey began, a shiver running up his spine, the hairs on his arm quivering with a far-away recognition that these were the translated words of what he immediately recognised as having the signature hallmarks of the declarative fragment of an ancient Bardic poem.

"The Sacred Book of Bran," Waterman replied with an even grin, adding, "and you're right. It's not in those leaflets and I doubt you've found the sacred book in your studies, have you?"

Bailey looked at Steve Waterman blankly.

"I know, I know." Waterman nodded his head vigorously. "It isn't what you expected, is it? Arrive at an out of the way old coaching inn. Meet an ex special services copper who happens to have inside knowledge of the goings-on in the far flung regions. Who throws in the odd quote from an allegedly old book that you've never heard of – and you with a Cambridge degree and the ear of the first Lord of the Realm Ecclesiastical! Beggars belief, eh?

"Don't look so worried, Rob! You'll have access to the book. In time. But first, there's the small matter of initiation. Did Commander Taft mention anything about this?"

Robert Bailey shook his head. "No, nothing."

"What about your Archbishop?"

Robert frowned, pausing for a moment. He looked a little pained. "He said something about an ordeal ... Yes, that was it. Something about having to accept, to take part in some sort of ceremony. I thought he meant a church service or something like that!"

Steve Waterman looked at him impassively and sighed. "I see," he said. "Fact of the matter is, Robert, you would have to agree to join a select group of what I can only describe as 'adepts'. People who have a hereditary link, for the most part, with what happened many, many years ago. You've heard of the Menai Massacre? You know of the genocide committed on the Iceni tribe? The Sacred Book of Bran documents these events in detail. It also details events going back thousands and thousands of years. It is not a book for the uninitiated, Robert. You would have to agree to an ancient rite of passage before you can access the tome. Fairly painless ... but extremely necessary if you are to succeed. If we are to succeed."

"I'd agree to anything," Bailey murmured, transfixed. "Short of committing a crime that is ..."

Waterman grinned knowingly. "Don't worry. We're not talking crime, Rob, but we are talking strange powers and you'll need to access some of that strangeness, shall we say, if we're to even think of completing this project successfully."

"Intriguing," Bailey laughed, thinking that Steve Waterman had been accessing a bit too much bong. He'd heard there was a low-level drugs culture in the area though he wasn't remotely interested himself. His books were his drugs of choice. He tuned back in to what Waterman was saying.

"I've lived here for a decade now and I know this part of Wales like the back of my hand. Tomorrow you head for Anglesey. In a week or so I'll have further orders and we'll discuss strategy.

"But meanwhile, take Taft's advice. Visit the standing stones, examine the dolmens, check out any antiques shops, get into the local pubs and listen out for anything that could help us trace the artefact. You speak Welsh?"

Bailey nodded.

"Good. Don't crack on that you can though. Best if you act the *saesneg*, Rob. People will talk in Welsh if they think you don't understand. We might get a lead, a hint, a name, anything. It's a cold trail and something has to give to warm it up."

14

Steve Waterman glanced at his cell phone before turning back to Bailey. "Commander has deliberately caused traffic hold-ups on the M56 and A5 so that my coach party arrives late. They're on their way now. We'll have to finish this off later. Meet me at the castle at midnight. It's a full moon tonight but here's a torch in case you need it."

Waterman handed over a black rubber-covered Ezra, turned on his heel and headed for the noisy depths of the hotel kitchen, leaving Robert Bailey staring hard at his glass half empty, desperately wanting to ask Waterman about the Sacred Book of Bran.

CHAPTER 3

Climbing to the windswept summit was both tiring and exhilarating and Bailey was grateful for the black rubberised torch as fleeting clouds temporarily obliterated the silver moon.

The trail was well worn, rough underfoot with small snuffling noises coming from overgrown hedgerows starkly outlined against the moonlit sky. The air was cool and fresh; tiny glow-worms dotted the edge of shallow ditches; he could smell the dandelions, nettles and wild garlic tumbling down a steep bank where the path twisted sharply as its gradient rose higher still toward the dark outline of the forbidding fortress. Fifty yards forward he could see a light flashing on and off in a regular rhythm. He was almost at the summit. He paused to catch his breath, taking a small swig of bottled water before ploughing onwards. He was there. The adrenalin rush making him stride forward straight into the arms of Steve Waterman.

"Steady on!" Waterman pushed Bailey away. "Don't you ever look where you're going, mate?" he hissed.

"Leave him alone," another voice commanded. Robert Bailey froze to the spot, his heart beating, knees shaking, hands sweating, throat constricted so much that he couldn't speak, couldn't think, couldn't move.

"Take him!" The disembodied voice ordered as a pair of unseen hands deftly covered Bailey's eyes with a rough, dark coloured cloth, twisting it several times to ensure no transparency and tying it tightly behind. Bailey began to hyperventilate, nausea creeping unbidden from his stomach, settling in his mouth and making him retch. He swallowed it.

Focusing on calming himself, he took three deep, long breaths, steadying himself and allowing his mind to feel the fear then let it go. He knew how to handle fear. It had been a constant companion for most of his life. If this was it, he was going to the next life with as much dignity as he could muster.

Gathering himself together, he stood rigid on the castle mound feeling the wind in his hair, registering the smell of summer in a light rain that began to fall. He bowed his head as if to gather courage. Listening carefully to where the sound of small movements was coming from he began to slowly orientate.

He turned to his left and began to swear and curse at Waterman with undiluted rage. All was silent for a second or two. Waterman carefully laid a hand on Bailey's shoulder and said, "It's not what you think, mate. Keep calm. It's just precautions. That's all. In an hour or so we'll walk back to the hotel but you must never speak of this to anyone outside of those here. We have to have your word before we can proceed."

Bailey was furious. Waterman did one of his lop-sided grins. "Both the Commander and the Archbishop know. Both have sanctioned this meeting. Both can be included on the inside, so to speak. Just so's you know, mate. There's nothing to get in a bother about. And you did give me your permission. We wouldn't be here if you hadn't. So stop acting the martyr."

Still furious, Bailey didn't move. He couldn't trust himself not to clock Waterman with a solid left-hander. "Best wait and see," he mumbled to himself. Save his energy for later when he may need it. Either way, Waterman had it coming he simmered. And that thought alone helped him to calm down a little.

The chamber was positioned down a steep staircase that led to an under croft not visible to the inexperienced eye. Constructed in the eighth century originally, on the remains of an ancient wooden hill fort that had been dated to 60 BC, there was evidence that its location had been a place of ritual as far back as 2500 BC. Strange small objects had been found in the shape of crows, yet their provenance was not indigenous according to the British Museum's research department. Indeed, there appeared to be a strong connection with Egyptian artefacts of a similar shape and size discovered on the Giza Plateau. It was a puzzle.

A puzzle the academics preferred to leave unsolved.

Taking Bailey's arm gently, Waterman walked him to the secret place, down the steep stone-cut stairs into a large, dank-smelling room illuminated by a single light. The scarf was taken off and Bailey blinked rapidly, his eyes adjusting gradually to the bright glow from what appeared to be an old-fashioned paraffin lamp.

The room was circular. No windows, yet the air was gradually becoming cool and fresh. In the middle of the stone-flagged floor sat a large round table made of ancient oak, edged with a black band of iron. The table was divided into segments, each segment painted a different colour that was now faded. Traces of bright blues, greens, yellows and reds could just be discerned. Grey and silver symbols dotted each segment. Bailey frowned intently. They looked like ancient Greek!

As his eyes adjusted, Bailey noticed u-shaped frames covered in faded red tapestry cushions, their tarnished gold-fringed tassels glinting in the soft light of the hurricane lamp, rippling slightly in the small breeze emanating from an iron grill set deep in the stone-flagged floor. There were three stools. Six segments in this round table. He saw a heavy red curtain set back in the far wall. He noticed too that there were three of them in the room. Steve Waterman, himself and one other.

"Your Grace!" Robert Bailey's jaw dropped.

Archbishop Odo patted the stool next to him. "Sit, Robert. We have much to discuss. But first, I want to know if you are willing to help us. Do not answer yet, there are many facts you need to be aware of before you decide. I must also remind you of your need to abide by the Official Secrets Act which you signed of your own free will when you joined my staff."

Robert Bailey nodded his assent. He remembered being totally bemused at having to sign that paper in the Archbishop's office all those years ago. He had decided then that it was all rather melodramatic. What sort of official secrets could be held by a prince of the church?

In the intervening years, however, he had understood. The Church Archives were an amazing repository of two thousand years and more of primary historical sources. There was sensitive information in the scrolls, parchments, hand-tooled volumes that could re-write some of the nation's history sufficiently to cause a suspension of historical study in both schools and universities. Sufficient, some would say, to re-write the history of the world!

At times, he had been tempted to write a pamphlet or two on the dichotomies he had found between reported history and recorded events, but he had been told mildly to refrain for now. To focus on the 1st Century scrolls, and when the political climate was more conducive, he could, with the Archbishop's blessing, visit St Catherine's Monastery in Egypt to dig a little deeper. And he had accepted that, due in no small measure to the tremendous respect he held for his boss.

Robert felt himself falling into a trance-like state as he sipped the cool tumbler of spring water handed to him. An incense burner threw clouds of white, fragrant mist over the chamber, obscuring the features of those gathered there. He felt himself sink into a relaxed, frozen, semi-awake state without fear, yet alert and accepting of what was happening.

A blurred outline of a woman appeared from behind the red curtain carrying a small metal container filled with burning coals. She carried a long thin metal rod on the end of which was an obscure object in the shape of a bird.

Robert held his breath. He knew what this was. Steve Waterman sprayed his upper left arm with a clear mist, freezing skin, muscle and movement in a second. Robert couldn't move his arm, couldn't move his body. The branding iron sizzled onto his bare skin as he calmly looked ahead, noting the Archbishop's concerned smile, his head nodding encouragement as Robert searched his cloudy eyes for reassurance.

"It is done," a female voice announced.

"It is well done," Steve Waterman said.

"In my beginning is also my end," the Archbishop said, his sonorous tones reverberating throughout the small chamber.

All was serenely calm.

Robert Bailey slowly came out of his trance-like state as Steve Waterman helped him to his feet. He was unsteady after the ordeal yet in no pain. He twisted his neck to look at his upper left arm. "What is it?" he queried lazily. "I can't see it properly."

"It's a bird," Steve Waterman grinned. "Look, I have one too, Rob." Steve rolled up his tartan shirt to show Robert the menacing outline of a jet-black crow.

"You are now a part of the Brotherhood of Bran," Steve Waterman explained. "Your Druidic training has begun."

CHAPTER 4

Commander Taft was furious. "Who sanctioned the story leaking out?" he demanded. "And where is our minor royal right now?"

"Prince John's gone walkabout again, sir." Ceris Pendragon, tall, lithe and very lovely, raised her perfect eyebrows expressively as she poured herself a black coffee from the large Thermos sitting on a black lacquered tray on Taft's cherry wood conference table. She checked out the plate of digestives, noting that all the chocolate ones had been taken before settling for a couple of rich tea offerings, dunking one of them unceremoniously into her mug.

"What?" she queried, raising her eyebrows in a challenge.

"Hope you don't do that in your department meetings, Pendragon," Commander Taft admonished, pretending to tick her off for this breach of etiquette.

"No, sir," she replied smartly. "I crumble them up first, and then dunk them in all together. Makes for quite a splash and a bit of a stir if I get my timing right!"

"Hmmmm." Commander Taft's attention drifted back to the case in hand and he looked directly at his Detective Inspector, raising his eyebrows to mirror hers.

"Get on with it, then," he half grumbled. "I haven't got all day."

DI Pendragon grabbed the remote, calling up the big screen that took up the entire far wall of the conference suite. She adjusted her iPad's control, setting into view footage of a wild, marshy area of ground in the centre of which was a small lake surrounded by reeds. A grey sky, vast and ominous loomed into view as light drizzle began to fall on the windswept scene.

"This is Lake Gwynfor," she began. "It was discovered after re-emerging from some heavy excavations on the island a year ago when a new road was being constructed." She paused, turning her bright blue eyes directly toward Commander Taft who waved his hand to signal for her to continue.

"Yes, I remember the media coverage." He tapped his fingers thoughtfully on the cherry wood veneer. "Building work was held up for twelve months, as I recall."

"Yes, sir," the DI agreed. "It was, because what emerged from that body of water was of huge importance to the archaeological record. Over fifty artefacts were fished out of the mud and at first it was thought that the hoard would be similar to one found previously in a small lake on the north of the island. It wasn't so much a lake at that point as a huge, deep puddle.

"Most of the artefacts were small and though interesting, not particularly significant to the furtherance of academic understanding. Small knives, slave cuffs worked in plain metal, spear heads, a ring that was dated as 1st century Romano-British and a finely worked brooch clasp with the Celtic knot design intricately engraved.

"However, there was one significant find in that very same cache that shook the academic world. Once it was dated, it proved to be the only known artefact that, with certainty, could be said to have belonged to the Druids of Anglesey."

Commander Taft narrowed his eyes as the picture shifted from Lake Gwynfor to a picture of small finds: knives, slave bracelets, a fine brooch, a small silver ring; then to a picture of a huge, mud-encrusted, wide-rimmed bowl with the fragment of a handle still attached.

"This," DI Pendragon announced, pausing dramatically on the last picture, "is widely regarded as The Cauldron of Bran." She paused again, for effect, her finger hovering over the next picture in the sequence as she put it up on the big screen.

"And this," she smiled, "is what it looked like once cleaned up. It took six months to carefully remove all the debris," she added helpfully.

A picture of the cleaned-up cauldron slid into view and Commander Taft sharply inhaled.

The artefact was made of pure gold. It was huge. Three feet wide, three feet deep, every inch finely worked with Celtic knots, strange, unrecognisable symbols, astrological details, all surrounded by the most delicately cut frieze of botanical reliefs.

The fragment of handle still attached was of plaited silver in the design of elongated mistletoe branches and mistletoe berries. It was absolutely breath-taking. It was the most superb work of art the Commander had ever seen.

In silence, Commander Taft and his DI feasted their eyes on the extraordinary image. Pendragon broke the spell with a small clearing of her throat. Taking a sip of her cold coffee, she looked straight at Commander Taft and said simply, "And now it's gone. Stolen to order, I'd say, from the British Museum two weeks ago. As you know, sir."

"Quite," Commander Taft acknowledged. "So what information do you have that tells you it was stolen to order?"

"This, sir." She reset the controls on her iPad, switched the remote control back on and projected another set of pictures onto the big screen.

CHAPTER 5

Number 10 Downing Street was ablaze with lights. At eleven thirty pm, this was unusual except when crisis loomed or extraordinary business had to be discussed. Both were on the agenda this particular evening.

Prime Minister Angela Astley twisted her shoulder length blonde hair back up into a neat French pleat, smoothed down her Chanel pink tweed skirt and called for order as the entire cabinet sat around the green room mahogany table, rather peeved at having to give up their Friday night jollies.

"Right," the 55-year-old self-made millionaire stated calmly. "Here's the situation." She proceeded to distribute one page briefing notes, telling her colleagues that each page would be counted in at the end of the session. No phones were allowed as her assistant had cheerfully collected them in moments before. "Tricky situation," she mused carefully. "Culture and Heritage. Are you ready?"

The room groaned as a Power-point presentation started up and the Minister for Culture and Heritage, Bev Jennings, bounced into position, her deep booming voice intimidating all into keeping quiet as she ran efficiently through the narrative regarding the missing artefact.

Still after still was projected onto the overhead screen. Angela Astley was pleased that Bev had stuck rigidly to the known facts. No speculation, no wild assertions, no room for awkward questions. Ms Jennings finished the presentation with the directive which all imprinted firmly in their respective minds that this was all we knew, further investigations are on-going and the Police were conducting rigorous enquiries. She sat down, clearly pleased with her performance as the Prime Minister warmly thanked her for her concise appraisal.

"By now, you all know about the missing artefact, found on the Island of Anglesey," she began. "Lauded briefly as the single material link we have to the ancient Celtic Druids. Some say the artefact has special powers!"

A mild murmur of laughter followed. "Regardless," she continued, "we have evidence that the artefact was stolen from the holding basement of the British Museum by no less than a Royal personage.

"Prince John is now under arrest pending further enquiries but I have to tell you, it does not look good." She paused, looking seriously at each member of her cabinet team. "We haven't located the artefact as yet," she frowned, "but we will. I am personally overseeing the proceedings and have already allocated resources, the best resources, to try and discover its whereabouts.

"I can't say more at this time as I have had to classify the operation Top Secret, due to the sensitivity of both artefact and person or persons involved in its disappearance." The Prime Minister held up her manicured right hand. "No, no questions, Home Secretary," she said seriously. "This is a briefing. If anything happens to me, the full facts will come out automatically. I've taken out a small insurance policy." She smiled.

Each member of her cabinet looked aghast. Everyone began talking at once. Except for one. She decided to confront him.

"Crispin." She leaned forward to catch his eye.

Crispin Farndon looked directly at the Prime Minister, his face twisting in a sneer that was impossible to disguise. "Prime Minister?" His fruity, cut-glass accent elongated each syllable in a disparaging tone.

"What are you thinking, Crispin?" The Prime Minister held his gaze steadily until, reddening slightly, he looked away.

Angela Astley folded then unfolded her arms. She placed both hands palms down on the mahogany table, scanning the room and its occupants carefully before settling back in her chair and smiling graciously at the assembled company.

"Well, that's all for now, guys." She shuffled her papers, shaking her head at the Home Secretary in a secret signal that said, "Later, this is too serious for everyone to have access to privileged information. I'll brief you privately." The Home Secretary blinked rapidly, acknowledging his understanding of the coded command as the entire cabinet noisily exited the green room.

"Stay," the Prime Minister commanded as Lord Farndon gathered his things together. "Crispin, we have to talk about the missing artefact. You're close to Prince John. We have to get to the bottom of it before matters are out of our control."

Crispin Farndon looked disdainfully down his long narrow nose at the petite Prime Minister. Leaning menacingly forward, hands balancing his weight on the waxed conference table, he leered provocatively toward her lovely face. "What's in it for me, Prime Minister?" he said smoothly. "I can give you the prince right now … for the right price," he smirked.

Angela Astley took a deep breath. She didn't enjoy this aspect of premiership. She didn't appreciate the daily slights, innuendo, vaguely veiled references to her anatomy, her hair, her clothes, and her female gender. The truth was, she was sick of it. She had spent the second half of her adult life as a career politician on a mission to improve the lives of the 67 million people who inhabited these islands. She had drive, energy, passion and most of all, conviction. An almost religious conviction. The Pistis Sophia. The wisdom of the world was female. She knew that.

It was her whole reason for being. In a still patriarchal society, however, it was hard sometimes to keep that sacred knowledge close. She glanced back at Lord Farndon and sighed. What was the saying? 'Keep your friends close but keep your enemies closer.' She gave him one of her brilliant, charismatic smiles as she pressed one of several direct line buttons beneath the table. Immediately, the door opened. A tall, elegant man in a bespoke hand-tailored suit swept into the room.

"Prime Minister," he said, respectfully.

"Commander Taft," the Prime Minister responded politely. "Please, take a seat, Commander. I think Lord Farndon is ready to co-operate. Isn't that right, Crispin?"

Commander Taft folded his long legs under the mahogany table, clasped his hands together and leaned forward, looking directly into Lord Farndon's eyes. "Your phone." He handed the gold-coloured mobile to the peer, who blanched.

"We've identified the current location of Prince John," Taft announced. "My people have picked him up and he's singing like the proverbial canary."

The Prime Minister glanced at Lord Farndon, noting how pale the peer had become. Taft nodded to the Prime Minister who responded with a cheery, "Do continue, Commander. I have the authority to redact if necessary. I hope I make myself clear, Crispin?" she said.

Commander Taft spoke. "Right then, sir." Taft unfolded his long legs, standing up straight and tall and looking at the peer with something bordering on pity as Crispin Farndon bit his lip, glancing furtively from the Prime Minister then back to Taft.

He let out a long sigh. "I'll tell you everything." He sat up straight. "I'm tired of all the subterfuge anyway. Will I be prosecuted?" He looked, momentarily, genuinely worried.

"If you co-operate, Crispin," the Prime Minister said gently, "and give Commander Taft here a full and frank disclosure of what has led up to this … point," she swept her hand in a wide arc, "we can grant special privileges. Isn't that right, Commander?"

The Commander nodded. "Providing it's very full and totally frank," he added. "No holds barred."

Lord Crispin Farndon shakily poured himself a glass of water from the carafe near his elbow. He looked uncertain until Commander Taft spread a set of grainy photographs in front of him. He looked furtively around the room as if scanning for an escape route before letting out a long, meaningful sigh that spoke volumes. He was trapped. And he had the sense to know it.

"As you know," he began. "Prince John is the second son of the late monarch. As such, he has many privileges, a direct line to His Majesty, a grace and favour apartment at Hampton Court and a small income of £80,000 per year. Small by the standards of the higher echelons, that is. When the dig on Anglesey revealed the ancient artefact, the cauldron, Prince John, having an interest in ancient history, became very excited. He contacted me as an old friend.

"We go way back, incidentally. At Eton in the same year, then Cambridge and the Guards. Knowing that I could influence the culture and heritage chaps via my position on the Board of Trustees."

"Of the British Museum?" Taft enquired.

"Exactly," Farndon nodded. "John just wanted to borrow the thing. He was totally fascinated by its provenance, which hadn't yet been proved, incidentally. He was convinced that it was the real thing.

"The sacred cauldron as described by Gerald of Wales, as recounted in the stories of the *Mabinogion*, as attested to by 1st Century scholars at Glastonbury and Dublin. He, or as it transpired, his brother, who is, as you well know, an expert on comparative religions, wanted to make a replica. I authorised loaning the artefact to Prince John and arranged for the conservationists involved in looking after the thing to be moved to other duties.

"We transported the cauldron to Edinburgh where a team of craftsmen created an exact replica. In a strange turn of events, the replica was destroyed in the casting process. Prince John and I took the decision to transport the cauldron back personally and His Majesty agreed that we could store it in the Jewel Room at Windsor Castle … temporarily."

Commander Taft looked unconvinced. "There is no replica?" he asked sharply.

"I don't understand, Commander …" Lord Farndon looked genuinely disorientated.

"We had a tip off," Commander Taft said evenly. "An anonymous caller spoke to the Met reporting that another major theft had taken place. Naming you, the prince and a security guard at the museum personally. What do you have to say to that?"

Taft was on form. Crispin Farndon looked agitated.

"Egyptian scrolls, sir." Commander Taft glared at the Lord. "Specific Egyptian scrolls, according to the curator, who, incidentally, is incandescent with rage and talking about taking out a contract himself on the perpetrators!" Farndon's eyes widened with horror. Commander Taft's tone of voice softened. "We can clear this up, sir, if you co-operate fully. I want names, numbers, addresses and reasons. Why the cauldron? And why the scrolls?"

The Prime Minister watched the proceedings with interest, noting how Taft managed Farndon with a masculine, no-nonsense, and uncompromising dexterity. She was enjoying the discomfiture exhibited. Mentally, she reprimanded herself for such uncharitable thoughts whilst tapping out a quick text to her Home Secretary. 'Game still in play: tell Odo to go ahead immediately.'

CHAPTER 6

Bailey was enchanted. The cottage rented for him by the Archbishop's staff was a little run down but it was surrounded by rolling green pastures. There was a small lake in the middle of a nearby field and he could just make out a circle of standing stones that he couldn't wait to examine. It was a short drive from the small village, close to the narrow straits and a stone bridge that spanned their grey swirling waters.

He took the government issued cell from his back-pack, glanced at the number code Waterman had given him and sat at the dated Formica-covered kitchen table composing in his head the text he was about to send. He couldn't think of anything to say. No developments, nothing happening, he thought to himself, tapping in 'No developments as yet' and sending it mournfully.

Daily update completed, he sat there, staring into space, his mind elsewhere, thinking, as he always did when distracted from his work, of her. She was always there. Always present at the core of his being. Nothing would ever change that.

His reverie was disturbed by the spluttering sound of an MG Midget screeching to a halt on the gravelled drive outside. A car door slammed. Heavy footsteps scrunched their way up the slight incline toward the small cottage. As the doorbell rang insistently, Bailey wandered to the peeling front door to see a male outline in the frosted glass panel.

"Waterman?" he hissed.

"Nice welcome, I'm sure." Steve Waterman offered his lop-sided grin showing that he didn't take any offence at the lukewarm welcome.

Robert Bailey stood to one side. "Come in," he said gruffly.

"You still haven't forgiven me, have you, Robert?" Waterman said sadly. "It was orders, Rob. Simple as. If you haven't yet realised that this operation is getting darker and more dangerous as each day goes by then you're not paying attention," Steve Waterman stated with a sigh, seating himself heavily at the battered Formica table still covered with Robert's breakfast dishes this late in the morning.

"Well, it's bloody hard paying attention when you're only getting half a story! All my questions are met with avoidance, prevarication, and calls to be patient. I'm sick of it, Steve. If it wasn't for jeopardising my job, I'd have thrown the towel in by now," Robert Bailey half shouted.

Waterman shrugged. "Our brief was to observe, record and report. On no account were we to intervene, interfere or instigate." He leaned forward on his elbows. "Orders came from the top – beyond the alphabet agencies, Robert – if you get my drift?"

Bailey wasn't sure that he did. "No," he said. "I think you're going to have to spell it out for me, Steve. I'm just a lowly librarian. Give me an old manuscript, a silent space to work in, a collection of very old books for reference and I'm your man. That's me, Steve. Not a sophisticated bone in my body!"

Bailey gave an ironic laugh. Still smarting from the manhandling on the summit of Dinas Bran Castle, he was not in a forgiving mood. He was tired of the cryptic allusions and careless assumptions coming at him from both Archbishop Odo and this ex-Special Branch Waterman.

"Look, Waterman," he sighed. "I've spent all my time since leaving Cambridge working for the Archbishop. Researching the Celtic connection regarding the foundation of the Church in Britain. I know there's an early link with pre-Christian so-called pagan belief systems, specifically Druidism, but until either a written document or a datable artefact comes to light, my research, my studies, have come to a dead end. And that, really, is where it's currently at.

"Fascinating as it is to visit the dolmen stones, cairns and what's left of the sacred groves here on the island, I'm not sure that there's very much more for me to do here. It's all becoming a bit dispiriting to tell you the truth, though this morning I did feel energised by the task … until you arrived, reminding me of all the nonsense up at Castle Dinas Bran!"

Waterman's lop-sided grin was sympathetic. "Do you remember anything about that night?" he asked.

"In the castle?" Robert Bailey replied.

"In the castle," Steve Waterman echoed.

"I remember you blindfolding me. I remember being taken to an underground chamber. I have a recollection that Archbishop Odo was present, but that can't be right! A red curtain … the sound of water flowing over stones … No, that's it. That's how I got this tattoo. Here, look!"

Robert threw off his shirt enthusiastically to show Steve the perfect outline of a fierce black crow expertly and delicately etched onto his upper left arm.

"Then … waking up next morning in your hotel, trying to find you to give you a piece of my mind only to be told you were out on business."

Robert Bailey shook his head as if the rapid movement would somehow return lost memories. "That's it," he said simply. "There was someone else there too, not you, not the Archbishop, not Commander Taft. It was a woman. She wore a red robe … there was incense everywhere, cloudy grey and white smoke, highly perfumed. It made me feel calm and strong. I remember the marking, the tattoo and there was no pain. Did I actually agree to that? She gave me a goblet of spring water. There was something in the water?"

Waterman nodded, his eyes never leaving Bailey's face. "There was something in the water all right, mate," he grinned. "Mistletoe."

"What? I was drugged?"

"Very mildly, Rob. Don't get in a panic. It takes a week to activate and that's why I'm here. Plan to stay for a few days and help you through it, sunshine!"

Robert Bailey's expression changed from anger to incredulity to rage as he glared at Steve Waterman's calm features, contemplating whether or not to knock the amused look off the man's large, grinning face.

'He's a lunatic,' Bailey decided, pulling back his fist ready to strike.

Waterman grabbed his arm, twisting it back on the grubby Formica table. "Not a good idea, mate," he said quietly. "I know you're pissed off and who can blame you? That's why I'm here. And when you've heard me out, if you still want to, I'll take it on the chin. That's a promise, mate. You can knock me for six then if it will make you feel any better."

"Oh it will … mate," Bailey glared right back. "It most certainly will!"

CHAPTER 7

"So ..." Archbishop Odo's massive bushy eyebrows frowned meaningfully as Commander Taft, immaculate as ever, gently steered him away from the diplomats, politicians, minor royalty and wealthy Arabs enjoying the summer garden party in the grounds of the ancient palace.

Box hedges, topiary sculpted into intricate geometric shapes bordered the white gravelled pathway meandering south to a small boating lake complete with a family of snowy swans gliding effortlessly across its glassy surface. Stone benches discreetly placed at regular intervals framed a half-horseshoe shape a short distance from the lake's shore while the scent of wild honeysuckle drifted past on the edge of a westerly breeze.

Commander Taft steered his elderly charge to one of the furthest stone benches. The Commander forced a grim smile and his eyes looked vaguely troubled as he turned to face the venerable old man.

"Is something wrong?" the Archbishop enquired anxiously. "Have you found it?" His rheumy eyes, once a clear, sparkling blue, were clouded with age and the immense burden of his considerable office.

"No, Your Grace," Commander Taft said bluntly. "I've activated one of my best men, name of Steve Waterman. He's received orders to assist your young protégé in every way possible."

"Ah yes, young Robert. Robert Bailey." The Archbishop smiled wearily. "What do you mean ... assist?"

"It's not as straightforward as we initially thought, Your Grace," Taft acknowledged. "The artefact has, quite simply, disappeared. We had intelligence suggesting that it had been returned to its original home..."

"On the island?"

"Yes, on the island. We're still searching. Both Bailey and now Waterman are actively involved in that search. The Anglesey police have been hugely co-operative too yet nothing has emerged, though I'm confident that Waterman will be able to discover some new intelligence. He is very experienced, Your Grace. But we have to be, for now at least, patient."

"Ah yes, patience." The Archbishop nodded sagely. "A great virtue and one sadly lacking these days with instant everything. A great virtue patience, my boy! But I cannot help but be very concerned. Who knew? Who would want it? And more to the point, what do they plan to do with it?"

"The Cauldron, Your Grace?' Commander Taft said quietly.

"The Cauldron, Commander! What else would I be talking about? We have to find it. If it gets into the wrong hands … if the inscriptions are decoded – and who knows if that is possible without a template to use as a reference point – all hell could be let loose, Commander. I'm talking total, absolute chaos. The foundations of our nation are at stake here, my boy. Do I make myself clear?"

Commander Taft looked squarely at the frightened face of the elderly man and bowed his head. "Crystal clear, Your Grace."

"Do you have any leads at all, Commander?" the Archbishop asked sharply.

"We've interviewed both Lord Farndon and Prince John. In custody, I might add. The picture that's emerging is that they've been had quite frankly." The Commander's regular features broke into an uncharacteristic smile at this point, leaving the Archbishop furious.

"I'm glad you find it so amusing, Commander," he spat. "Perhaps I should have a quiet word with the Prime Minister and suggest that someone more senior and, let's say, more serious, take the case on."

Commander Taft looked at his black highly polished shoes before meeting the angry prelate's hard stare. "You must do as you think best," he said. "I'm vaguely amused because we've been trying to pin charges on Prince John for quite some time now. The missing art works in particular," he finished.

"Oh never mind those," the Archbishop sniffed. "Minor bits of paintings anyway, those National Trust portraits."

"And landscapes," the Commander interjected.

"Yes, yes, all right and landscapes, too. But compared to this…" He took a long, slow breath. "Well, it's no real comparison at all in the great scheme of things," he finished mournfully.

"No, Your Grace."

"Patience," the Archbishop said quietly.

"Indeed, Your Grace," the Commander responded. "Excuse me, Your Grace." Taft rose from the stone bench and walked a short distance before answering the insistent ringing on his cell phone. "Pendragon?"

"Sir." Ceris Pendragon's mouth was still half full from a lunch of chocolate biscuits and half a can of coke she'd found in the small office fridge. The Commander raised his eyes to the heavens while he waited for her to swill the remains away without choking. "Sorry, sir," she mumbled finally, taking a deep breath and clearing her throat.

"Well, get on with it," the Commander grumbled. "I haven't got all day."

"No, sir. I mean, yes, sir," Ceris responded zen-like, her head full of the news she wanted to share with her boss. "Sir," she began, a small note of excitement in her muffled voice. "We've arranged for the curator's written findings and diagrams to be taken to the island tonight as instructed. Yes, the curator at the British Museum, the one who was studying the artefact. Anyway, Waterman's found someone who may be able to decipher the symbols and, if so, that will give us a head start on trying to work out why anyone would want to steal it. Maybe even who would want it. Yes, it's a line of enquiry.

"Secondly, I've just received the transcript from the interview with His Highness. Looks like Lord Farndon was telling the truth, sir. He was just helping an old pal, though the House of Lords want to speak to him. If he's suspended from the Lords he's going to have to resign from cabinet so that's a result of sorts, sir. But we can forget Farndon as far as anything more interesting goes.

"And thirdly, it seems Prince John is up to his neck in it, sir. He's working for someone … we don't yet know who … and he's terrified. So much so, he'd rather stay locked up in a stinking cell than cut a deal.

"His solicitor has told him to say nothing. MI5 are all over the place. His protection officers are standing like guards outside the cell and we've only got six hours left before we either charge him or let him go. What do you want me to do, sir?"

Ceris Pendragon leaned against the window in her high-rise office. Her head was throbbing from too little sleep, a twelve-hour shift and a sugar rush on its downward curve. The glass was cool on her hot forehead as she gazed blankly at the modernist skyline of glass, steel and chrome outside, as grey clouds scudded against a darkening sky and a light, persistent rain transformed itself into a darkening torrent.

Commander Taft glanced over to the stone bench he had just vacated. Archbishop Odo was still sitting there, lost, it seemed, in his own thoughts. His refined, ascetic features were profiled against the backdrop of the ancient cathedral's mellow stone.

"Set up a meeting with Waterman. I'm driving to Anglesey tomorrow," he said sharply. "And Ceris?"

"Yes, Commander?"

"Find out everything you can on the druids. I want you to brief me before I drive up. In my office, six thirty sharp tomorrow. I plan to leave by eight. And Ceris? Let the minor Royal go. I've a meeting with MI5 after I finish here. Should be more productive."

"Sir." She groaned inwardly. Another long night beckoned. Not that she had anything else to do, she quickly told herself. Her life was her job and her job was her life. It was all she'd ever wanted. To rise through the ranks and become the best she could be.

Her secondment to Special Operations was a dream come true, though she sometimes wondered about what could have been. What might have been. With Robert. Her serious, funny, quiet, brilliant ex. She sighed. He had wanted to settle down. She had wanted to fly. It was better this way. Wasn't it? The thought, unbidden, entered her weary mind as she grabbed her coat and car keys and headed for the lift.

CHAPTER 8

The weekly audience with the King was usually a pleasant interlude in her ridiculously busy schedule, she thought, as she was ushered smoothly into the audience chamber of Windsor Castle. Balancing a neat bob of a curtsey, Angela Astley took the green velvet chair offered and waited expectantly to be invited to begin.

King Alfred, named for his great ancestor, had come to the throne unexpectedly some twenty years previously. Small of stature, with a penetrating gaze and formidable intellect, he was known throughout Europe as the Scholar King. He was the first of his line to receive a doctorate in comparative religions from Imperial College, London. And he had earned it. Not for him the dubious gifts universities offered to illustrious personages. His Majesty was visibly excited as he leaned forward, pressing her hand in a firm greeting before languidly leaning back into his slightly larger, slightly higher chair.

"My dear Prime Minister," he began. "I want to know of any further developments. I've had the Archbishop on the phone sounding distressed. He thinks that matters are out of control. Some Commander or other appears to be not taking it too seriously from what I can surmise."

The Prime Minister shook her head emphatically. "No, sir. Commander Taft does have matters under control. There's intelligence just in to suggest that there are people who can help us. People on the island. We have someone who can hopefully translate the glyphs and symbols there, and we're hopeful that matters will be resolved within the coming week." She paused, expectantly.

"I don't think you understand, Prime Minister." A dark, menacing shadow overlaid the delicate features of the King. His eyes narrowed and his voice dropped to a barely audible hiss. "I don't want the cauldron found. I don't want it translated. Indeed, I would be happy to see the thing at the bottom of the Irish Sea. Do I make myself clear?"

After a few seconds of loaded silence, she spoke. "I don't understand. If we can find the cauldron, decipher the symbols, link it to any extant manuscripts that we have in the national and international archives, surely, the progress of knowledge, of understanding … You, sir, are a renowned academic…" She trailed off, bemused, saddened, and disappointed.

"I want it destroyed," he replied.

The Prime Minister scanned his impervious features, intrigued yet unsurprised at the turn of events. "I see…" she calmly stated, as the monarch leaned forward, his fists clenched, eyes blazing directly at her. She refused to be intimidated and he didn't like that one little bit.

He exploded. "Have you any idea what would happen if it was decoded? Have you any idea of the impact such knowledge would have on society? We're talking about the dismantling of the current social order, Ms Astley. And no, I'm not over dramatising matters. Do you have any idea what sort of society gave rise first to the Druids and then the early Celtic Church? It was chaotic, ungovernable, superstitious … pagan! And it was also written, two thousand years ago, that a descendant of the Royal Druid line would save Prydain -"

"Prydain…?" The Prime Minister pretended ignorance.

"Ancient Brythonic, Prime Minister. This land was once called Prydain. It's an ancient Celtic name, which became corrupted through usage to Brydain. After further corruption it became what we know it as today – Britain. And as for deciphering the thing, try the castle archives here. We have manuscripts dating back to the first century. Many of them taken from Glastonbury during the Reformation. I have studied these documents most carefully.

"Indeed, Prime Minister, we know all about the Sacred Cauldron of Bran. It is written that the cauldron was disposed of in 60 AD with the massacre of the Druids on the Isle of Anglesey. At that point, a new world overlaid the old. A world of class systems, written laws, organisation, rationality. The early beginnings of the modern era were born where every man knew his place. And that structure has been maintained, Prime Minister – with certain tweaks of course."

He raised an eyebrow, referring to her own position as a female premier. "They were dangerous times," the King spat. "Do you have any idea what it would be like to return to a time where the established order was based upon … magic?"

The Prime Minister scanned his face. She was both saddened and amused. Sad that such an erudite, scholarly man couldn't see beyond the construct and amused because, as always, this was about preservation. The preservation of the status quo.

She knew what the game plan was. Create an uncomplaining serf class in the time-honoured Roman model. Distract with bread and circuses. Divide and conquer. Those who would rise from the plebeian class would be the warriors, the industrious and the sociopaths. The future managers, educators, law makers would be drawn from their ranks while the majority of the population learned to be grateful for having plentiful food and plentiful game shows. Bread and circuses. Just as it was in ancient times.

The new religion was sport. The new gods wore football shirts or running shoes, cycling shorts or tennis wristbands. To touch the cup, the banner, the shirt, the flame, a quasi religious experience. To worship the new gods all you needed was a phone, a tablet, a computer and you could be part of an organised mass hysteria. You could belong.

A discreet tap and a younger version of the King entered, wearing a frightened expression as he bowed and stood nervously, framed like a canvas in the open oak door.

"John," the King frowned. "Good of you to join us, brother. Now, tell the Prime Minister everything you've told me."

Angela Astley composed herself. She felt an overwhelming urge to record the proceedings but having nothing on her except a neat beige coloured Osprey, containing her phone, keys and lipstick, she inwardly kicked herself, willing her formidable memory to focus and record instead.

Prince John moved a chair close to his brother's and furtively glanced at each of them. "Lord Farndon isn't involved in any of this," he nervously stated, looking directly at the Prime Minister.

"My brother, with his vast knowledge of the subject, realised early on that the cauldron, or bowl as it was first thought to be, was of a size and shape described in an ancient manuscript believed to have originated at Glastonbury.

"Lord Farndon allowed me to take the cauldron to Edinburgh where its provenance was duly established. A replica was made but destroyed in the casting process. We tried several times to reproduce the original artefact ... to no avail. It was as if the cauldron had intelligence. As if it didn't want to be reproduced. We planned to return the original to the British Museum but..."

Angela Astley could barely contain herself. The two brothers looked at each other meaningfully. She threw them a furious look. "Quite. So we can return the original, the Sacred Cauldron of Bran, to the British Museum. I really don't understand what the reluctance is here," she finally snapped.

She was irritated and annoyed at their prevarication and the fact that they thought so little of the people of these islands that they could, without conscience, remove one of the most valuable, indeed the only single example of a solid link to a heritage and a history long forgotten. A cultural icon beyond material value.

She willed herself to calm down but the disgusted look on her fine features and the haughty, disdainful tilt of her delicate head froze the two men into submission. She was ferocious in her clipped, stern, uncompromising attitude to the two men. All thoughts of deference to their position as far away as the Holy Grail.

"Get on with it," she commanded. "I want to know everything! What have you done with it? What have you done with the original?"

"That," King Alfred shot a look of fire in the Prime Minister's direction, "is the question, is it not? What do we do with the original?" He paused meaningfully, then sighed. "It's gone, Prime Minister. We had it. We've lost it. It's disappeared.

"This morning, it was in the jewel room, under lock and key. Two hours later ... vanished. No trace of it anywhere. Nothing on CCTV. The strong room door still locked when we opened to check on it. No one has been in or out of that part of the castle ... It's a mystery ... except ..."

"Yes?" Angela Astley was on the edge of her seat with barely disguised anger and thinly veiled apprehension.

"There's a legend, a story, one of those old Celtic tales that talks of future events. It's in an unpublished Welsh Triad and it's linked with the object being a repository of strange powers. Something about it relocating, of itself. Absurd. There's no other explanation however … unless …"

"Yes?" the Prime Minister barked, jumping to her feet in obvious irritation.

Prince John cleared his throat ready to speak. "Unless, Prime Minister," the royal began, "unless there are powers we know nothing about. Impossible." He shook his head, eyes glazing over with what could only be described as fear.

"If you find it, Prime Minister, you must destroy it," the King said suddenly. "There is a power in that object that defies the laws of man and nature. I felt it myself when I was studying it. Yes, Prime Minister, I made drawings, took measurements and countless photographs from every conceivable angle … there is something very, very strange about the artefact. Very strange. You must have it destroyed before its essence is released into the world."

She listened to what he was saying with care and attention. The anger was still festering and bubbling just below the surface of her consciousness when she suddenly and without warning remembered an evening shortly after she had taken over her premiership. An evening of pomp and ceremony; a grand state dinner here at the castle followed by a tour of the original part of the great fortress built shortly after the conqueror had constructed the mighty monolith in the 1080's, his second great fortress after the building of the Tower of London.

Ever sensitive to atmosphere, vibrations and coincidences, Angela Astley had paused outside a small turret room as the rest of the party walked on, laughing and talking animatedly, not noticing her absence. It was in the doorway of this bare and dusty half circular space where she'd had one of her 'sensitive episodes', as she liked to call them.

She had been transported back in time to 12th Century Windsor. A young woman, her hair tucked into a saffron yellow cap that covered her ears, was writing, hunched over a portable desk. No, she was busily copying something. She could see the manuscript, written in what looked like Greek to her untutored eye. The woman looked to be in her 30's, possibly younger, studious, carefully replicating each letter with total concentration, complete focus.

The woman had looked up from her work and smiled. She had smiled at her, Angela Astley, newly minted Prime Minister. It was the year 2020. Almost one thousand years separated them. And she had smiled back. The woman had pointed to a vast wooden chest that stood in the corner of the room; four foot in height and six foot in length, bound by bands of iron vertically studded on either side of a finely wrought, intricately engraved locking mechanism.

She understood.

She looked at the King who was listlessly staring at the ornate fireplace. A large bowl of dried flowers in its centre stared right back. Prince John fidgeted annoyingly with the tassels on a rectangular tapestry cushion behind his half-slumped back as she quickly came to a decision and turned in her chair to face His Majesty directly.

"No," she began. "I cannot countenance the destruction of so valuable an artefact, even if we do discover its whereabouts. Surely, knowledge is power, Your Majesty?" she queried.

His Majesty threw a contemptuous look. "You obviously don't understand, Prime Minister. This is not negotiable. Not negotiable at all. Do you know the legend of the ravens?"

She nodded. "In the Tower of London?"

"The very same. Legend has it that when the ravens leave the tower, the kingdom will fall. The Celtic name for ravens or crows, as they're commonly called, is Bran. Like the castle in Wales. Like the mighty druid warrior Bran."

"Castle Dinas Bran?"

"The very same, Prime Minister. And it was Bran who was buried on the white hill where the tower now stands, facing France. Legend also has it that while he remains in situ, no invasion will topple the kingdom."

"Legend also has it that King Arthur removed his remains as he saw himself as the great protector, Your Majesty," Angela Astley retorted immediately.

"The surviving Druids returned Bran's remains after the defeat of Arthur," the King replied slowly, his brow furrowed, slightly stunned that she knew of the legend. He made a mental note to look deeper into his Prime Minister's background. He continued, "Until yesterday, the crows or the ravens kept watch over the tower and over the kingdom."

A silence filled the room, as Angela Astley comprehended the importance of what was being said. "Until yesterday?"

"Yes." The King fixed her with a penetrating look that sent an icy shiver up her spine. She had realised her mistake too late. She would have to be very careful now, she thought, as, serenely, she manufactured a highly convincing look of concern for the benefit of the assembled company.

She had to get hold of the cauldron, she thought to herself. If it was still there, in the jewel room. If they had removed it for their own ends then there was little hope of deciphering and understanding its message until it could be located.

It was all they had. That, and the chest, the large oak box. She knew it was real. All her instincts told her it was sitting there, in that small, semi-circular room, waiting, just waiting to be found. As she listened with one ear to the furious ranting of the monarch, she formulated a plan that she fervently hoped would work.

CHAPTER 9

Ceris Pendragon half choked on her breakfast of chocolate digestives and lukewarm coffee. Spinning around in her Ikea computer chair she grabbed a box of supermarket tissues and mopped up the detritus half-sprayed across the screen of her Apple Mac.

'NO HAVEN FOR RAVENS!' The headline screamed from The Times.

Meanwhile The Daily Mail blazed: 'TOWERING APOCALYPSE NOW!'

A breathless article followed, outlining the historic significance of the ravens to the Tower of London, the state of the nation and predicting a national apocalypse that was inevitable and seemingly imminent.

She switched on the television. Breakfast programmes on two of the main channels wittered endlessly about it. Experts, so-called, sitting on lurid green and orange sofas pontificating about meaning, history and what the politicians should do. There were cameras outside Downing Street waiting for the Prime Minister to make a statement.

The Culture Secretary, Bev Jennings, was filmed walking from her front gate to her ministerial car waving cheerily as she deftly seated herself, her driver speeding away while expertly dodging two cyclists who had wandered into the road.

Ceris tapped her boss's number on her contacts menu, wondering whether or not she should just send a quick text instead. Commander Taft picked up on the second ring, leaving her still in a state of uncertainty, not ready for so quick a response.

"Pendragon," Commander Taft barked, making her jump.

"Sir," she stammered.

"Well, get on with it. Haven't got all day."

"No, sir. Yes, sir. Have you seen the papers, sir?"

"Wi-Fi's a bit iffy up here, so I'm told. No. Why?"

"It looks like it's all kicking off, sir ..."

As she explained the developments, Commander Taft listened very carefully, his eyes focused on a grubby patch of yellow Formica. Waterman looked at the serious expression on his boss's face and switched off the noisy electric kettle spluttering ominously on the tired laminate worktop. The Commander scribbled a quick note. Waterman scanned it then tapped several digits into his mobile, giving Taft the thumbs up sign as he snapped the cell phone closed.

"Get over to Number 10," Taft said at last. "The Prime Minister's expecting you. There's a warrant waiting there for you to search Windsor Castle. The Prime Minister will accompany you. When you find the cauldron, there's a large oak chest. The Prime Minister has intelligence that suggests it may be relevant to our enquiries. I want it transported here immediately. Security's been arranged, there's an armoured van and I want you to stay with it. Double-check the Jewel Room, Pendragon. I've arranged for forensics. Don't let that box out of your sight. Understood?"

"Understood, sir."

"And Pendragon."

"Sir?"

"You are not to comment on any of this. If anyone asks, you have no comment to make. The only person you speak to is the PM. No one else. Do I make myself clear?"

"Perfectly, sir," she said.

"And Pendragon?"

"Sir?"

"I'm placing the King and Prince John under house arrest. Archbishop Odo is on his way to Windsor. I'm hoping we'll get a full and frank confession ..."

Ceris was dumbstruck. She mumbled her farewells to her boss as an armoured car arrived outside the office window.

Six motorcycle escorts surrounded the vehicle which was soon joined by a large, heavily guarded truck and six more motorbike escorts.

Two Special Forces personnel swept into her office, flashing their intelligence service identity cards. She just had enough time to grab her phone, her bag and her keys before they efficiently moved her out, into the lift and down to the large reception area and its automatic plate glass doors.

The convoy and its occupants sped seamlessly into the early morning dawn as London awoke to the news that a sacred pact between the ancient and the modern had been broken.

To the cynical it would be amusing. To the materialist it would be an over reaction. But to the thinking person, the scholar, the poet, the writer, the artist and, too, those who believed that there was more to this world than the tangible, it was devastating. A tear in the fabric of time. The ravens, symbolic of the protection of the great Bran, had abandoned these shores. It was, to the initiated, a portent of doom.

Cameras flashed, sound mikes were pushed into her face as Ceris stepped out of the lead limousine. "No comment," she said, head held high, pushing her way through the throng of eager news reporters.

The Prime Minister, disguised in a dark wig, wearing a cheap raincoat and carrying a plastic shopping bag, slid out of the rear entrance as the armoured truck with its blacked out windows screeched to a halt. Ceris helped the Prime Minister negotiate the high step as the protection officers scanned the alleyway. Nothing. They were clear. Sirens blaring, traffic came to a halt as the convoy sped its way from Westminster to Windsor.

Angela Astley, looking remarkably composed, changed out of her cheap raincoat, pulling on a pair of Nike jogging pants and slipping a matching hoodie over her slim shoulders. Replacing her heels with a smart pair of contrasting trainers, she shoved the discarded clothes into the carrier bag and managed a couple of stretching exercises.

She sighed sadly as she saw, through the blacked-out windows, people standing on the side of the roads looking angry, frightened, bewildered. She glanced at Ceris and frowned. "You have an interesting name." She half closed her eyes.

"Ceris, ma'am? Oh, it's Welsh …"

"No, not Ceris, though it's a very nice name of course, my dear, but I understand you're a Pendragon?"

Ceris laughed, "Yes, ma'am. Another Welsh name. It means …"

"Oh, I know what it means, my dear. Head Dragon. Do you know the significance of that?"

Ceris wasn't sure. Although Welsh by birth and background, she had been brought up in Dublin, where her parents had owned a small travel business running organised tour holidays, mainly for rich Americans who wanted to find their roots. "It just means dragon's head." She shrugged, adding mischievously, "It does sound rather aggressive though. Highly appropriate given my line of work, ma'am." She smiled as the mighty fortress emerged from a background of dark cloud overlaid with grey, misty rain.

CHAPTER *10*

Robert Bailey stared hard at the curator's notes and diagrams. His head was ready to explode, his eyes itching from too much time spent gazing at the strange runic type symbols, swirling Celtic knots and intricate embellishments.

"Here's a brew." Waterman banged down on the yellow Formica table, now covered in papers, a purple mug with 'Croeso' emblazoned in red, white and green. "Anything?" he cheerfully grinned, noting the thunderous expression on Bailey's face.

Commander Taft entered the small, dingy kitchen and sat directly opposite an unhappy Bailey. "Right then, Robert," the Commander said brusquely. "Leave the papers for a moment and come outside. There's someone I want you to meet."

Bailey groaned inwardly. He was not having the best of days and his head continued to throb as if he'd had an excess of alcohol the night before. Except, he hadn't. Waterman had warned him. The mistletoe drug had exploded in his system after the requisite seven days and seven nights. A thin grey veil stood between him, his reality and something else, somewhere else.

Outside, sitting on a stone wall, a small, slight woman in a long red dress gracefully stood up, holding both hands outwards. Bailey walked toward her, in a dream. She took his hand, leading him gently down the short gravel driveway to a gap in the hedge at its bottom.

Slowly, they walked through the gap and into a large, flat field, a rusted metal gate at its far end. In the centre, a small lake was surrounded by granite standing stones that appeared to enclose the glass-like stillness of the water. A boat, a coracle, with a thick rope looped around a smaller stone was waiting. She stepped in, holding his hand, pulling him in. Taking the single paddle, she expertly pushed the small craft into the water, seamlessly driving it forward, toward the tiny island.

Commander Taft watched. Steve Waterman stood beside him. In silence, they waited together until the craft had landed on the distant shore. They turned and slowly re-entered the cottage, Commander Taft's eyes wearing an unusually worried look.

"What will happen, Steve?" The Commander frowned.

"He'll have the second part of the initiation, Commander. Don't worry. Branwen knows what she's doing. He won't be able to make sense of anything until he understands the old ways. The Archbishop was right, sir. If Rob is going to solve the problem, he has to come at it from a first century not a twenty-first century angle. And the only way he and we can do that is to understand, truly understand, the old ways."

"But didn't it take twenty years training back then? How on earth can anyone learn twenty years worth of ancient lore in a few hours? It's ridiculous! And what about those stories? You know, the ones about human sacrifice?"

Waterman shook his head ruefully. "Sir, history is written by the victors and Julius Caesar was both victor and conqueror. It was his story. Early propaganda, designed to cast the natives in a less than civilised light. Yes, there was capital punishment for serious crimes against the person or the community, but no, sacrifice was certainly not part of the culture. And you're right, sir, we can't, in a few hours, imbue Bailey with twenty years worth of study … but what we can do is unlock the part of the brain, the part of the mind that deals with symbols, metaphor, poetry and meaning.

"Branwen and the others will take him into a deep trance state. If successful, he will return with bardic gifts, maybe even druidic gifts, sir. It's hard to tell … but we do have to try."

"Yes. I see that," Commander Taft acknowledged sadly. "Though it's all a bit above my pay grade." He half smiled.

"Yes, sir." Waterman offered his lop-sided grin. "It's above mine too!"

"Tell me." Commander Taft eased himself onto one of the matching plastic chairs. "How far involved in all of this are you?"

"Started not long after I retired from the service, Commander. One day, I'd just bought The Bridge and was renovating, redecorating ready to open for the season when in walks this stunning brunette. Petite, like a pocket Venus with the bluest eyes I've ever seen. I just fell into them," he laughed. "She told me that I had been chosen. The Community had decided that I was the reincarnation of Elisen, one of the three ovates who guarded the Arch Druid of Prydain in the first century Common Era. I know, I laughed too." Waterman grinned back at Taft.

His voice taking on a more serious tone, Waterman continued. "I was very taken with the lovely Branwen, as I'm sure you can appreciate, sir. And when she invited me to come to a gathering with her one autumn night, well, I couldn't refuse … I was intrigued.

"Every week, I met Branwen who taught me all she knew of the healing arts. Herbs, plants, berries, how to measure, strain, and blend. I had to memorise as much as I could. I surprised myself, you know, sir. I managed to memorise most of it. Anyway, after a year of that, Branwen introduced me to a colleague, Tegid. Tegid was a master of herbal medicine and I spent another four years learning all I could from him. After five years of instruction, I was welcomed into the community."

"You became a Druid?" Taft was incredulous.

"No, I became a Healer, Commander. It's not just about healing the sickness of the body; it's about healing the whole. The mind, the body, the social, the economic, the political, the environment … the list goes on and on. I became, I'm still becoming, as I haven't learned all there is to know of course … part of the knot.

"The Celtic knot has no beginning and it has no end. Each strand interlinks with the next. It is representative of the world. Everything is dependent on everything else. There are no straight lines in nature, Commander, just as there are no straight lines in Celtic art. We are all part of the intricate circle of life."

Commander Taft was at a loss as what to say next. He cleared his throat and mumbled something about getting some fresh air. He needed to think. This assignment was straining every nerve in his body, he thought to himself.

Never one to feel self-pity, Taft was surprised at how unsure he was beginning to feel here on this island. It was as if he'd stepped into a different world, a world that had no anchor. Yes, he thought, that's it exactly, I feel adrift … and out of control … nothing made sense to his trained, logical, particular, perfectionist self.

"They're here, sir." Waterman popped his head around the front door with the news. "Your Detective Inspector's on her way. About half an hour away. She says there's congestion on the Menai Bridge but it's beginning to move, sir."

"Thanks, Waterman." Commander Taft flipped his cell open, punched in a special code and was immediately transferred to Archbishop Odo's private line.

"Taft?"

"Your Grace."

"What is it, my boy? Rather busy here, don't you know."

"I need some clarification, Your Grace. I don't know what we're doing any more …"

A long silence followed, punctuated with a heartfelt sigh from the venerable old man. "Let me sit down, Commander. Legs not as steady as they used to be. One moment."

Commander Taft heard the distant sound of a heavy door closing, a chair pulled across tiles, a rustle of clothing as the prelate sank into a leather chair. He wandered down the driveway to a small stone wall. He carefully sat down, noting the gap in the hedge further up where Bailey and Branwen had disappeared earlier on.

"Commander," the Archbishop wheezed. "What is it exactly that you don't understand?"

"Just about everything, Your Grace." Taft sounded miserable. He was completely outside of his comfort zone. Part of him thinking that the whole operation was some sort of sick joke, part of him knowing that it wasn't. It was deadly serious. And he had absolutely no idea how to proceed.

By now, both royals would be under house arrest. By now, the curator's documents, notes made by the King and the strange wooden chest would be in an escorted truck with Pendragon.

By now, the Prime Minister would be hard-pressed to maintain national security. By now, Robert Bailey would be in the middle of a bizarre initiation rite. And still, they had no idea where the artefact, the original ancient cauldron, could be. And here he was, in a dilapidated old cottage on the Isle of Anglesey, keeping company with an ex-employee, waiting for the bookish Bailey to return, hopefully unscathed, from a small island in the middle of a tiny lake.

He gave a deep, meaningful, heartfelt sigh that Archbishop Odo, on the other end of the phone, truly understood.

It was, as the wise Archbishop knew, a question of belief.

CHAPTER 11

Angela Astley was finally alone. She poured herself a large glass of chilled Chablis and curled up on her worn, comfortable, cushioned Chesterfield, her mind buzzing. She knew she wouldn't be able to sleep. She'd pay for it tomorrow, registering that tomorrow was now today as she squinted myopically at the grand carriage clock on the elegant Adams fireplace in front of her.

"What a day!" she mused. "And what a dilemma, too," she thought, though was it really? Wasn't what she had worked tirelessly for these past twenty years now almost within her grasp? She leaned her tired blonde head against an overstuffed chenille cushion, a small smile dimpling her pale cheeks as she recounted the scene, earlier that day, in the castle.

"What had he expected?" she thought. The King, practically dancing with indignation as the heavy oak chest was taken out to the waiting vehicle. A frightened Prince John looking deathly white as he tried, unsuccessfully, to console his elder brother. What had he expected? The King, angry, unhappy, disdainful; while the stiff, formal, palace lackeys looked down their noses in furious disapproval; some hissing at her and Pendragon as they swept out of the ancient doors, both of them paying scant attention to their nasty, indeed sexist, comments.

The uniformed police officers, standing to attention, keeping guard over the two royals, their faces impassive, courteous to a fault, professional and alert.

Ceris had managed to unlock the ancient box. "Part of the training, ma'am," she'd said wearily after two hours of careful prodding and prying. Inside, a three-foot leather-tooled container engraved with strange symbols in silver and gold. Inside the container, a tightly rolled scroll, impossible to extract without damaging it. Excitedly, the Prime Minister told Ceris to leave it in situ. It would require an expert to carefully extract the artefact.

And as for the cauldron, was it real? She would know in a day or two. To her eyes, the photographs were impressive, detailed, thorough, and clear from every angle. It did look like the real deal, but she was no expert and she knew that proper provenance had to be established before the next phase could be implemented. But without the actual artefact, that would be almost impossible. With Security dismantling the Jewel Room and surveyors poring over various old castle maps in search of hiding places, there wasn't any more that could be reasonably done right now. Patience, she thought to herself grimly.

Her mind drifted. She remembered a conversation many years ago. She was being interviewed by the party for a prospective parliamentary candidate nomination in Somerset. Stephen Odo had been chair of the committee and she'd sensed that he was determined that she should receive the nomination. He would do everything possible to secure a majority vote in her favour.

She had, at the time, no idea why. She wasn't the most outstanding candidate. There were others far better connected than she was, with more money, assets, connections, background, family. She had fought for the nomination. She had out-performed, inspired, amused, and spoken knowledgeably and with passion. She had convinced the committee, dazzled them with her erudition, affability and media presence until not one of the twelve members had voted against her. A coup, she had been told later. Unprecedented.

At the welcome reception a few days after, she had personally thanked Stephen Odo for his unstinting support while confessing to him that she didn't fully understand why they had chosen her and not any of the other candidates. It had been a good field, exceptional some had said. Why her?

She smiled as she recollected his response.

"You want to change the world, Angela," he had said, smiling but serious too.

"I too want to change the world, my dear, but I've learned that to truly change things for the better, you have to change the political, the secular, if you like. You have to upgrade the spiritual side of life, meld it with the secular. Not have, as we have today, a separation of roles.

"If you go back to the origins of our society, we lived a life not based on consumerism, or materialism, life was governed by the seasons and by the wise men and women who had power. The power to stop wars, the power to arbitrate in disputes of family, land, and division of labour. Gifted individuals would receive age-old training to become the leaders of society. But it was a leadership not based on property or possessions – indeed, it was considered very bad form for them to actually own anything. All was Community.

"The Community looked after each person and each person contributed, in any way they found useful, to that community. But make no mistake, it wasn't anything resembling communism. Oh no! Far from it. People had choices, life was respectful, people believed wholeheartedly in a higher power and celebrated life; not, as we do today, denigrate it. Today, we are concerned about the environment, nature, global warming, urban regeneration, rural poverty and poor education in our inner cities, young people who have no hope, no jobs, and no future.

"The politicians are promoting the old model. It's a model that took shape with the Roman invasion, then again in 1066 with the Norman invasion. Prior to those times, Britain, or Prydain as it was known, was a very different place. A place that celebrated life, not depressed it as we see today.

"I want to re-invent that world, Angela," he had said, his eyes sparkling with conviction. "I want humanity to cast off the wickedness we have inherited. A wickedness that most do not see, are not even aware of. Save for a constant, deeply felt sense that life isn't supposed to be like this."

He had been a lowly vicar at the time. Responsible for three parishes, he had a formidable reputation for community initiatives. Almost single-handed he had raised money through grants, European funding, business fund-raisers, to create a range of community enterprises that had eventually seen the county emerge from terrible unemployment, rural deprivation and underachievement in its schools and colleges to become a beacon of sustainable enterprise and growth.

He had risen swiftly through the ranks over that period, becoming Archbishop of Canterbury just three years previously. The same time as she had become Prime Minister. Their careers had progressed in startlingly similar ways over the years. Her mind drifted back to that conversation.

What had Stephen said? She was tired. She couldn't quite remember. It was on the edge of her consciousness but just out of reach. That was it, something about a new order. A New World Order. Stephen was convinced that the time would come when a better world would emerge.

A world that should have evolved but hadn't because of an ancient wickedness. And it started in the First Century of the Common Era. He had always said that 2020 would be a watershed but she hadn't pressed him on that. Now she wished she had. She must remember to ask him about that, what he meant. She drifted in and out of an unsettled sleep, the questions pressing on her mind unbearably.

†✝†

Deep in the cathedral, Archbishop Stephen Odo ritually washed his wand of office and meditated on the forest of stone soaring up to the magnificent roof. He was vaguely concerned. The conversation earlier with Commander Taft had unsettled him a little. He was always sensitive to the inner conflicts of others and he could sense that the Commander was experiencing a crisis of belief unprecedented in his ordered, predictable, organised life.

As always, he'd listened carefully to what the Commander was saying. As always, he read between the lines. The policeman didn't understand what was happening. He felt that what they were doing was dangerous. Anything could happen. It was disordered. Robert Bailey could be harmed. And wasn't mistletoe an illegal substance?

The Commander was agitated, ready to call a halt to the proceedings. It had taken the Archbishop over an hour to reassure him that all would be well. It wasn't dangerous and it wasn't illegal. Robert was in safe hands and he had nothing to worry about.

In fact, mistletoe extract was used as a compound in many pharmaceutical drugs. Bailey would enjoy a system cleansing as well as an esoteric experience. The key was supervision. Bailey would be supervised throughout.

He was minded to telephone Branwen to ask how he was but shook the thought away with a grimace. Branwen would be ill pleased. Indeed, he knew she would deliver a harsh lecture. She saw herself as the true heir of the Brythonic and had little time for those who had gone over to the other side.

Taft had talked about contacting the Home Secretary and the Archbishop was interested to discover that Taft had an indirect line to him. The Prime Minister had insisted that he report, via Sir Rufus, to the Home Secretary or to her. Archbishop Odo agreed that was a good idea, knowing that all three individuals were as desperate as he was to find the cauldron, translate the symbols and move things forward as swiftly as possible. Containing the royals however, was proving to be more difficult than anticipated. No matter. He was confident that the King could be persuaded once he had briefed him thoroughly.

King Alfred was, at heart, a scholar not a monarch and he knew, more than anyone, how fragile his inheritance truly was, coming as it did from the Georgian succession, a German antecedent that was rooted in the history of the Saxon hordes who, like the Romans and the Normans, had collectively uprooted the indigenous culture of these islands.

No, he could be managed. He could be used as a pawn to avert the threat of retaliation from America, from Europe. He would remain Head of the Commonwealth nominally, until such time as a new wave of missionaries could be sent to those lands to return them to the fold.

He prayed for guidance, knowing that tomorrow would bring the promise of that New World Order he had talked so animatedly about to Angela Astley all those years ago. It was time to put into place the ancient prophecy.

Renew the kingdom under its original, ancient laws. Remove the panoply of state and replace it with the wisdom of the elders in fulfilment of the ancient covenant between the Creator and Humanity.

The ancient covenant that had been broken in 60 and 61 AD with the massacre of the Druids and then the extermination of the Iceni Tribe. Queen Boudicca and her daughters had perished; the Druids too had perished during that terrible time.

Yet one Arch Druid had survived. One who had been travelling on foot from Anglesey to Glastonbury, keeping far away from known roads, travelling across the ancient paths through forest, grove and valley, climbing hill and mountain on his sacred journey. He and the other Druids had foreseen events.

As Arch Druid, he was tasked with gathering up the ancient lore, knowledge and wisdom to pass on to the next generation. It was on his instructions that the sacred cauldron had been ritually submerged in Lake Gwynfor. He was Bran the Blessed. It was his legacy that had to be protected, handed on in readiness for the prophecy's fulfilment.

"Was Robert Bailey the one?" Archbishop Odo asked himself. "Could Robert continue the sacred task?" He knew he couldn't answer that question yet. All would hinge on how he emerged from the initiation on Anglesey. And there was no way to predict the outcome.

Then there was Angela. Angela Astley, Prime Minister. A true Warrior. Boudicca and Bran. Bran and Boudicca.

It was time to defeat Caesar.

CHAPTER *12*

Lord Farndon poured out two stiff measures of single malt and handed one to Prince John. "What's happening, John?" the peer asked anxiously, checking to make sure the door was firmly closed before slowly circling the rosewood table loaded with old framed photographs of half forgotten family members.

Prince John tapped his foot to the beat of a tune unheard as he met Lord Farndon's gaze. "Looks like Alfred and I are under house arrest!" he spluttered, spilling some of the malt whisky in his agitation.

"Yes, yes, I gathered that," Crispin Farndon replied, a little peeved at being told what was so blatantly obvious.

"It's bloody unprecedented!" Prince John raged, his small features reddening, his foot tapping away manically.

"Yes, yes," Lord Farndon replied, a note of sympathy just evident in his well-modulated voice. "Let's cut to the chase, John," he said after a moment or two. "Did the King manage to decipher the thing? The cauldron? He had enough time, didn't he? Two weeks you said?"

"He was working on it the whole time, Crispin," Prince John said sadly. "He had all the manuscripts brought into the library and the cauldron set up on a small platform so that he could work on it from every angle. Day and night, night and day, he scribbled away."

"Did anyone help him?" Lord Farndon was intrigued to know if anyone else was privy to the situation.

"No. Not to my knowledge, though I hardly saw him over that time. Do not disturb event, if you see what I mean."

"Quite," Lord Farndon sighed sorrowfully.

"Look Crispin, old chap, can't you get the PM to intervene?" Prince John implored. "She simply doesn't have the power to keep the monarch locked up here, or anywhere else for that matter. Alfred has rights, as do I, and the whole shooting match is completely unprecedented!"

"It isn't actually." Lord Farndon permitted himself a wry grin. "Know your history, John? Think about one of your ancestors perhaps. Does the name Charles ring a bell? Or James II maybe?"

"Oh come on!" Prince John exploded. "That was aeons ago. Quite, quite different."

"Was it?" Lord Farndon mused. "Was it, though? Think about it, John. Then it was about King versus Parliament. Protestants versus Catholics. The individual versus the collective. The collective won. Parliament won and the monarchy, since those times, has provided the nation with a symbolic version of ruler-ship. Nothing more and nothing less. What if there are moves afoot to dismantle the current balance of power between sovereign and country, nation and citizen? What if there's a deliberate attempt to remove the King and replace him with … something else? Think, John. Think!"

Prince John stopped tapping his foot and took a long, slow drink from his whisky tumbler. "There may be something in what you say," he said quietly. "My brother seems to think there's a coup being planned but I just told him he's being paranoid, fanciful even. The business of being cooped up here and constantly monitored getting under his skin perhaps."

The Prince leaned forward and held Crispin Farndon's eyes. "Do you have any evidence, old friend?" he asked softly. "I plan to have supper with my brother later on. Is there anything I should be telling him?"

Lord Farndon took in a deep breath, meeting the prince's gaze firmly. "I'm being watched too, John, so I have to be careful here. But, unlike you, I'm not under house arrest so there are places I can go, people I can see without too much interference. I do have to be careful, however. I will visit you again in a few days. I need some time to check out one or two ideas. One or two suspicions that have been bothering me of late. There's something going on with Astley, the Prime Minister. There's something not quite right with her involvement here – taking away that old chest earlier today. I'm intrigued. What was in it, John?"

Prince John wore an expression of terror.

"What is it?" Lord Farndon gasped.

"The chest. The box," Prince John whispered. "It was hidden, deliberately hidden away in the oldest part of the castle. The key kept with my brother's most important documents. He told me that its contents are never looked at but, instead, an account of what it contains is passed down to each generation who succeeds to the throne. This knowledge has been kept hidden for almost two thousand years, Crispin. It relates to what happened in 60 and 61 AD. In what is now Norfolk and on Anglesey. The Iceni and the Druids.

"The massacre of the last Brythonic tribe with Boudicca leading the warrior class was a historic watershed, Crispin. When the Romans conquered, they suppressed all knowledge of law giving, community rulership, elective leadership, which had existed for generations. The role of women, once equal if not superior to men, was devalued and demoted. At the same time, the Romans marched to the seat of European learning. A place where Kings and Princes, Queens and Thegns sent their young to be trained. Twenty years it took, Crispin, and they graduated as Druids. The most learned men and women in Europe and beyond. Their knowledge, it is said, had a direct transmission through the ages from the legacy of the ancient Egyptians.

"The mother college, the national seat of learning, was on Anglesey, Crispin. The Druids were destroyed. Except for one. Bran, son of Llyr. Bran the Blessed as he became known. He survived."

"But what do the documents in the chest say?" Lord Farndon, on the edge of his seat, was captivated.

"In strictest confidence?" Prince John asked, shaking.

"Of course, John," the peer responded. "You have my word."

The prince moved over to the window and pressed a cream painted panel on the curved, upholstered window seat. As the small rectangular panel shot back he quickly put his hand inside the opening and twisted something unseen. He removed his hand and pressed the panel again. It immediately shot back into place without a sound. Lord Farndon raised an aristocratic eyebrow and gave a small nod. They could talk freely now. Any listening device would emit the most awful static hum to those on the other end of it.

"Right." Prince John took a deep breath. "Best to begin at the beginning I expect."

Lord Farndon nodded his agreement as he poured them both another single malt.

"There is a prophecy," Prince John began. "It's called 'The Prophecy of Bran', and it was written by Bran the Blessed just before the massacre on Anglesey and the massacre of the Iceni in Norfolk. Bran decided, according to the document, that it was time to write down the ancient rules, the various aspects of learning, including philosophical, astrological, natural science and -" He drew a breath. "- Magical doctrine.

"The massive store of druidic knowledge was, for the first time in history, written down in a series of scrolls. The cauldron, with its intricate details, was ritually disposed of until such time as the land, the country, would awake from the sleep of foreign rule.

"It was prophesied that both Bran and Boudicca would live again. The Druids believed in reincarnation," he finished with a nervous laugh. Taking a deep breath, he continued. "The prophecy states that there are triads at play in this land. A group of three: events, persons, incidents, catastrophes, which this land is fated to endure.

"Bran's manuscripts predict many events that have already happened. Abdications, executions, the birth of a great bard in Shakespeare and how his family line would die out with his granddaughter, Elizabeth. How a new line of Bards would emerge with the War Poets of the First World War. He predicted three world wars Crispin. Two have come and one is coming, according to the manuscript. The first two wars could not be prevented. The third can."

"How?" Lord Farndon whispered.

"By recompense, Crispin. The completion of the triad. There has to be a retribution for the massacre of the Iceni, for the massacre of the Druids, for the killing of a warrior Queen. Queen Boudicca.

"According to the manuscript, until this land is re-balanced, re-dedicated and tribute is paid, we will be at the mercy of another invasion.

"Whether it's an invasion of the mind, the body or the soul, I do not know. If it is a physical invasion, again, I do not know. The manuscript is unclear. But an invasion there will most definitely be.

"The manuscript also tells us that those who rule are not sacred keepers of the land. They are the product of the Roman story and the Conqueror's story. It is their descendants who maintain a power in the land that is not their own and they must be overthrown to be replaced with indigenous rulers, those of the Brythonic Blood, the rightful heirs to the kingdom. The third story, the Celtic story, will complete the sacred Triads.

"The manuscript goes on to tell of a sacred cauldron that holds the secrets to this end. By deciphering the ancient language of symbols, the means to achieving right over might will be discovered."

Lord Crispin Farndon's mouth hung open in sheer incredulity. "Are you saying that this 'prophecy' is at the heart of what is happening here? With you and the King holed up in this old castle? It's ridiculous!" he said, banging his whisky glass down on the side table next to his overstuffed chair.

"Yes, I expect it does sound vaguely ridiculous, as you say, old friend," Prince John murmured, but there was a hardness in his eyes that spoke of something else entirely. "The ravens have gone, Crispin," Prince John said quietly. "They've gone. This is the first sign of the end times, according to Bran's prophecy."

"What is the second sign?" Lord Farndon asked in a voice as quiet as his friend's.

"Bran's castle, the island, the sacred tree

The warrior, the ovate, the red dressed she

Justice for Prydain, Druid and Iceni"

Prince John slumped back in his chair. He looked exhausted.

Lord Crispin Farndon looked pensive. "Very cryptic. Leave it with me, John," Lord Farndon said crisply. "I have connections. We can't have the ancient order overturned by a silly woman who thinks she knows better than everyone else!"

"I'll get on to my chums in the Guards. The Home Secretary is an old school friend. And what about the public? They won't stand for a regime change if that's what you think is going to happen."

"I don't know, Crispin." The prince suddenly looked very tired and very overwhelmed. "There's a part of me that would gladly see the back of all this aristocratic nonsense and I know my brother has moments when he feels he'd like nothing better than to retreat into a monastery, or at least a well-equipped library. Maybe, just maybe, it is time for change, Crispin."

Lord Crispin Farndon concealed a look of utter contempt as he surveyed his friend's sad face. The man was not a fighter, he thought to himself, and neither, if the truth be known, was his brother. Both products of an over-indulged childhood and adolescence; kept protected, cosseted, apart from the wider world. They had never had to fight for anything in their lives and, at that moment, it showed, he thought to himself.

But he was ready to act. If not for King and Country then for himself, his position, his wealth, and his legacy of land, money, paintings. The paintings! He thought about them with a deep frisson of pleasure. On the black market they would bring in an absolute fortune, enough to buy back that blessed cauldron when it surfaced.

"Is the cauldron really authentic, John?" he asked the prince carefully.

"Yes. Yes, it really is, Crispin. It had a strange aura surrounding it … difficult to put into words … but it was as if it knew you." He laughed nervously. "I touched it once, just lightly, just in passing really, and I was frozen to the spot. All manner of strange, whirling images came flooding into my mind: soldiers, horses, battles, screaming voices. My brother had to pull me physically away from it. I felt ill for the rest of the day …" He looked away, his eyes clouded with a dark memory.

"But what did your brother want it for?" he asked carefully.

"Research I think," the prince nodded. "You know he's obsessed with ancient philosophy and religions. He has an idea that there's something, some symbolic designs on the cauldron that have a connection with Egypt. He's desperate to go there and test out his theory.

"Whilst we're under house arrest, that's not going to be possible, so he's having some Egyptologists visit him here, under supervision of course. He's hopeful that once the PM sees how serious he is, she'll agree to him making a visit to Cairo. We'll have to wait and see."

Lord Crispin Farndon was intrigued. "What does your brother know about an Egyptian connection, John? I thought that all the documentation showed was 1st Century to 8th Century records, commentaries, narratives … why Egypt, of all places?"

The Prince shook his head and frowned. "All I know is that he became hugely excited, quite beside himself actually, when he spotted some faint engravings on the interior of the cauldron. Something to do with straight lines as opposed to curved lines. Must admit I wasn't paying much attention. He can, as you know, old chap, get carried away when he's researching anything to do with early history.

"He did say one thing that struck me though…"

Lord Farndon nodded for him to continue.

"He said something about the coffer in the great pyramid. The one in the King's Chamber. How it was now evident that it hadn't been used as a sarcophagus, but as a marker, a secret marker to an undisclosed area within the pyramid itself. He desperately wants to go to Cairo himself and check out his theory."

Lord Farndon narrowed his eyes. He could feel a eureka moment coming on. Somehow, he had to get to Egypt too. And urgently.

CHAPTER 13

The small kitchen appeared even smaller as Commander Taft, Steve Waterman and Ceris Pendragon sat around the old Formica-covered table sipping mugs of coffee. Outside, the light was fading, lending a mysterious quality to the fields and hedges in the distance. Taft and Waterman had wandered down to the gap in the hedge earlier on, but nothing could be seen on the far lake. All was quiet. Not even a bird in the sky or the sound of the wind rustling in the trees.

Ceris looked at her watch. "It's getting on for ten, sir." She seemed surprised. "How time flies when you're having fun!" A cryptic remark as she wasn't having fun at all. She was tired, anxious, and jittery and her stomach was in knots.

"I didn't know you and Robert Bailey were once an item," Commander Taft said.

Ceris said nothing, staring intently at the bottom of her mug instead.

Steve Waterman looked at them both, suppressing a small smile. He took pity on the obviously embarrassed Ceris and offered to pour her another Americano from the huge pot he'd made half an hour earlier.

"No, I'm fine thank you, Mr Waterman," she said quietly.

"No, Steve. Please call me Steve. Mr Waterman makes me feel very old indeed!"

She smiled at him and he smiled back, taken with her lovely features and open, honest countenance. She turned to Commander Taft.

"We were in university together, Commander," she said lightly. "And we became … close. We carried on seeing each other for some time afterwards but there came a point where we either married, settled down together … or … not. It was the 'not' that ended it sadly. Robert wanted to stay in Canterbury; I was launching my career in the Met. I couldn't give it up …" she finished, looking at the bottom of her mug.

Commander Taft lightly touched her arm. "I understand. It's a hard call when you're in this game."

"It is, sir," she acknowledged, with a tremulous smile. "I really wanted to do this. I knew I had to give it everything I had and that included Robert. It was the hardest thing I've ever had to do," she finished.

"Would you do it again?" Steve Waterman asked, curious as to her response.

"Do you know Mr … Steve," she laughed, "I really don't know. I've missed him terribly over the years and no, there hasn't been anyone else … Not even looked, though I've had offers," she said archly. "I can't see how we could've made it work. One of us would have had to compromise and neither of us could. It was checkmate, game over … I had no idea, though … that it was Robert who was the Celtic Scholar sent here to decode the artefact."

Steve Waterman stretched his huge arms, placing his hands like hams, flat, on the kitchen table's faded surface. "Looks like fate's intervened here, young Ceris," he twinkled. "Looks like the old gods are throwing you two together for a purpose, if you ask me."

Ceris offered another tremulous smile as she excused herself, leaving the room mumbling about some important emails she had to send urgently. She paused at the door, instinct telling her there was something coming that she needed to hear.

"Well, we're not asking you, Waterman." Commander Taft looked vaguely irritated at Steve Waterman's statement. He was jittery too. He knew, from what Archbishop Odo had told him, that the initiation would take a week to complete. He had to get back to London and he was worried about leaving Ceris here as his deputy, given recent revelations.

"Look here, Waterman," Commander Taft said brusquely. "I have to get back to London first thing in the morning and I need you to keep everything under control. Can you manage with Ceris here? Or do you want me to take her back with me to London? I'm minded that there could be some emotional difficulties once Robert Bailey discovers she's here."

Steve Waterman rubbed his chin, deep in thought. "I think she should stay, sir," he said finally. "Robert will need a friend or two."

"Are you sure?" Commander Taft wasn't convinced.

"Yes, sir, I am sure. Robert can cope with more than you think, sir. And if my instincts are correct, it might just make a difference to him."

"A difference?" Commander Taft looked puzzled.

Steve Waterman looked earnestly at his boss and nodded his huge head. "Yes, sir, a difference. Robert hasn't had many true friends in his life and Ceris, though they've been estranged for a while, is connected to him. After the initiation, Robert will feel these connections more and more strongly, and even if his love for her remains unrequited, the bond between them will exist as long as time exists, sir. You see, he will feel no resentment, no hurt, no anger, just acceptance, and with that comes a purity of power, with that comes the ability to see things as they truly are. He will have become, at the very least, a seer. At the very most, a Druid."

"Didn't realise you were poetic, Waterman," Commander Taft said gruffly, evidently moved by Steve Waterman's speech.

"No, sir. Nor me." Waterman laughed openly at himself. "But I have a hankering after the bardic life."

Commander Taft roared with laughter, forgetful of Ceris, still standing at the kitchen door, trying desperately hard to hold back the tears that had threatened to tumble down her pale cheeks. She excused herself, finding solace in the small box room that had been allocated to her on her arrival that morning. She flopped onto the thin, narrow bed, pulled the pillows over her head and sobbed quietly into them, whether for herself, for Robert, for the future, she knew not.

She fell into a disturbed sleep in which strange shadows played against tall trees.

A small clearing, fringed by the tall trees, came into view. A canvas canopy set up in the middle of the clearing acted as a shelter from the rain falling rapidly onto the forest floor. She reached out. A hand clasped hers, pulling her forward into the clearing. A sound, the wind sighing high in the treetops; stars, cold white light dazzling against the darkness up above.

A familiar face smiling at her in total recognition. A warm embrace melting the anxiety and fear deep inside her. She looked directly at the beloved features. "Robert," she breathed softly and he held her so close it was as if they, the stars, the forest floor and the clearing were one and the same.

She awoke with a start. Outside, all was dark and silent. She looked out of the small bedroom window, half-closed curtains fluttering in a small breeze. Commander Taft was setting off in his big, black Audi, the white light from its headlamps throwing the gravel driveway into relief. She heard Steve Waterman cheerily waving him off then re-enter the small cottage, snap shut the fragile glass-panelled door, switch off any remaining lights and pad heavily into the other bedroom.

She lay there, thinking about the past few days, the retrieval of the chest from Windsor Castle, the Palace lackeys sneering and spiteful as they were escorted out of the castle precincts, the long road trip from Windsor to Anglesey, the security detail escorting them, the Special Forces personnel standing guard outside and on the perimeter of the nearby lake.

What was it the Prime Minister had said?

"Call me if you need to talk. You only have part of the story, Ceris. The day will come when you'll need to know all of it. I can help you but you must not communicate this to anyone. Commander Taft doesn't need to be involved in the next stage. Do you understand?"

Ceris remembered feeling angry. She was loyal, dependable and had a good relationship with her boss. She respected him enormously. She debated about whether or not to tell him of her conversation with the PM. Now Commander Taft had driven off into the night. She felt sleep pulling her downwards, its softly subtle grasp conquering any other thoughts as she murmured to herself that she would think about it all tomorrow.

✝✝✝

Steve Waterman grabbed the Ezra torch from beside his bed, pulled on his old Wellington boots, threw an old waxed jacket over his huge frame and silently climbed out of his ground floor bedroom window.

Puffing with the exertion, he carefully crept noiselessly down the gravel drive flashing his torch at the security detail in a coded signal. They nodded. They knew who he was. They knew where he was going.

Waterman walked to the gap in the hedge and stood silently for a moment, waiting. His eyes adjusting to the dark and the lashing rain, he squinted into the distance. A flashlight on the small island in the middle of the lake blinked on and off several times. He strode down to the shoreline. Two security men were already in position as the coracle approached.

Branwen stepped out first, her long red dress now partly covered with a wool cloak held fast by a large Celtic brooch. Steve Waterman carefully helped her to disembark, smiling rapturously at the sight of her. Her small, delicate features were serious as she turned to Waterman and nodded silently to him. He turned back to the small boat, physically lifting an unconscious Bailey with a mighty sweep as the security guards rushed to help.

Between them, they managed to half-walk, half-carry Bailey to the cottage as the rain, now coming down in torrents, swirled around the lake's edge. Drenched, cold, tired, exhausted, they staggered towards the cottage, entering it just as a flash of lightning exploded in the inky sky, obliterating the stars, releasing negative ions into the already highly charged atmosphere.

Branwen took control after they had deposited Bailey in his bedroom. He was sound asleep, fully dressed apart from his trainers. Branwen carefully covered him over with a faded quilt and closed the thin curtains. They tiptoed back into the kitchen, slumping exhausted onto the matching plastic chairs. The security guards returned to their positions.

Steve Waterman looked carefully at Branwen. "Well?" he asked, barely containing his curiosity as he quietly organised a mug of tea for her and coffee for him.

"Is she here?" Branwen asked quietly.

"In the spare bedroom," Waterman whispered. "She's leaving first light though. Commander Taft wants her in London."

"Does she know?" Branwen mouthed, wide-eyed.

"No. Not yet. It's all happening too fast. She's brought the ancient chest. The Sacred Book of Bran is rolled up inside a leather container, too difficult to extract without specialist knowledge. Robert will know what to do. I've had all the necessary tools sent over for him to extract it without damaging it. We have the photographs of the cauldron, taken by the King, some of his notes and more curator notes, too, on the Egyptian connection," he added.

"Good," Branwen replied. "You're thinking ahead."

Waterman looked pleased with himself.

"I want to take her to the island, Steve," Branwen announced into the companionable silence.

"Is that a good idea?" Steve responded, his brows furrowing in a look of concern. "She's not ready," he said, astonished.

Branwen shrugged expressively. "Maybe not, old friend, but we are. We are ready and she needs to learn about her heritage. What her ancestry owes to this land. What her people expect of her. Like Robert, she too is part of the future Prydain. Robert is of the scholar class, she is of the warrior class, both have to have their initiations, Steve. Robert has had his. She must have hers. It is written."

Steve shook his head. "Branwen, you can't make unilateral decisions like this! She has to give her consent and I doubt, from what I know of her, which admittedly is very little, that she would consent. I think you're misreading her quite frankly. Which isn't like you..."

Branwen stared at him until he felt very uncomfortable. "Who would she listen to, Steve?" she asked after a minute's silence

"She'd listen to Taft," he said confidently. "But Taft has strong reservations about this island and mistletoe business … if either Odo, Astley or Sir Rufus ordered it, however …"

"Yes, he'd have to make sure she complied. I see that," she replied thoughtfully. "I want you to continue supporting Robert. I know he can be difficult, but you do seem to have a way with him, unlike me."

Steve gave her one of his lop-sided grins in acknowledgement as she continued. "There's someone I need to consult about this next step ... Don't ask me any more ... I need to focus, think of a way to get her to comply ... "

"You're not going to force her, Branwen?" Steve Waterman stared hard into her deep blue eyes. The delightful yet determined Branwen stared silently back.

CHAPTER *14*

Commander Taft had made good time, arriving at MI5 Headquarters in London in a little over four hours. He was surprisingly alert after the long drive through the night and pleased that he had arrived promptly for his meeting with Sir Rufus just before the 7:00 am deadline.

He made his way to the ground floor executive bathroom, extracting his shaving kit and a fresh shirt and tie from his laptop bag. Looking hard at himself in the mirror, he felt centred, determined, he was ready to have it out with Sir Rufus if necessary, though his instinct told him that it wouldn't come to that. He was a thoroughly decent man, a superb manager, a most agreeable boss. Taft's instincts were usually accurate.

Taft finished tidying himself up, packed away his kit and strode toward the executive lift. He unblinkingly held his eyes steady as the retina scan clicked into action, allowing him into the rarefied atmosphere of Level Three, an area of the service classified at Privy Council level; headquarters of the Dissonance Office and Sir Rufus' current pet project.

Taft allowed himself a small smile. Sir Rufus was one of the new breed. Progressive, articulate, decisive and unwaveringly patriotic. Taft was convinced that he would call a halt to the experiment now. All the data points collected showed that the public didn't want change; they were content with life as it was. Change couldn't just be manufactured against the will of the people, surely? Strangely, Taft suddenly felt a little unsure of himself. He paused, straightened his tie, and knocked politely on the grey painted door at the far end of the corridor.

"Enter!" a disembodied voice commanded as Taft twisted the glass doorknob, thinking to himself how ordinary everything looked inside this iconic building. More bland than Bond he sniffed, finding the doorknob sticky and grubby on his freshly washed hands.

Sir Rufus was tiny. Five foot five inches tall, thin, wiry, late fifties with greying hair receding at the temples, he looked very much like a clerk, or a bank teller.

It was part of his persona, Taft knew, to look incongruous, yet beneath that ordinary exterior there lurked a first class mind that still retained a passion for the Classics from its university days.

Taft exhaled. Sir Rufus stood by the vast window, his back to Taft, looking out onto the panoramic view of early morning London.

"Sir," Taft said, standing to attention.

"Sit," Sir Rufus barked without turning around. "We're going to go ahead with the mission, Taft."

He swivelled round, facing Commander Taft head on. "I've had a long talk with both the Prime Minister and His Majesty. Both are agreed that we have to see matters through to their rightful conclusion. We can't continue this current social experiment any longer. It's become far too dangerous. Too divisive. Too … Roman, if you like. There's a body of lost knowledge in that book, Taft. If we can access it we have a chance to turn matters around.

"Rome fell, you know. All civilisations fall, Taft, once they become too complex, too secular, and too materialistic. And that's where we are today. The new gods are eating up our world and we have to put a stop to it. We need to learn the lessons of history."

He sighed and sat down suddenly. He looked tired and grey, deep lines like fissures in his normally smooth face, his eyes watery from reading or lack of sleep – probably both. The office door opened. Archbishop Odo entered, carefully negotiating unfamiliar terrain, his hands a little unsteady as he seated himself, uninvited, next to Taft.

"Archbishop," Sir Rufus welcomed him warmly. "Just telling Taft here about developments."

"Ah yes. Indeed," the venerable Archbishop responded. "We need to discuss matters further, Sir Rufus."

"Are there further developments?" Sir Rufus exhibited surprise.

"No, no, Sir Rufus. Not yet at least. Though once the Sacred Book is deciphered we will most assuredly have further developments. But for now, all is as it was 24 hours ago."

"Not quite," Commander Taft offered, carefully scanning his boss' face. "Robert Bailey returned from the island late last night, early hours of this morning." He looked at their faces, both eager, both anxious, both curious.

"And?" Sir Rufus asked, impatiently.

"Evidently, he slept for several hours, extracted the scrolls from the leather casing and is, as we speak, currently deciphering them. I'm told everything looks positive. Steve Waterman is supervising the security detail, my deputy is gathering intelligence and preparing an interim report which she should have completed by the end of this week."

"Excellent!" Archbishop Odo was beside himself. "If this is true, Commander, then we can confidently move matters forward. What do you say, Rufus?"

Sir Rufus folded his thin arms and took a moment to think. "I think we need to secure the island first. This is a long-term project and it's going to cause some serious dissent. People don't like change. What we are doing here is moving the whole of society in a totally different direction. It is going to be painful. There will be difficulties."

He paused and looked hard at Commander Taft. "We need to mobilise a secret army, Taft. One that will protect the new knowledge. The new gods if you like."

Archbishop Odo looked offended.

Commander Taft ignored him and looked directly at Sir Rufus. "We have the Book, sir, but we still don't have the Cauldron," he said carefully. "Surely that makes a difference?"

"Yes, it does. Of course it does," Archbishop Odo interrupted. "But we know it must be on the island."

"The Prime Minister told me a story about how the cauldron, if misused, would re-locate itself." Sir Rufus tapped his teeth with a pencil as he spoke. "Which could mean that, if the legend is true …"

"It's worth a try," Commander Taft responded.

"Hasn't the whole area been reclaimed?" the Archbishop queried.

"And more to the point," Sir Rufus said archly, "can we trust this Robert Bailey?"

Commander Taft looked at both of them carefully. He had a duty to pass this new information on, he knew, yet he was strangely reluctant somehow. Telling himself firmly to 'get a grip', he turned to his boss and cleared his throat.

"There's something else you need to know," he began. "My deputy, Ceris, Ceris Pendragon …"

Archbishop Odo's jaw slackened. Sir Rufus squinted his eyes, intently studying Taft's features as he explained.

"I've recently discovered this …" He handed over a buff-coloured file to Sir Rufus. He quickly and expertly scanned its contents before handing it over to the Archbishop who fumbled for his reading glasses as he wandered off toward the large window where the early morning light was better.

A calm silence permeated the large space as the Archbishop quickly absorbed the handful of documents. His breathing was audible as he grasped the significance of their content. He turned back to see Sir Rufus pouring coffee from a large thermos flask. A tray of croissants had miraculously appeared from somewhere and Commander Taft was energetically tucking in to his second helping.

The Archbishop sat down gingerly. "So," he began. "She's a Pendragon?"

Commander Taft swallowed. "Yes, Your Grace. It wasn't until we did a further check that we realised she belongs to the original tribe. She's a direct descendant of Uther Pendragon."

"Does this mean that she is of the indigenous Warrior Class?" the Archbishop asked, a serious look on his normally benevolent features.

"Yes. It does." Sir Rufus leaned forward, clasping his slim hands on his thin knees. "I suggest we send her for further training, Taft. Six weeks should do it, given her rank and physical fitness. Hasn't she already had fitness training with the Marines?"

"Three months ago, sir," Commander Taft nodded. "All my people went on the Brecon Scheme. I've already organised some SAS counter-terrorism training in Cairo. She left this morning. And yes, she came first in all categories on that particular course … except one."

"And which one was that?" Sir Rufus asked, a small smile crinkling his eyes as he spoke.

"Empathy," he smiled back at his boss. "It's true, sir. She doesn't do sympathy, empathy, none of those so-called 'female' virtues that we hold to be inviolable. It's a wonder, all things considered, that she ever managed to have a relationship with Robert Bailey. I'm still trying to work that one out …"

"Genetic," Sir Rufus barked, making the Archbishop jump.

"Genetic?" the Archbishop repeated, lost for words.

"Exactly." Sir Rufus nodded. "Young Ceris can trace her lineage back to the 1st Century AD, as can Robert Bailey. Both come from two separate tribes: the Iceni in the case of Pendragon, the House of Bran in the case of Robert. I had the Royal Heralds do a bit of digging – they've lists, documents, old scrolls going back to the year dot on British history. Most of it not in the public domain, of course, given the fact that Ancestry.com has become such a popular tool. The establishment were rather concerned that the natives could rebel if they knew the full story, and so …" He raised his hands in the air in a gesture of fait accompli as both the Archbishop and Commander Taft looked on, awestruck.

"Sir," Commander Taft said at last. "What I don't understand is this desire to push through the project. I thought it was just an experiment. People are content as they are. If we go further on down this road of changing the status quo … Indeed, overturning it … It could result in anarchy. It's a dangerous game, sir," he finished off, unhappily.

Sir Rufus looked kindly at him. "I understand your concern," he said gently. "But matters themselves are fast becoming dangerous. The present order, when we look at all the statistics over the past twenty years, shows us a society on the brink of meltdown.

"Crime has never been higher. Poverty is endemic. Violence has become a casual affair with people posting muggings, sexual imagery, and sexual violence on line as if it's of no consequence. Man has become predatory, nasty and vile.

"Religion, once the opiate of the people, is sneered at. Ethnic minorities, women, children, the elderly, live in fear. A crisis of drugs, porn, obesity, unemployment, homelessness, and debt and relationship breakdown threatens the very fabric of our society. Indeed, we know from several hard-hitting studies that it is just a matter of time before that fabric disintegrates.

"And *when* that happens, not *if* it happens, we enter a dark, dangerous world similar to that of the so-called Dark Ages. The seeds of social and economic anarchy have already been sown, Taft. And their harvesting is within our lifetimes. We have spent the last ten years gathering data points, seeking solutions. Nothing will work without a complete re-boot of the system. The system has failed. We cannot allow it to destroy us now.

"We thought that Europe was the answer. By being in Europe, we could be part of something bigger, something better, and something more meaningful. Humanity must have meaning if it is not just to survive but thrive in these difficult times, in any times if you glance at the history books. The experiment has failed. Our History has failed us, Commander.

"Two thousand years of adopting the Roman Way has failed. The academics know it, the industrialists and the business people know it, the educators know it, and the politicians know it. Even the King and the Royal Family have finally accepted that this is the end of the road for their world as they know it. It is they, Commander, who have finally consented to this change. It is they who fear a future based on the current model. And it is for them, and for our very future survival that we must act.

"We must. We have to find an alternative if we are to continue civilisation in this country and not kill each other with the tools of modern nihilism.

"If we gradually dismantle the prevailing Social Order and replace it with something natural born, not adapted or adopted to these shores, perhaps, just perhaps, we can make the world, our world, a better place.

"If we don't act soon, very soon, Commander, I doubt if we will have a society to make better at all."

Sir Rufus' face was serious. His impassioned speech had left both Archbishop Odo and Commander Taft shaken. The Commander knew his boss well. He would not say these words unless they were exact, unless they really did reflect the current state of play. Unless they were based upon the most hard-headed research from a collection of venerable institutions.

Archbishop Odo nodded silently to himself. He had known for quite some time that this day would come. He had foreseen it himself all those years ago, in the days when he was a lowly clergyman trekking around his three rural parishes in the heart of Somerset. In the days, weeks, months and years he had helped to promote the meteoric rise of his dear friend, Angela Astley, Prime Minister of the United Kingdom. She too was an old soul, he thought to himself. And she still had a big part to play in the unravelling drama. All the old souls did, he mused to himself. Once they knew who they were.

☦☦☦

Steve Waterman tuned the television set manually. It was an ancient, cathode ray set, circa 1990's with a grainy picture and a volume control that didn't work properly.

"It's a bit loud," he grinned. "Nothing I can do about that. Should be all right if you tune out the low level buzz."

He eased himself onto the sagging sofa sitting next to a red-eyed, unshaven Robert Bailey, who kept turning his head toward the open doorway as if anticipating the entrance of someone unseen. Waterman stole a sideways glance. "Here we are." He shifted forward eagerly, tapping the brick of a remote in the direction of the small screen as the theme tune from the six o'clock news started up.

Robert Bailey leaned forward too, a small smile dancing around the edges of his mouth.

"You look pleased with yourself," Waterman challenged.

"Yeah, pretty much," Bailey responded non-committedly.

"Ceris?" Waterman enquired with an amused tone.

"Sort of … Maybe … Maybe not…" Bailey responded. "Not sure just yet, said she needs time to think things through … I don't know, Steve, she's had ten years to 'think things through'. Maybe I just need to face facts and stop hoping she'll come back to me. She's changed, Steve. She's become what she always wanted to be and it fills her up. I'm not sure there's any room left in her for anything else. Anyone else. I think I need to face facts, see her as a friend rather than what I'd hoped for. I wasn't very strong before, Steve. I think, for the first time in my life, I am now. I've changed, too, you see."

Steve Waterman nodded helplessly. He knew that feeling.

Bailey fiddled with the ancient remote control on the dusty coffee table in front of them both as he took a deep breath and turned to face a wordless Waterman.

"Anyway," he continued, "more to the point, I think I've cracked some of the symbols in the manuscript but it's going to be a big job, Steve. I need to get back to Canterbury to the library, where there are no distractions. Can you ask Commander Taft? You know him better than I do. I can't do much more here."

Steve stood up, towering over the seated Robert Bailey, his face impassive yet determined. "That's impossible, Robert," he said quietly. "We're moving you to Beaumaris in the morning, then to an isolated manor house on the Marquis of Anglesey's estate. Everything you need will be there by the end of the week. Branwen and I will be there with you too.

"I've appointed a temporary manager for the hotel so I can focus completely on matters here. Branwen will assist you with organising the research, though I don't know if or how that's going to work out. You'll understand why in a minute," he finished, glancing over to the TV set balanced carefully on a plastic chair.

A ticker tape with 'Breaking News', streamed across the bottom of the television screen. Both sat bolt upright when the picture shifted to the familiar exterior of Number Ten Downing Street.

Angela Astley stood in front of a jumble of TV station microphones. She was composed, elegant, and immaculate in her grey Chanel suit and perfectly coiffured hair.

To the side of her stood Commander Taft, Archbishop Odo and Sir Rufus, all wearing serious expressions as she announced that the country was, from this moment, on high alert.

She declared a nightly curfew, from eight at night until six the following morning. She stated that all ports of entry were closed to the public, all passenger flights would be diverted from the following week.

She made clear that a series of detention camps were to be opened, one for each county, where the Military Police, recently given complete autonomy over national jurisdiction, would have the power of arrest and detainment over any member of the public caught infringing any civil codes or committing any criminal act.

She declared that Parliament was suspended until further notice whilst a national assessment day was to be held, online, for every person over the age of fourteen. She announced that the King was under pressure from international partners to remain but would be reducing his role in the life of the nation considerably. He planned to move his family to Glastonbury within the next few days where he wanted to devote his remaining years to the re-building of its mighty cathedral.

A state of emergency had been declared. And Angela Astley looked directly into the television cameras, her brilliant smile one of absolute triumph.

CHAPTER 15

Lord Crispin Farndon seethed. He hit the off button on the television remote with a vicious stab as he paced up and down his elegant second floor Kensington apartment.

There was only one way through this, he thought, and that was to 'take out' Angela Astley. There was no other way, he surmised. The woman was destroying the country, had all but eradicated the nation and he raged at the implications of it all.

He stopped pacing to glance up at a portrait hanging over the hand-carved marble fireplace. A portrait of his ancestor, the Earl of Gowrie, a hedonistic firebrand who had created the founding fortune of the family through 17th Century slavery and piracy. "What would he have done?" he asked himself furiously and, knowing the answer, proceeded to rally his thoughts, calming himself down in the process.

He wanted desperately to show the Prime Minister who was 'boss'. He hated her with such a passion it made him feel quite dizzy sometimes. His anger often melted over into tears of abject frustration. But who could he trust? Who would listen to him? Who might be on his side? He was friendless. Not even the Home Secretary would take his calls anymore.

There was always John of course … the frightened younger brother of the King now spending his days wandering aimlessly around the streets and lanes of Glastonbury whilst his brother worked night and day to rebuild the ancient cathedral with the help of old Odo.

Why were they rebuilding it? He stopped his pacing about and sat on the velvet cushioned window seat, hearing the sound of the great curfew bell announcing eight pm. A strange sadness overtook him. He needed human company, but to go out now risked the wrath of the Military Police and the possibility of incarceration in one of their containment camps. The thought re-fuelled his anger as he continued to pace up and down the airy apartment.

Reaching for the tumbler of single malt, he stretched out on the large, deeply cushioned velvet sofa and sipped the amber liquid contemplatively. Why were they rebuilding it? He needed to find out.

It wouldn't cause a fuss if he phoned, would it? It was an innocent question, a matter of curiosity surely? He resolved to visit. First thing. As soon as the curfew could be broken, he'd head over there and find out what, exactly, was going on.

He needed to know everything. If he was going to make sure Angela Astley learned the hard way, that he and his class had an ancient right to rule, based upon conquest, hereditary precedence, tradition and class. Who was she to overturn the old order, the very foundation of the nation that had once created an empire that ruled most of the known world?

Revenge was a dish best served cold. This he knew. And he would make sure, with every fibre of his being, that she would feel its icy hand when the time was right. He allowed himself a small, tight, evil smile as he imagined the look of fear and helplessness throwing dark shadows over her lovely features.

The buzzing from the door phone interrupted his reverie. Startled, he placed his tumbler on the rosewood coffee table, knocking over an exquisite silver vase filled with white flowers, the opaque liquid pooling on an old copy of Vanity Fair. He jumped to his feet, his heart racing, hands trembling. Was it the Military Police? The thought, unbidden, flooded his mind, leaving him incapable of action until it buzzed again. His mobile screamed into the silence. He automatically pressed the green logo.

"Farndon?" A brusque, modulated, confident tone.

"Speaking."

"Open the door."

"Who are you?"

"You know who I am. Open the door."

"Yes, yes. All right, then. There. It's open."

Lord Farndon stood in the centre of the large, high ceilinged room trying hard to control his breathing, which was coming in short sharp breaths. He wiped the palms of his hands on the side of his immaculate grey trousers and took a grateful gulp of the single malt as the front door of his apartment silently opened.

Two military police officers stood to attention, their faces hard and impassive in the fading light. Commander Taft stood between them.

"Am I under arrest?" Farndon stuttered nervously.

"No," Commander Taft replied carefully.

"Then?" Farndon shook his head, uncomprehending.

"The National Assessment, Farndon." Commander Taft's voice held a hint of amusement. "It appears that you're one of the thousand and we're here to escort you to the College of Initiates." Commander Taft was, by this time, finding it hard to keep a straight face.

"You can't be serious!" Farndon burst out. "This is the most ridiculous thing I've ever heard!"

"Isn't it just." Commander Taft allowed himself an amused shake of the head. "Who would have thought it, Farndon? But there we are. We have the evidence, the proof if you like. You are one of the thousand selected for the National Assessment by virtue of psychological profiling, multiple-choice questionnaires, DNA testing and College of Heralds research. No question about it. Pack a bag, just a change of clothes and a toothbrush will do – everything is provided once you get there."

"And where, exactly, is 'there', Commander?" Lord Crispin Farndon was virtually apoplectic by now.

"All in good time, Farndon. All in good time."

Both military policemen took a threatening step forward as Lord Farndon sharply made for his bedroom door. Commander Taft settled himself on the comfortable sofa, straightening the exquisite silver vase and its contents of miniature white lilies with a satisfied smile.

Taft glanced with interest around the gracious, high-ceilinged room, admiring the obviously valuable oil paintings, bronze statuettes set elegantly on Regency sideboards scattered around the rectangular space. A floor to ceiling window, draped fussily with swags and pelmets enclosed a padded velvet window seat that looked directly toward a recently empty Kensington Palace. Once a home for Royal relatives, now darkened, almost forbidding, its spacious rooms shrouded in white sheets covering expensive furniture and objets d'art.

London was shifting, mutating. By day, modern, dynamic, bustling and busy. By night, dark, forbidding, the sound of the Thames never far away; its dark, swirling waters rushing forward to the sea, marking time itself with its ebb and flow. At night, you could feel the history of the place. The centuries swirling behind you. All that history. All the events, great and small, this great metropolis had witnessed.

Commander Taft thought about the recent statistics that had emerged from Whitehall. Crime had fallen nationally by 60%. Domestic incidents by 80%. Illegal immigration by 100%. Civil disturbances were at a record low. Youth crime was the same since the introduction of the New Curriculum in parallel with the extension of the school day from nine to six.

In the six months since the start of The Interregnum, society had become more docile, more fearful, it seemed to him. And he couldn't shake off the thought that it wasn't meant to be like this.

Where was the joy in life? Where was the freedom to simply be?

He mentally shook himself, knowing that there was no way back now. Did he want to go back? Think of those statistics, man, he argued with himself. This is the first phase of the grand plan … It will get better … Patience, as the Archbishop often reminds me, is a virtue. And one I badly need to work on these days.

He shook himself from his reverie as Lord Farndon emerged from the bedroom carrying a large canvas holdall. He looked defeated and a small part of Taft felt a little sympathy for him. He was beginning to feel a little defeated himself.

"Sergeant Dennis and Corporal Smith will escort you, Lord Farndon," Commander Taft said kindly. "There's nothing to concern yourself about, sir. In fact it looks like you will be one of the more fortunate ones. Your profiling revealed that you are in the top ten per cent of subjects nationally. An impressive achievement and one that means you will receive the highest level of training from the Initiates."

"What if I don't want this training, Taft?" Lord Farndon scowled menacingly. "What if I've no interest in this nonsense you, Astley, Odo and the Intelligence clowns are determined to promote? What if the experiment fails, Taft? Have you thought about that?"

"And what if it doesn't?" Commander Taft said quietly. "What if, in a few years time, we can re-create a better world, become a model civilization that others can emulate? What if, after all the hard work that Robert Bailey and his team have done completing the translations of the Druidic Texts, we have the template for that better world? I understand your fears, sir. I really do. At times, I too have those same doubts. But we've come this far. We have to give it a chance. Even your friend Prince John sees that. And his brother, too, acknowledges that there is a force now at work that cannot be contained. A force for the greater good we earnestly hope."

Sergeant Dennis took one arm and his corporal the other as they led the reluctant Lord out of the grace and favour apartment. Commander Taft waited a moment, listening for footsteps in the outer hall before turning once more to the perfectly proportioned window in front of him. He could see the lights going out all over London as a stealthy darkness crept like a shadow over the buildings, roads, shops, and the imposing palace in the distance. He could smell the darkness descending. A damp, pungent aroma reminiscent of stagnant water and uprooted trees.

A brief flash of understanding sparked for a moment, before, like a shooting star on an unknown trajectory, it disappeared. But the image persisted. Stagnant water. Uprooted trees. He knew it meant something. He knew he would remember the thought but not, as yet, understand the meaning. No, the meaning, the comprehension was just out of reach. He couldn't grasp it. Not yet. But he would. Patience.

"Sir!" A breathless Ceris Pendragon powered into the room clutching a tooled leather folio case bursting at the seams, her energy sparking and pulsing the air like electricity. Commander Taft frowned at his deputy, folding his arms across his designer-suited chest, briefly noting her more confident posture, her assertive glance, holding his. Fearless, respectful, determined. He allowed himself a slight raising of the eyebrows. It wouldn't do to let her know that he was immensely proud of her.

She was almost ready to take on the gathering hordes, the mercenaries, assembling over the waters under the banner of Rome. The details were not yet in the public domain but it would not be very long before rumours seeped out and the ominous whisperings began.

They had to locate the Cauldron. Robert Bailey was going frantic, Waterman had told him in confidence, over the lack of progress in finding the artefact. He was ready, Waterman said, to remove himself from his role as Chief Custodian and begin digging up the island with his bare hands if necessary! Steve Waterman appeared genuinely worried about him. He must speak with him soon, he reflected.

Ceris stood silently, waiting for her superior to emerge from his reverie, calmly taking in her surroundings and marvelling at the elegance, the understated wealth, the exquisite good taste reflected in Lord Farndon's carefully choreographed environment. Her eyes drank in the Gainsborough portraits, the Burford hunting scenes. Was that a Turner seascape? Her glance shifted to a cluster of smaller portraits grouped together in an alcove by the large window. A handful of still lives. A portrait of a springer spaniel with his moist, chocolate eyes looking directly at the viewer caught her interest as she knitted her brows together, opening her mouth slightly in sudden astonishment.

"Sir!" she blurted out, causing Commander Taft to shake himself suddenly from his thoughts.

"The pictures, Commander! I do believe they're the missing National Trust ones! The ones that Waterman was trying to locate. The ones that disappeared from those heritage properties in North Wales."

She pointed excitedly at the seascape. "Wasn't one of them thought to be a Turner? I'm sure that's a Turner, sir, and I'm positive Steve Waterman mentioned that the most valuable one stolen was an early example of the artist's work."

She exhaled sharply. "Wasn't there something about a gang, a cabal, in the Berwyn Mountains, not far from Steve's hotel? Something about them stealing to order? And what's this, sir?" She pointed to a bundle of brown wrapping paper lying discarded in a Japanese lacquered bin at the side of a small desk. "Look, it's a compliment slip. It must belong to one of these. 'Benedictus', it says, 'Rome wasn't built in a day. Remember Aristobulus.'."

Commander Taft frowned. He looked first at the potential Turner and then at Ceris, rubbing his chin thoughtfully. "Who on earth is Aristobulus?" he asked. "Benedictus? Does this have something to do with the art thefts we've been chasing?

"I'm no art expert, but someone knows something about the missing artefact that we don't. This has to be a link, Pendragon! And just to add another speculative thought … maybe we're not being told the full truth by his Lordship.

"Not a word to anyone. I need to speak with Sir Rufus and organise an audit of this place. And take a convoluted route back to your apartment, Pendragon. I've a feeling we're being played … there are still a handful of the criminally inclined out and about after curfew. … So carefully does it."

Ceris couldn't help grinning back at her boss. The last person who had tried to intimidate her as she jogged around the Serpentine last Sunday was still in hospital. She'd gone to visit him yesterday and taken a bowl of fruit as a token of goodwill. He'd been astonished, slyly asking her if she fancied him. She'd laughed until her sides ached before telling him gently that no, she didn't want to be his girlfriend. She was simply doing what warriors do, claiming both right and might. In victory there was magnanimity. The fruit was a symbol of that. He didn't understand. She didn't expect him to really.

There was a small yet noticeable swathe of the population still clinging to the old ways. Violence for the sake of it, abuse both physical and emotional, fragile egos desperately clinging on to their version of normality, the old put-downs, biased assumptions, one-upmanship, narcissism.

She was looking forward to her upcoming secondment. Training the trainers: a regiment of operatives was about to go elite and the National Assessment Centre had chosen her to lead the initiative. Why, she wasn't really sure. And she was reminded of a conversation with Angela Astley, former Prime Minister, now My Lady Protector. Hadn't she said to contact her if she wanted anything, needed to understand anything? Ceris shook the thought away.

"Sir?" Ceris looked directly at her boss as she emptied the contents of the tooled leather folder, handing him a heavily embossed document bearing miniature waxed seals. "You need to look at this, sir. It may have some bearing on matters."

Commander Taft took the document over to the fading light coming through the long window and scanned its contents before seating himself heavily on an ornate Regency chair and placing the document on its matching small table.

"Where did you get this?" he whispered.

"Branwen," she replied.

"Does Bailey know about it?"

"No. She has lost faith in Robert and believes that we've made a terrible mistake. Not in the translations and academics, but in allowing him access to the sacred texts. The Druidic texts. She believes that he has lost all modesty, has become arrogant and wilful. And that such behaviour marks him not as a wisdom keeper, but as a fool."

"Have you read it?"

"Yes."

"And?"

"Well, it's clear that Branwen's community feels very strongly that a wrong turn has been taken and they desperately want the College of Heralds to find a new Arch Druid. What do we do with Bailey, though, in the interim? He's hardly likely to wander off into the sunset singing a happy tune."

"Can we get Waterman to contain matters over on the island until we come up with a plan? What do you think?"

Ceris felt strangely flattered that her boss was genuinely interested in her opinion, she puffed her chest out and stood a good inch taller. "Well, sir. I think we need to try to sort out matters before the whole situation becomes unmanageable. Branwen is keeping her distance, I'm told, whilst Waterman is acting as peacemaker between all factions. However, we need Branwen on side. She is the one with the access. Once Robert has finished the translations – and we believe he is just a few months away now from completion – he could be sent back to Archbishop Odo and Canterbury, without too much fuss."

"Would he go?" Taft queried, unconvinced.

Ceris shrugged her shoulders. "I don't know, Commander. A little while ago, I would have said yes, of course he would.

"Now, I'm not sure. He's changed. He's lost his shyness, his vulnerability, he's become assertive, confident, arrogant even, and very, very decisive according to Steve Waterman. He's a very different Robert Bailey, sir. One I'm not sure that I know anymore … Or if I ever did."

"Can we trust what Branwen and the others are saying, though? Maybe, just maybe, this is a power play with Branwen and her tribe trying to gain the upper hand. We need to find that blessed cauldron, Pendragon! Look, cancel the plan. I'll go to Glastonbury and speak to the King and Prince John. Archbishop Odo is still there, I believe.

"You go to Anglesey and talk to Waterman. Remember, you're due in Cairo again shortly, so forty-eight hours max. I have to say this, Pendragon. Written complaints, gossip and hearsay don't quite cut it in my book. Horse's mouth is the way to go. I want you to get to the bottom of this. Forty-eight hours and I want a full report. If in doubt of the veracity of any statements, send for escorts and we'll bring them here for interrogation.

"This is serious. I'm minded to get Alalladin here to help out … He has a doctorate in Comparative Religions and Philosophy from Oxford, and he's one of ours. I'll have a quiet word with Sir Rufus and see what he suggests."

Ceris carefully returned the document to the folder, noting her boss' frustration. She dashed to the door, her eyes glimpsing a thin panel of painted wood tucked away on a high hanger above a half hidden alcove. She paused, looking again at its faded greens, blues and reds, its dark, ominous, brooding presence. "Commander," she said softly. "What is this?"

Commander Taft glanced up to where she pointed and stared hard at the unmistakeable outline.

"Castle Dinas Bran," he breathed. "How very, very interesting."

CHAPTER 16

A year had passed. Robert Bailey was furious. Steve Waterman was unrepentant. And the lovely Branwen, archly amused.

"I'm in charge here!" Robert Bailey seethed, banging his fist on the waxed manor house table still cluttered with the detritus of breakfast.

"As far as we're concerned, Robert, Commander Taft's in charge, not you," Steve Waterman replied, shaking his head patiently.

"Who has been responsible for the translations, Steve? Who has compiled a working narrative from over a thousand fragments of parchment and papyrus? Who has directed the translation team, Steve?"

"You have," Steve Waterman agreed. "And done a magnificent job too from what I understand. But you have to stop lording it over everyone, Robert. Your ego is getting in the way, and that wasn't the plan. Was it, Branwen?"

"Ha!" Branwen sneered, locking her eyes as deep as dark blue pools onto the glinting ones of Bailey. "Your ego is in the way, Robert. You cannot see. You cannot hear. You cannot feel, with that ego of yours. It is killing you. It is killing all of us. This new order is supposed to change the old order, the old beliefs. You are reinforcing the old ways with your contempt for everyone.

"I've had enough, Robert. No more. No more insulting behaviour from one who, just a year ago, was clinging to my hand begging for understanding of the old ways, the Brythonic ways. Now, you can barely hold a civil tongue in your head. What manner of man are you, Robert Bailey, that you feel you can speak to me so disdainfully?"

Branwen, small, delicate, her long brown curls framing her perfect features, threw the contents of her breakfast mug in Robert Bailey's face. He gasped for breath as, satisfied with his reaction, she turned on her heel and sashayed out into the early morning sunshine, humming a discordant tune under her breath.

Steve Waterman offered him a tea cloth. Robert Bailey picked up Branwen's empty mug and smashed it on the terracotta-tiled floor.

"She's something else, isn't she?" Steve Waterman grinned as he swept up the shattered pottery.

"She's a pain in the backside," Bailey retorted as he slid onto the wicker chair, holding his head in his hands.

"You know what this is?" Steve leant back in the chair opposite.

"No, explain it to me, Steve. I don't understand women. Never have done. Never will."

"Very simply put … You're both in a power play for supremacy. Branwen has been top dog for twenty years; born and bred in the old ways, she can trace her line right back, through the Welsh Triads and ancient books to Taliesin and before. You're trying to take her place. And, Robert, you really should know better."

Robert Bailey sighed, slumping forward in his chair, a look of despair on his even features. He had let himself go this past twelve months. He'd put on weight, rarely shaved, constantly wore the same faded woollen fisherman's jumper and dated cords. His hair had grown to his shoulders. He was the very picture of a seventies-style hippie, a transformation that needed addressing before Archbishop Odo saw him again. Before Commander Taft saw him again. He thought fleetingly of Ceris, but his heart had hardened toward her these past few months and had left him feeling both confused and angry.

Steve Waterman pushed a fresh mug of coffee toward him across the vast manor house kitchen table and sat heavily on an opposite chair.

"Why are you doing this, Robert? Why are you so determined to turn Branwen and the others against you? Is it because you have the academic learning and they don't? Or is it because you just want to control everything and everyone? We're all very concerned about you, Robert. Very concerned. So much so, I've asked Commander Taft to intervene before matters get out of hand. You're making life impossible for us, Robert, and I honestly don't believe that is your intention. Is it?"

Robert Bailey looked squarely at Steve and weighed his words carefully before replying.

"I'm scared, Steve," he said simply. "Really frightened."

Steve Waterman held his tongue, nodding slowly to Robert to continue.

"It's all happening too fast, Steve. I spend the day busy on the translations and directing the work of the others to speed things up. I do appreciate how urgent this work is. But my nights are filled with strange, strange visions, dreams, omens, and portents. It's as if the whole of History is unravelling before me.

"I see battles, lonely warriors climbing snow-covered mountains, sacred gatherings filled with meaning and symbol, here on the island. Roman soldiers screaming and slashing, covered in blood, sliding in pools of the stuff as they manically hack down men, women and children who are without swords or shields.

"I hear poetry. Strange, beautiful songs, praise-hymns to warlords and leaders, spoken in ancient Brythonic. I see Mead Halls and drinking horns and, often, I see him. He beckons to me to go with him but I am terrified that if I do go with him … I will never return. Never return, Steve. And I can't get past that point.

"Every night, it's the same. Every night he beckons to me. And every night I wake up in the early hours with no recollection of having gone to sleep. Or even to bed. I wake up sitting at my desk, in my room, every morning. Every morning, Steve."

"You haven't slept?"

"Not for months now. I can't remember the last time I woke up, refreshed, in my bed."

"Did you tell Branwen?"

Bailey shook his head silently. "I felt such an idiot," he sighed. "What could I say? 'Hey, Branwen, I'm having a nervous breakdown.' Help me."

Steve Waterman was calm. His whole demeanour expressed understanding, empathy, sympathy. Robert Bailey felt strangely reassured. It was as if a weight had been lifted off his shoulders. He suddenly felt desperately tired as a wave of utter exhaustion swept over him. Steve Waterman saw it.

"Come on, mate." He grinned in his lop-sided way. "Let's get you up the old apples and pears. I think you just might sleep now. Properly. Without any strange goings-on. I'll come and check on you each hour to make sure."

Steve wasn't about to be persuaded otherwise as he prodded Robert toward the steep oak staircase, heavily worn treads displaying two hundred years evidence of previous occupants heading in that weary direction. Robert silently acquiesced. He was in no fit state to demur as he half-dragged himself to his airy rear-facing room, silently allowing Steve to dislodge his filthy trainers and cover him over with an old but clean satin-edged blanket. He closed his eyes, drifting at once into a deep, dreamless sleep.

Steve Waterman returned to the kitchen. "It worked," he said with a worried frown.

"As I said it would." Branwen stood erect, all five foot of her dominating the space, hands on slender hips, long brown curls lightly bouncing in the breeze from the open door. "I have to take him there, Steve," she stated firmly. "We thought he was strong enough to meet him on his own. But it is clear that he is not. I doubt if we have the right one, if he is the right one, Steve. I have had many doubts this past year regarding Robert Bailey."

"But we know he is of the line, Branwen," Steve Waterman hissed, dismayed.

"Ha!" she scoffed. "There are others."

"Yes, there are others. But have they been authenticated yet? No. Didn't think so. He's the only one we have at the moment. He's all we have, Branwen."

"Perhaps. For the moment, Steve. Yes, he is. But I have doubts. And reservations. He hasn't the strength for the task ahead. Can't you see that?"

Steve held his silence. He had faith in Robert but could see that Branwen's concerns were also valid. Robert had no people skills; he upset people without thinking of the consequences. But was that such a bad thing? Who had ever heard of an Arch Druid – in training or otherwise – who had won a popularity poll?

There was strength, a different but no lesser strength, in being true to oneself and not pandering to others' expectations. He felt a twinge of sadness that Branwen couldn't see that what she perceived as a damning weakness in Robert Bailey, he saw as a form of strength.

He shook himself from his thoughts to gaze adoringly on the exquisite Branwen. She laughed playfully, as she turned on her heel and drifted out of the open kitchen door. He grinned, in his characteristically lop-sided manner, before registering the muted vibration of his mobile twirling insistently amid the detritus of the cluttered table.

CHAPTER 17

The early morning mist was lifting as Commander Taft's Audi swept into the visitor car park. Walking slowly toward him, Archbishop Odo lifted his right hand in both benediction and greeting, puffing with exertion as he attempted to hurry toward him.

The early morning air was cool. A slight aroma of incense hung on the prelate's robes. The taste of Autumn in a light breeze wafted past as he crunched his way through a mound of dry leaves, golden brown, orange-baked in the pale weak sun.

"Welcome. Welcome, Commander. I can't tell you how relieved I am." He shook his head, a worried frown deepening the lines on his furrowed brow.

"Your Grace." Commander Taft shook his hand decisively, concerned at the 75 year old's look of exhaustion.

"Oh, don't mind me, Commander." He patted Taft's arm. "Just a bit overworked and understaffed, that's all. We've finished, you'll be pleased to know. The translation, that is. Very strange, Commander. Very strange indeed. But, forgive me, where are my manners. You must be tired after your journey. I have organised a light breakfast for us both, so follow me. Here we are..."

They entered a low arched doorway, its ancient oak frame splintered and jagged to the touch. Inside, a vast, vaulted ceiling soared over a rectangular room dotted along its length with long refectory tables and matching benches. All was quiet, except for the shuffling movements of someone in a friar's habit laying one of the tables with two wooden plates, two knives, two spoons and two wooden goblets. The Archbishop sat heavily on the wooden bench and began tucking in to the Eggs Benedict the friar had dished out.

"Eat, Commander!" he ordered. "A long day ahead and we will both need our strength. Thank you, Brother Francis," he said to the friar hovering nearby. "We can manage perfectly now."

The silent Brother Francis reluctantly left the large refectory, closing the huge arched door behind him with a small sigh. The Archbishop raised his eyebrows, "We must keep our voices low, Commander," he whispered conspiratorially. "This place has many ears."

Commander Taft nodded his agreement, surprised at how good the Eggs Benedict were. He was ravenous and ate heartily. While he waited for the prelate to finish his meal he hoped that at some point he would be offered coffee. The wooden goblet filled with spring water, while refreshing in its own way, didn't have the requisite caffeine kick needed for so early an hour.

"Tell me, Commander. How is everything in London? How is the Lady Protector? I haven't heard from Angela in over a month now. I expect that she is inordinately busy, of course, but I do worry about her, Commander. She was a protégé, you know."

"I haven't seen her, Your Grace," Commander Taft replied. "I understand that she is overseeing daily COBRA meetings with the Chiefs of Staff and Sir Rufus. There are rumours, nothing more than rumours as yet, that some sabre-rattling is making a bit of a noise over the channel."

"Yes, I've heard the rumours, too." The Archbishop finished his toast and took a delicate sip of spring water. "What do you think, Taft?" he enquired, his tired eyes fixed on the Commander's face.

"It doesn't look good, Your Grace," Commander Taft acknowledged seriously. "I understand that Sir Rufus is concerned that what looks, at the moment, like a small skirmish in the making, might turn out to be something else entirely."

"That bad?" The Archbishop wore a look of deep concern as he led the way through an arched central door in the refectory, to an equally large rectangular room bathed in the early light of a crisp autumnal morning. "The Scriptorium," he announced with a small hint of satisfaction. "Perhaps what we have discovered will help resolve matters, Commander. Here, let me show you."

The Archbishop opened a large, leather-bound volume, exquisitely tooled in gold lettering with a large Celtic knot design taking up the entire front cover. It looked as if it too was worked in gold, surrounded by a fine silver-embellished border studded with small colourful jewels. Garnet, turquoise, sapphire, ruby and pearl. A work of incomparable craftsmanship. Commander Taft held his breath as Odo carefully slipped on a pair of cotton gloves and opened the large, heavy book.

"There," he said softly. "Just here, Commander. We have a direct reference to the Cauldron of Bran. Incidentally, this is considered to be the first vernacular book written here in the 1st Century AD – or CE as we say these days. This book also tells the story of Britain from the point of view of the original tribes, their concerns, their wars, their belief systems and their prophecies.

"What is very interesting is that Robert Bailey's recent transcriptions of The Great Work parchments and scrolls corroborate this. His work on the Sacred Book of Bran not only echoes the words here, in the Commentaries, but also takes the British Story forward, onto another level. We begin to understand just why the Romans felt they had to annihilate the Iceni and commit genocide on Anglesey. Wiping out all but one of the ancient line of Druids."

"All but one?"

"Yes, all but one. The Chief Druid, Bran, son of Llyr. Bran the Blessed as he is known, Keeper of the Old Faith.

"It was he who foresaw the two events: the massacre of the Druids and the massacre of the Iceni. It was he who travelled on foot to Glastonbury to bear witness. It was he, the first person in the history of Britain, who established this scriptorium, purely for the purpose of setting down on parchment the entire knowledge of the Druids. A knowledge that, from the dawn of time itself, had been transmitted orally to the next generation by custom, tradition and wisdom. The wisdom being that only those who could memorise and learn vast amounts of knowledge through the oral transmission process had the intellect, the aptitude and the stamina to become initiates. To become druids.

"And according to what Robert and his team have transcribed thus far, the great Bran was the last in a long line of Royal Arch Druids stretching back to ancient Egypt. To before the time of the pyramids even, when that vast desert country was a lush, green land.

"We did not know this, Commander. This was lost knowledge."

The Archbishop pored over the text as Taft gathered his thoughts. "Where do we go from here, Your Grace?" Taft quietly asked. He felt as if they were heading toward some sort of impasse where the ground was moving beneath their feet very slowly, imperceptibly, so slowly that it was barely registering, yet moving it was. And he felt unnerved. Everything was strange. New uncertainties had replaced old ones.

Increasingly, society was becoming inward looking, suspicious of everything and everyone. The nightly curfews didn't help. The theatres were closed, cinemas only open in daylight hours, restaurants the same. People didn't bother venturing out at weekends any more. Online shopping was more normal than going to the city centres or supermarkets for the majority of the population. Insularity and loneliness combined with a low level disinterest in anything outside of hearth and home. Commander Taft found it all very worrying. Archbishop Odo caught his mood and looked up from the Sacred Book.

"Where do we go from here?" the Archbishop echoed. "Why, we go forward, Taft. Surely you see that? This is an Interregnum. Nothing more. Nothing less. Once we have all the translations: Glastonbury, Robert Bailey's, the completion of the training of the Twelve, we shift from this half-way house affair that we have at the moment and put into place the New Covenant. Hasn't this been explained to you?"

Commander Taft didn't reply. His eyes were fixed on the door to the scriptorium as it slowly opened, its hinges creaking with the sheer weight of its thick oak panels and iron furniture.

"What the blazes are you doing here?" Commander Taft's tone of voice was incredulous.

He had left strict instructions in the Daily Notices diary for security details to be doubled whilst he was away. Under no circumstances were they to go walkabout or change the routine, yet here they were. Impossible. He was furious.

They were silent. All looking at him with compassion and, was that respect?

A dishevelled Robert Bailey stood next to an exhausted Steve Waterman while Branwen stood calm, composed and silently apart from the others. No one said a word. A small, male figure slipped like lightning through the half-open door and walked purposefully toward the group. Taft took a couple of deep breaths as his boss, Sir Rufus, folded his arms and told everyone to sit down. The noise outside of several pairs of running feet startled everyone until Sir Rufus explained that he'd ordered armed guards to surround the precincts. Security was paramount. He had important news. A hushed air descended on the gathering as the Head of National Security began.

"At Curfew tonight, an announcement will be made on national television by My Lady Protector. I am here to brief you on its contents and to answer any questions you may have. It is imperative that you speak to no one of this briefing, or its subject matter, in the interim."

He nodded to Robert Bailey who, longhaired, bearded and dishevelled, got up from his chair to address the room.

"Some of you may already know that the translations are complete. The Sacred Book of Bran has proved to be the most challenging of tasks and the most rewarding. Giving us an insight into the workings of the Druidic mind, culture, history and belief system.

"A body of knowledge lies in these pages. It was never before revealed to the uninitiated, as it had never been written down. Until Bran the Blessed, after his weary journey from Anglesey to the Abbey, devoted the last years of his life to recording the ancient knowledge. Here. In this sacred space.

"It was 60 AD when he arrived here. He was kept hidden in a secret place on Glastonbury Tor as the bloody massacre of the Druids took place far away on Anglesey. As we know from the historical record, Tacitus in particular, the Romans then marched south to obliterate the Iceni.

"Queen Boudicca gave herself as a blood sacrifice by committing suicide. Thirty years earlier, as the records state, the Blessed Saviour too had also sacrificed himself. These two momentous events we believe to be connected.

"However, on this aspect of the translations, and as we are still working through several complex archaic connections, we have very little hard evidence as yet.

"The Royal Arch Druid of the Brythonic, Bran son of Llyr, was thought to have fallen. The Romans never mention his name again. The daughters of Queen Boudicca were captured as trophies and sent to Rome as tribute, then sold into slavery. We now know, from a recently discovered written record, that one of the daughters survived, returning to these islands and marrying into the family of Bran.

"Her line is of great significance, but more of that later. Suffice to say, the Romans had won. Ancient Prydain became Britannia, becoming of course what we know today as Britain. Fast forward to the 16th Century. A Welshman, a Tudor, from a family whose origins are deeply rooted on Anglesey, decides he wants a Reformation.

"The Dissolution of the Monasteries is widely believed to be the result of Henry having a nasty tantrum because he couldn't get a divorce. In part yes it was, but in many other ways it wasn't. And the documents show us why.

"The documents also show us that the male members of the original Tudor line, prior to both Henry VIII and Henry VII, were Druids. The uncle of Henry VII, Jasper Tudor, was, as a young boy, sent to both Anglesey and Armorica, the original name for Brittany, to learn the old ways. This was the tradition of those times. On Anglesey he learned the sacred arts. In Brittany, the warrior arts.

"He was of the aristocratic Warrior Class and learned in the art of war and the making of peace. He told stories of the old ways, of how a thin veil separates this world from the next, of the magic of nature, the music of the spheres, of how the trees absorb the bad in the world and transmute it into oxygen, the very air that we breathe. They knew this. They knew many things about the sciences that we are not aware of here in our modern age.

"They explain how the forests, the birds, the flowers and streams speak their own language. To know that language is to have the ear of the creator. To have the ear of the creator is to be a lord of this world and a prince of the next.

"Jasper was both an adept and a killing machine.

"Henry VII understood this complex paradox. Like his Uncle Jasper, who had brought him up, he too had esoteric knowledge. He too had studied some of the Druidic teachings. However, Henry was a fearful soul, not suited to either war or peace. Not gifted, like his uncle, in the higher arts. No, Henry was interested in power, security and, most of all, money.

"He decided that in order to retain his throne he had to create a Roman-style Britain, not the Celtic Prydain that Jasper had schemed for, worked for, battled for. Jasper believed wholeheartedly in a Brythonic heritage and he had dedicated his life to securing a true Brythonic King to rule a truly Brythonic land. Jasper was the mastermind behind the success of Bosworth. It was his sword that cut down Richard III, his hand that placed the crown on his nephew Henry's head.

"Imagine how he must have felt when his nephew, newly installed on the throne of England after a battle that Jasper had managed to win for him, through superior tactics and strategy, turned to his uncle, the man who had put him there, and said 'No'.

"So, Jasper retired here, to Glastonbury, and completed his part of the great work, adding another chapter to the Sacred Book of Bran. He tells of his disappointment that the Brythonic heritage would never be seen again. He made an observation, which still resonates down the centuries, that 'The Plantagenets and the Popes rivalled each other in debauchery'. Jasper despised them both. He began to despise his nephew, Henry VII.

"Henry named his first born son Arthur. A symbolic name that spoke of a Brythonic future, not a Roman one. Telling Jasper that his great nephew would restore the old ways once the kingdom was settled. We learn from this archive that Jasper remained unconvinced."

Robert paused and glanced around the room. All were silent. "Your Grace," he said quietly before seating himself. The Archbishop slowly got to his feet and cleared his throat.

"Thank you, Robert," he twinkled, smiling benignly at the assembly. "And so ... the reformation ... Yes, it was about divorce and yes, it was also about selling-off the abbey lands for profit.

"But think for a moment on that word 'dissolution'. To dissolve, to liquidise, because that was the fundamental purpose of it all. And why? You may well ask. The reason, my friends, was very simple and very clear. We have evidence from the Windsor Castle documents in particular on this point, haven't we, Robert?"

Robert Bailey nodded in agreement.

"Laws, charters, written land documents," the Archbishop continued, "tribal boundaries, community law scrolls, economic and social rules, bills of rights of the individual, Royal Arch Druid Proclamations. All of these documents pre-date the Roman invasion, the coming of the Saxon hordes, even the Battle of Hastings.

"Legally, this country belongs not to those who have traditionally held it for hundreds, for more than a thousand years. No, my friends, we have legal documents proving that the Brythonic nation of Prydain holds that right.

"And we have proof, too, that the dissolving of the monasteries was designed purely to get hold of that ancient documentation and destroy it."

"So, Bran was the last Druid, the last Brythonic to hold the land for his people?" Commander Taft was intrigued.

If so, who was left to inherit both spiritual and temporal kingdoms? All eyes looked directly at him as a gradual dawning overcame his normally serious features. His eyes widened as the realisation hit. "No!" he mouthed, astonished at his own stupidity.

"Yes." Archbishop Odo spread his hands in open benediction, "I am the inheritor of the Royal Arch Druid line. The Archbishop of Canterbury is the heir to the spiritual kingdom of these isles. The hidden origin of this office goes back millennia, Commander. To the original crucible or cauldron, a metaphor for the first time, the first fusion of time, matter, and energy. When life was created. And it is through the power of the Sacred Cauldron that this land and its people will be renewed. This is what we are working for. All of us. Renewal."

The room buzzed as the Archbishop took his seat and Steve Waterman slowly rose to his feet, carefully focusing his eyes at a point slightly above the heads of the assembly. He was so tired.

Night after night of watching Robert as he slept the sleep of the tormented had finally caught up with him and he felt unusually incoherent.

The lovely Branwen poured him a glass of water. Taking a suede pouch from her leather cross-body bag, she sprinkled a small amount of powdered leaves on the liquid and told him to drink it down in one. "It will energise," she said sagely. "And give you calm."

Waterman did as she advised, feeling the electrolytes in his blood slowly but surely recharging. He took a deep breath and began.

"Commander Taft informed me of intelligence suggesting that some of the paintings, stolen from National Trust properties, to order it would appear, had surfaced in Lord Crispin Farndon's apartment in Kensington. One of those paintings, an early 16th Century oil on canvas of Dinas Bran Castle, was sent for analysis to the Royal Academy where an under-painting was detected. Not unusual it would seem, as the RA said that the re-using of canvas and board was common practice at the time. Well, anyway, Professor Stone, an expert, reconstituted the under-painting and digitally enhanced it. This is what he discovered."

Steve Waterman handed out a series of photographs to be circulated around the table, each of them showing an image of a crow, a Celtic cross, a circle of standing stones and a pyramid shaped hill tapering off into the distance. In the foreground was a map, curled at the corners with indecipherable symbols painted in red and blue. Steve Waterman paused, calmly taking in the puzzled expressions and shaking of heads.

Commander Taft spoke. "What does it mean, Waterman?"

Steve shook his head and nodded to Robert Bailey.

"It's the missing link," Robert smiled. "It means that we finally have access to an archive missing for hundreds of years. Proof of the real reason for the Reformation. Not just a removal from Rome, but a removal from the pre-Roman foundations of the nation. It is all there. We have several references to it in the documents recently translated. It is all there, I am convinced, in Whiting's Archive.

115

"A team of specialists have cordoned off Castle Dinas Bran and we believe that the archive was secreted there shortly before Whiting's arrest and subsequent execution. This is confidential of course. We are working towards recovering the archive but it is still early days."

Steve Waterman spoke, "So, what is it with this archive?"

"Whiting's archive?" Robert asked him.

"Yes, I don't understand why Henry VIII wanted the archive and why Bishop Whiting was executed for not handing it over.'"

"We don't have the full picture yet," Robert replied, pushing his shoulder length hair off his face. "What we do know is that Cromwell was ordered to bring trumped-up charges against Whiting. He was convicted before he had his trial. That is in the records, ostensibly for not agreeing to the divorce, but he did agree. Again, that's in the historical record, as is his agreement for his own abbey, Glastonbury Abbey, to be dissolved.

"No, what Henry wanted, and Cromwell couldn't get for him, was a massive archive of documents proving that ancient Prydain was a land that couldn't be subjugated. That it was a land dedicated, consecrated even, to a higher power, a higher authority. A sacred land, closer to the gods than to mortal man. And it terrified him. It terrified Henry, because if the archive became public, entered the public domain, then everyone would know that there was no divine right of kings, there was no way he could be God's representative on earth. And there was proof. Yes, hard evidence, real proof, in that archive!

"There are those who have known of this. Hidden, secret societies whose roots go deep into this ancient tradition. One example. And there are many. You've heard of William Blake, the artist and poet?"

Everyone nodded agreement.

"You've heard, or read or even sung his famous words 'Jerusalem'?"

Again, everyone nodded.

"Think about what those words actually say. Because that is what we are doing here, today, in this Abbey of Glastonbury. We are building a new Jerusalem.

CHAPTER *18*

Cairo was blisteringly hot. The temperature gauge wasn't working in the Nissan hire car but Ceris had a fair idea that it must be in the high thirties as the sticky sweat trickled down the back of her neck, making her light cotton tee-shirt damp. She wound down the driver-side window for some air, only to be blasted with the heavy, thick traffic pollution emanating from the thousands of ill-serviced cars, trucks and motorbikes streaming forward in no particular order on the road leading from the airport to the Mena House Hotel.

From the haze of grey hovering like a horizontal blanket over the city, she could just make out the outline of two of the three pyramids in the distance. She held her breath, the wonder and incongruity of their setting amidst crumbling concrete tower blocks, single storey shanties and dust-covered palm trees threatening to overwhelm her senses. A cacophony of blasted horns and screeching tyres trumpeted her arrival, while men shouting "Yalla, yalla!", fists shaking good-naturedly, it seemed, at a decrepit old petrol tanker, broken down on the highway at an angle that one car could move around, but not four abreast jostling with each other for pole position.

She had always loved Egypt. Had holidayed here twice in the last few years, but this was not a holiday. This was business. She turned into the tightly cornered forecourt of the hotel, noting the beautiful lagoon-shaped swimming pool surrounded by perfectly manicured gardens with sprinklers gently misting the verdant grass, the exotically purple blooms.

The room was small but tastefully furnished with a large, high double bed covered in silk damask with matching curtains and a chair upholstered in the same blue green paisley colours with a delicate hint of gold thread running through. An en-suite bathroom had both bath and shower, ornate gold plated taps, thick white fluffy towels, a matching bath robe and mule style slippers sat neatly on top while a range of coloured glass jars revealed a selection of hand soaps and bath crystals.

"How very old fashioned," she said aloud and was quietly delighted.

Her window had a view of the gardens to the side of the hotel. A perimeter fence somewhat spoiled the vista as she noticed that on the far side there was a steep sloping hill topped by a watchman's hut.

Showered, freshened, Ceris changed into calf-length cream linen pants, a long sleeved white cotton shirt and sandals. She picked up a lemon pashmina bought at the airport. The nights, she remembered, became chilly once the sun set. She was ready.

†T†

"Your Majesty," she said.

"Alfred," he replied. "Please, no formalities, my dear. We have to remain incognito as far as possible, though I do believe your Commander Taft has organised extra security. Just in case. At least, that's what Sir Rufus has led me to believe."

He looked up and down, his eyes darting about the elegant atrium dotted with silk upholstered sofas and low intricately carved tables.

The vast space was empty, apart from a waiter who, smiling broadly and displaying a set of perfect white teeth, set down a tray of tea and a plate of bite sized cakes in front of them. Ceris blinked. She had felt a little overawed, mildly apprehensive. After all, this was the King! He was still, despite Astley's manoeuvrings as Protector, head of state. Abdication was anticipated, but hadn't transpired as yet, as far as she knew.

She could clearly see from his severe expression and his negative body language, legs crossed away from her, body folded at an awkward angle, that he was ill at ease, distracted. He looked disinterestedly at the small cakes, occasionally lifting a china teacup to his pinched lips to take a delicate, frowning sip.

"I hope you like Earl Grey, Miss Pendragon. It's all I ever drink these days, apart from a good Islay of course."

"Earl Grey is perfect, Your – Alfred," she replied, a note of firmness and no nonsense in her tone. He looked surprised. It was noted.

She had no intention of fawning to him, no matter how illustrious his pedigree. She was acutely aware that this initial meeting would set the tone for the next few days. They had a job to do and she was determined that it would be completed both professionally and thoroughly. She could be pleasant, of course, but he needed to know that she wasn't here as anything except a highly qualified and experienced trouble-shooter. And he was here to find his missing link.

If discovered, it would mean that his research findings were correct and Robert Bailey's flawed. There was much at stake.

The discovery of so many hidden documents had shaken the country to the core. There was a growing consensus convinced that a re-boot of the system was the only way forward, the only way to create a sense of a civilised society in a world that had become too brutal, too harsh, too frightening. Even Angela Astley's cabinet were, in the main, supportive of her sweeping legislation, which had torn down the centuries of class and privilege. The closure of the elite public schools a year ago now, the abolition of the House of Lords following shortly after, reducing the aristocracy to unprecedented hardship as their assets were stripped and handed over to local communities for wealth creation.

BBC World News had interviewed the newly designated Lady Protector on Magna Carta Island in the Thames. Ceris wondered what Alfred thought of her performance as she nibbled one of the small cakes.

"Did you see the interview last night, sir?" she enquired, debating whether or not to indulge in another of those small sweet delicacies.

"Yes. Yes, I did." He sounded tired. "She is very impressive, Miss Pendragon. I can understand why the country follows her. She does genuinely appear to have the best interests of the public at heart."

"Do you think she is … one of them, sir? I mean, do you think she is of the Druidic line?"

Ceris was genuinely interested to know his opinion. Here was a very learned man indeed. An expert of the first order who had an international reputation for scholarship in 1st Century ecclesiastical history. He frowned. He wasn't used to being asked questions. Ceris could feel that, but she remained silent.

He took a deep breath. They had to trust each other, he thought to himself. At least this so called new order that Astley promoted didn't have a problem with freedom of expression. Indeed, people were encouraged to express their opinions and debate had become a substitute for the bread and circuses of cookery programmes, dancing programmes, even sport on the television.

"I'm not sure." He shook his head sadly. "Of course, I've had detailed intelligence gathered but it's very inconclusive. She was very well supported by Archbishop Odo, I do know that, but when I questioned him, he told me that Ms Astley was very much a political animal. Indeed, he had supported her candidature for that reason alone. I had the impression that Odo saw her as his opposite number in a sense. She was tasked with a political reformation whilst he was tasked with a spiritual, religious style of reformation. I'm sure that is how he sees matters, Miss Pendragon."

"But how do you see matters?" she said, looking at him directly and steadily.

"Well, I have no intention of playing Henry VIII to Odo's Thomas Cromwell if that's what you think! No, I agree with the old chap actually. He's right; we have replaced the adoration of statues and relics with the adoration of a king or a queen.

"Humanity should not bow down before false gods, whether made of plaster or made of flesh. The problem is that man hasn't yet sufficiently evolved to be able to throw off his false gods. Whether you worship a football team, a famous actor, a favourite food, a king or a queen – it's all the same. It's utterly unreal. But it does serve an important purpose. It makes people feel that they belong. That they're not alone."

Ceris pondered what he had said. She was both surprised at his candour and impressed by his openness. A still small voice told her to be careful, though, as she opened up her cell phone to retrieve the incoming text.

"But what do you honestly believe, sir? My own opinion is irrelevant, as you know. My job is to make sure that you have all the access and security you need to facilitate this operation. Though I really would appreciate any insights you may have, sir, as I must admit I remain a little confused with the ways events are unfolding."

King Alfred looked at her steadily. He was wondering if she had been authorised to quiz him as to his views. Perhaps they were hoping he would say something incriminating? He shook the thought away. He was becoming paranoid. Old Odo had told him that it was truth they were after, not agendas. He believed him. The man had no axe to grind, even if he was convinced that this Bailey character had found all the answers needed. Even though the cauldron itself remained elusively out of reach. He took a moment to consider her question and offered her a thin, watery smile.

"My dear Miss Pendragon. As you know, I briefly, very briefly I may add, had the Sacred Cauldron of Bran in my possession before it disappeared. We made a copy of course, but it was just that, a replica, though handcrafted and finely wrought by master craftsmen. Sadly, it disintegrated, as did other attempts to replicate the artefact.

"I studied the original diligently. It was in my possession for two weeks before it disappeared. I made copious notes, drew various diagrams, measured each angle and referred to several ancient documents written in old Celtic, or Brythonic, as well as Latin, Greek and Norman French.

"One design on the interior of the artefact was repeated many times. It was unusual, in that it was not of Celtic origin. All the design features on such a work of art are symbolic, you see. All the designs were typically Brythonic: swirls, images of nature, berries, flowers, trees, mountains and water.

"Did you know that there are no straight lines in nature? Just so. There were no straight lines in either the construction or the design content of the cauldron. Even its handle was of finely wrought silver, plaited to look like a creeping vine.

"Except, and this is what is of huge interest to me, on its interior, delicately engraved on the inner rim, the design features sharply changed. The contrast was startling, Miss Pendragon, because here there were no curved lines, no swirls of Celtic knots, no bunches of curved berries. Straight lines. In the shape of pyramids, obelisks and rectangular mazes. Each one punctuated with the hieroglyph of Thoth, an ibis sitting on a perch. Thoth is the god of wisdom, my dear, and the god of writing in the Egyptian pantheon."

He paused to take another delicate sip of his Earl Grey. Ceris was transfixed. He smiled indulgently at her.

"What I'm hoping to find on this little trip, my dear, is something I believe I decoded from my study of the cauldron. If the design is in fact a true representation of their ancient belief system, as I believe it is, then those symbols give us a map of sorts. I have an idea that if I am correct, if my research is correct, we could find out where the Druids came from and why they came to our shores thousands of years ago.

"It is my understanding that if we can find a connection, however small, that connection is here."

He paused and looked directly at her. "Tell me," he said quietly. "You were the one who recognised the painting in old Farndon's apartment weren't you?"

Ceris nodded. "Yes, I thought it odd that such a fine piece of art work should be hung in an area of the apartment that no-one would notice. There was something almost furtive about its location."

He pursed his lips, staring for a moment into space as he pondered her explanation. "Do you know what happened to it?" he asked carefully.

"Oh yes, it's common knowledge, I believe. A senior expert at the Royal Academy discovered an under-painting, pre-dating the landscape itself. Evidently, there was a map, finely drawn, at the foot of the under-painting. Which is why we're here." She frowned slightly, wondering why he had asked her. To her knowledge, he had received the same briefing as she had prior to arriving in Cairo. "Haven't you been told all of this, sir?" she asked, a little troubled.

"Yes, yes of course, Miss Pendragon. I'm just a little unsure of what, exactly, you've been told. You see, the markings on the map in the under-painting show a series of lines that look remarkably like the course of the River Nile. Now we know that no one had charted the course of that great river in the 1600's, which was when the under-painting was completed.

"The map also shows the hill on which Dinas Bran Castle is located as having a pyramidal structure. Something that had been noted in 10th Century commentaries retrieved from Glastonbury during the Reformation and taken to Windsor Castle for safekeeping.

"What is unclear, however…" He paused and tapped his fingers on the ornate coffee table. "What is particularly unclear, Miss Pendragon, is the connection. And there is a connection I'm convinced of it.

"If you look at the course of the River Dee, which runs through the Vale of Llangollen where Dinas Bran Castle dominates the highest hilltop, you will see certain similarities with a section of the Nile as it would have flowed four thousand years ago, when the river flowed past the Giza Plateau.

"Several studies have shown us that the course of the river in those days flowed in a similar arc to the Dee. Indeed, we have papers in the Windsor archives that record Sir Walter Raleigh travelling by ship to Alexandria, making his way to Giza, where he not only consulted the adepts, but drew a map of the plateau that records this fact.

"On his return to the London court, he went to see his great friend the alchemist John Dee and consulted his great library in Mortlake. John Dee was born in Wales, indeed his surname is the same as the river itself. In his library he had many old early map scrolls. Raleigh and Dee found a connection. The flow of the River Dee below Castle Dinas Bran was a mirror image of the flow of the River Nile at Giza."

Ceris remained transfixed as she fought down an overwhelming sense of foreboding. If what he was saying was true, then Robert didn't have the full story. Indeed, how could he? The missing cauldron, this new information about the map, the connections the monarch was making … she couldn't think clearly any more.

Remembering the cell phone still resting in her hand, she glanced at the text sitting there, waiting to be read. One thought still puzzled her but there was no time now to ask him about it. Why and how did the cauldron disappear? And had it truly disappeared? She was not convinced that it had. She was not convinced that an inanimate object could, of its own volition, relocate itself. That was just too weird. Yet this assignment was becoming all too weird. She wished Commander Taft were here. He would know what to do.

"Are you ready, sir?" she asked, refocusing gradually. He nodded absently as she led the way to the waiting car. Six security agents monitored their exit from the hotel, talking all the while into their cuffs as two other blacked-out SUV's screeched to a halt, one in front, one behind their vehicle.

Their doors opened to a blast of ice-cold air-conditioning. Ceris hastily arranged her pashmina around her thin shoulders while King Alfred blew his nose delicately into a snowy white handkerchief embossed with his royal crest. He raised his eyebrows playfully. He was very keen to get going, she thought.

The plateau was eerie. A light wind rippled against the folds of her pashmina as she waited for King Alfred to carefully disembark from the blacked-out SUV. Her heart flipped and her throat dried as she saw the magnificent monolith: stark, forbidding, magnificent, set against a backdrop of ice-white stars. She could see the out-of-focus arc of the Milky Way rising high above. The soft breeze caressed her hair as unbidden, tears welled up in her eyes. She sniffed and cleared her throat as a feeling of utter terror swept over her.

"What is it?" the King asked her.

"I don't know, sir," she replied honestly. "I don't know. I feel totally overwhelmed. It's as if - "

"It's as if you've come home?" he said kindly.

She didn't answer him. She steeled herself as they entered through the jagged gash of an entrance. This was nothing like coming home.

Two security agents followed them, one of them switching on the flickering electric light, the other carrying an LED torch, its brightness throwing a stark white light into the smooth-stoned interior. Carefully, they climbed the steep grand gallery, noting the strange notches and grooves evenly carved along each vertical side.

"Strange, isn't it?" he asked. "These grooves either side. They look as if they were installed to carry some sort of mechanism. Though what, exactly, no one could say. Another mystery. It's a long climb, my dear. One has to pace oneself."

The long, narrow gallery sloped upwards as they climbed slowly up to the centre of the pyramid. Its unusual starkness, lack of embellishment, was strangely puritanical in a land where decoration, colour, cartouche and hieroglyphs were representative of a lost yet dazzlingly evocative world.

"Careful, there's a very steep step just ahead. You have to climb rather than step over it, Ms Pendragon. Here, let me help you."

Ceris allowed herself a small smile as she practically leapt over the huge, deep slab of stone. Her body had recently engaged in far more strenuous activities. The King was suitably impressed as he struggled to gain purchase. She kneeled down, grabbed his arm and helped him to haul himself up.

Sweeping the grey dust off her pants, she followed him. The two security guards reluctantly followed behind, both sweating from the exertion, though, strangely, the heat inside always maintained the same temperature whether night or day.

"Almost there." He breathed heavily and Ceris was alarmed. His face was red, sweat beading on his temples, his breath ragged, coming in short sharp gasps. He crept into the low entrance chamber, coughing and spluttering as he heaved himself up from the floor and staggered like a drunken man, his hands and arms flailing against the flickering beam of her torch. She noticed a tiny tattoo on the exposed portion of his wrist, protruding from his pristine white shirt. It was a small picture of a raven. She knitted her brows, puzzled as he lurched to one side. As if in slow motion, he was slumping to the hard stone floor.

"Sir!" she shouted. One of the guards rushed forward, catching the King just before he collapsed into the swirling dust. He was pointing toward the jagged-edged sarcophagus, his voice pleading with her as she held his hand to soothe him.

"Put me in the coffer," he begged, his eyes beginning to roll back in his head. "At once, Miss Pendragon. You have to put me in the coffer. Please, please." His head rolled to one side.

She nodded to both guards. "Take no notice," she said. "Here, let's get you in the recovery position. You're unwell, sir. We have to get you an ambulance. Do it! Do it now!"

A cold silence enveloped them as, carefully, the security detail helped her to roll him into the correct position beside the ragged-edged coffer. Ceris' watch banged on the granite object setting off a tonal sound that reverberated throughout the chamber. She noticed that it was F sharp. The sound was F sharp! Strangely, it both comforted and chilled her in equal measure.

He wasn't moving. They should get him out, to a hospital. She scrabbled in her pocket for her cell phone. The security guards stared at her, waiting for instructions, immobile. Her phone didn't work. Neither did the guards'. There was something in this place that appeared to block all signals. Still the tonal F sharp reverberated, rising until it filled the entire structure like the sound of a massive bell.

"One of you call an ambulance." She shouted to be heard. "Go, now, get some help, I don't think he's breathing." She knelt, leaning close to his thin chest. Hearing his shallow breath she crouched closer. "Yes, he is breathing. Wait, he's trying to say something."

"The raven," he whispered. "Help me. We must go there."

"You're going to the hospital, sir. Never mind about a silly bird."

She clambered nimbly to her feet as he slowly lost consciousness, his face waxen, his thin voice mumbling something incomprehensible about how the raven was the ibis and the ibis the raven.

Ceris glanced quickly at the security guards. "He's rambling," she shouted. "He's had a nasty shock. He's just a bit out of it. Take no notice. Come, sir, we have to get you to a hospital. Get him down to the entrance between you. I think you'll have to carry him."

They did as instructed, half-carrying, half-dragging him through the narrow aperture and down the great step into the grand gallery. Ceris paused, scanning the chamber for any clue as to what it all meant, the sound of F sharp gradually receding as it echoed down the passageways.

She swept her torch in a wide arc over the flat-topped roof. Two of the ceiling stones looked cracked. She shivered. Nothing. She swept her torch up once again. What was that? Carefully, she pointed the beam of her torch to a discoloured patch of stone on the ceiling. Taking out her cell phone, she selected the photo option and clicked. Spinning around, she heard the sound of retreating footsteps. Who was it? The security detail were, by now, almost by the entrance door. Like lightning, she scrambled through the narrow aperture and back into the area of the great step with its access to both the Grand Gallery and the means of escape.

The strident wail of a siren further assaulted her ringing ears as an emergency vehicle in the distance screeched up the incline to the stony plateau outside.

CHAPTER 19

"Why am I here?" Lord Crispin Farndon was not amused. Indeed, he was positively snarling at the young police officer assigned to mind him in Old Scotland Yard. "I was told I would be going to Glastonbury," he sniffed. "For training. I'm one of the elite, don't you know? Top ten per cent."

"Indeed, sir," Constable Almansari agreed politely. "If you'll just wait a moment. He should be with you in a minute."

Farndon scowled at the young policeman who seemed totally nonplussed by the experience. He stood guard patiently by the peeling green-painted door. When the door opened Commander Taft entered, briskly nodding to the young constable to go and take a break. He slid his elegant frame into the standard issue blue polyester chair and opened a buff coloured folder.

"Why am I here, Commander?" the peer seethed. "Why have you brought me to this god-forsaken place? I was told – you told me – that I was to be sent to Glastonbury. I was quite looking forward to seeing His Majesty and Prince John after I'd got over the initial shock. And I know they were looking forward to seeing me." He pouted his mouth like a petulant child.

"Ah yes." Commander Taft raised his eyebrows. "That was before we discovered the paintings in your apartment. Several of which belonged to National Trust properties. We have witness statements from the Berwyn area naming you as the recipient. Stolen to order it appears." He looked steadily at the peer before continuing. "I'm particularly interested in one painting. A landscape, 17th Century I believe, of Castle Dinas Bran. Last seen in the Marquis of Anglesey's collection twelve years ago when it was lent for exhibition to the National Gallery. Can you tell me how and when and, more particularly, why you acquired it?

"It's no use blustering your way through this, either. We have all the evidence we need to convict you on nine charges of receiving stolen goods, bribery and corruption, with a possible case of fraud and money laundering pending further enquiries. You're looking at ten years in prison."

Lord Farndon blanched. "You can't do that," he shouted.

"I can actually," Taft replied calmly. "And I will. We have evidence. Hard evidence. We've retrieved the paintings, interviewed the thieves, and run a paper trail, which culminated directly at your door. There's nothing more to be said. It's done." Taft slowly turned the pages inside the buff folder as he waited.

"Ten years?" the peer croaked.

"Minimum," Taft replied. "And it's no use asking for a solicitor. You're about to be charged under Defence of the Realm legislation. Anti-terrorism laws to be more precise. Habeas Corpus has been suspended in the Interregnum. But you knew that, didn't you?"

"What do you want from me?" Farndon asked, his voice unsteady as he weighed up his options. They seemed, at the moment, to be very limited indeed.

Commander Taft narrowed his eyes. His handsome face was stony, devoid of any emotion at all. "I want to know who put you up to it. I want to know who the prime mover in all this is. It's not you and it's not that cohort of yours in the Berwyn Mountains. It has to be someone with a deep knowledge of symbolism, history. Someone that you're beholden to for whatever reason. We found a reference in your apartment to someone called Aristobulus. Tell me who this person is."

"I don't know, Commander," the peer said calmly. "Truly, I don't know. I acquired the paintings, had them x-rayed, and he sent me notes like the one you saw wrapped up in brown parcel paper. There was only one that he wanted and I was told to keep it for him. Someone would collect it, someone called Benedictus. I was expecting him tonight."

Commander Taft rushed to the door, barking into the corridor. "Get a surveillance team out to Farndon's place now! Code One. Get going!" he roared.

The peer shook his head and laughed. "You really have no idea, Commander, do you? This isn't about you, or me even. This is about moving things in a proper direction. Away from the nonsense fermented by that dreadful Astley woman and her cheerleaders. It's about challenging that decrepit old pagan Odo with his ridiculous views on community and country. This land was made great through my people, Commander Taft, not by left wing, slap-happy neo-hippies like that current shower inhabiting Downing Street and Canterbury."

The peer shook his head as he folded his arms defensively.

Taft watched him closely. "Then you give me no option, sir," he said sadly. He buzzed for Constable Almansari to re-enter the room. "Take him down," the Commander instructed the young policeman wearily. "Book him in the cells for another twenty-four hours. I'll see him again tomorrow."

The young constable silently ushered Farndon out of the bare grey interview room. Commander Taft sat for a moment gathering his thoughts, trying to piece the parts of the puzzle he had into some sort of order. He decided that he needed to speak to Steve Waterman. There was something odd. It was not linking together.

Waterman knew the background to the thefts; indeed, he had found the connection between Farndon and the King's brother, Prince John. Perhaps he needed to interrogate the brother further. Something's not quite right here he decided as he scrolled down his cell phone to find Waterman's number in the contacts box.

"Sir." Constable Almansari breathlessly re-entered the interview room. "Lord Farndon wants to speak with you. He says he'll tell you everything if you can guarantee an amnesty. He's terrified of going to prison from what he's just told me. He's convinced he'd be murdered within a week if he were sent to a high security unit. And I told him it's very likely that's where he would end up. Hope I'm not out of order telling him that sir ... but he says he wants assurances before he speaks with you. In writing."

"Tell him I can give him those assurances, Almansari. Tell him I have a document here that he can sign, that I will sign to that effect. Tell him he's doing the right thing, constable. Give me fifteen minutes, then bring him back here."

131

"Waterman?" Commander Taft paused, listening to the background noise in the manor house kitchen. He could hear the domestic sounds of a washing machine entering its rinse cycle, the sizzle of something cooking on a hob nearby.

"One moment, Commander, let me switch off the noise here. Can't hear myself think!"

Steve Waterman deftly switched off the washing machine, turned off the halogen hob as the aroma of half-cooked sausages, bacon, eggs and beans drifted his way. He moved heavily to retrieve his cell phone lying on the large kitchen table, picked it up and wandered over to the steamed-up window, wiping it half clear. An uninterrupted view of fields and trees met his half-awake gaze as he searched the horizon for a glimpse of the elusive Branwen. He hadn't seen her for several days now. Where was she?

"Right, sir. How can I help, sir?" he asked, a note of concern in his deep cockney voice.

"I have Farndon in custody, Waterman. He's agreed to tell all. I plan to interview him in a few minutes but I want to know what you know regarding the Prince John connection. What conclusion did you come to? I've read your report, Waterman, thoroughly. It doesn't appear to make any other links though – apart from Farndon and the Berwyn mob. Is there anything I should know? There's no evidence of redaction from what I can see. Yet something doesn't add up. And I don't know what that something is. Not yet at least."

Steve Waterman thought carefully. The Berwyn gang had been rounded up a year ago, charged and sentenced, with a handful of stolen art works recovered from one of their isolated properties high up in the fir tree plantation that topped the ridge.

He had reluctantly questioned Branwen, he recalled. One of the works of art had been discovered wrapped in hessian potato sacks in a crumbling outbuilding next to an abandoned cottage that she had inherited from a distant relative. A great aunt, wise in the old ways she'd said, dreamily. She had laughed at him, telling him she had no interest in money or stupid paintings without life or energy. And he had believed her. He had wanted to believe her.

Perhaps that was the connection Commander Taft was looking for? He still felt reluctant, hesitant even, to mention it.

"Waterman?" Commander Taft was getting impatient. His head was hurting, he was overtired. A feeling of foreboding tugged at the outer edges of his consciousness as he heard Steve Waterman swallow.

"Can I get back to you, sir? I need a moment to think."

"Is there something you're not telling me, Waterman?" Commander Taft's voice was suspicious.

"I'll call you back, sir. There's something I need to check out first before I can give you an answer. Something that's only just occurred to me."

The line dissolved. Commander Taft was annoyed and not a little intrigued as his cell phone buzzed within a few seconds of Waterman hanging up. He looked at the screen, his sense of foreboding intensifying as he pressed the green icon slowly.

"Yes?" he said impatiently.

"Pendragon, sir," a faint voice announced over a line charged with static and something else. Something else entirely.

"Well? Haven't got all day, as well you know," he said grumpily, a note of hesitation in his normally clipped tone.

"Yes, sir. Very bad news to tell you, Commander." She paused for a moment, willing herself to find the correct words. Unable to put it off any longer she took a deep breath and said quietly, "I'm very sorry to have to tell you, Commander, that His Majesty is in intensive care. He had a massive stroke in the great pyramid. We managed to get him to the university hospital where they worked tirelessly on him for several hours. He's stabilised, but it doesn't look good. The prognosis is critical."

"Get to the Embassy," Commander Taft instructed her calmly. "I'm sending someone out to you on the next plane. Did he find what he was looking for?"

Ceris paused before answering, her voice muffled in the five second telephonic time delay. "I have his notes here, sir. I went straight to his hotel room as instructed.

"One of the notebooks has disappeared, Commander, and it looks like it's the one that he was talking about to Bailey after the meeting at Glastonbury. Security's interviewing the hotel staff as we speak."

"They won't find it," Taft responded tersely. "I'd wager it's long gone. I'll speak with the intelligence people at the embassy. Find out if they have an idea. I'm confident they will. This was a disaster just waiting to happen. Right, tell me what you know. And I mean everything, Pendragon."

CHAPTER 20

Branwen looked stunning. Her long brown curls were swept up in a French pleat, a handful of escaping wispy tendrils framing her perfectly oval face and startlingly blue eyes that looked almost violet in the white light of an African morning. She wore a red cotton dress, modest yet fashionable, skimming her slim petite frame and setting off her alabaster complexion to perfection. Languidly, she monitored the passing pedestrians as she sat at the pavement café in the ancient souk, Khan el Khalil, in the old part of Cairo.

It was people-watching heaven as tourists, some wearing shabby football shirts, some wearing smart linen or cotton outfits, whiled away their Friday afternoons to the sound of the call to prayer from the many mosques in the vicinity. She sipped her mint tea, avoiding the eyes of men who paused to stare at her with interest.

Taking a fine thin scarf from her leather shoulder bag, she carefully constructed a head covering, sat back and continued with her watching. Carelessly, she listened to the sound of an oud playing mournfully a street or two away.

She nodded to the waiter who hurried over. She gave him a ten-pound Egyptian note as he turned to pull out the chair for her guest. "Ceris," Branwen said politely.

"What do you want?" Ceris said sullenly.

"I will bring tea?" the waiter suggested helpfully.

"Tea would be good," Branwen agreed.

Ceris sat silently for a few moments staring at her hands, which were scratched and bruised from the events a few days earlier at Giza. Branwen noticed them, delved into her leather bag and extracted a small pot of something that smelled of arnica. "Rub it on every few hours," she advised, passing the pot over to Ceris. "The bruising will soon disappear." Ceris didn't move. The tea arrived. Both were silent.

"And you have authorisation?" Ceris finally asked after a silence that had become uncomfortable.

"I have it here," Branwen replied, taking out a brown A4 envelope, Government Issue, stamped and signed by the Ministry of Dissonance. "Sir Rufus himself has authorised it," Branwen said quietly. "Commander Taft isn't happy, I understand. He thinks you should have a free choice."

"As do I," Ceris replied icily, staring angrily into Branwen's darkening eyes.

"I accept that, Ceris," Branwen acknowledged with a tilt of her head. "Yet, if you would but hear me out, you will understand that we need you to do this. It's not dangerous. If anything, it will unlock a part of the so-called 'rubbish DNA' that scientists believe serves no purpose. It worked for Robert. It will work for you."

"I understand that, Branwen. I also understand that I have to comply. What I don't understand is why you all want me to do this. What purpose could it possibly serve? I am not an academic like Robert. I am not some sort of druidess like yourself. I am a Counter-terrorism officer in a branch of the service concerned with acts against the state. It doesn't make sense!" Ceris looked away, her shoulders slumping in a sign of defeat. Branwen leaned forward, forcing her to re-engage.

"Look, Ceris, all I need for now is your signature. The rest will follow. We're to return to Anglesey very soon and by this time next week the initiation will be over. There is nothing to fear. And as for it not making sense, what if I told you that you have been selected as Assistant Head of Dissonance? Sir Rufus himself has authorised your promotion. You're now two ranks below Commander Taft!"

Branwen passed the brown envelope over for Ceris to scrutinise its contents. She knitted her brows, scanning the papers with deep concentration before taking the biro offered and signing each one with a bold flourish.

"Thank you, Assistant Commander Pendragon." Branwen offered a tight-lipped smile. "It's perhaps not the best way of going about matters, but you will understand its necessity once you've experienced the initiation."

She looked directly at Ceris, noting the young woman's ambivalent expression, and took pity on her. "You see, Ceris, you have a history, a pedigree if you like. A very important pedigree that can be traced back to the 1st Century Common Era. Anno Domini if you prefer. It's all here."

Branwen extracted a travel-worn, dog-eared folder from her capacious shoulder bag and passed it over. "Take your time. Read it," she advised. "I'll be back in an hour, so, please, don't disappear." With that, she calmly walked away.

Ceris let her tea grow cold as she read the contents. Several genealogical pages stamped with the College of Heralds watermark swam before her eyes. A photocopied extract from a document of the first century marked Glastonbury Archive and a stapled translation recording land holdings, tithes, and lists of bondsmen, made little sense.

A deed of ownership of what appeared to be vast tracts of land in Norfolk attached to an old parchment map – both photocopies – with a translated note declaring that these proved ownership and thus inheritance, part of the settlement of someone named Arvadica.

Another document detailing how Arvadica, at the age of twelve, had been sent to Brittany to learn the art of war at the court of the Count of Brittany. Another telling a tale of high adventure, where, after escaping from the processional triumph in Rome, Arvadica had joined a force of five thousand fighters in Germania, defeating the Romans at the mouth of the Rhine. She escaped, returning to Glastonbury where she lived quietly, marrying a man much older than herself to ensure the bloodline continued. They had two daughters. His name was Bran.

She had escaped from Germany just as she had escaped from Rome. Arvadica was the sole surviving daughter of Queen Boudicca and, according to the College of Heralds, she was the ancestor of Ceris.

Ceris sat stock-still. All colour washed from her face as she processed the information silently. She turned to the final page in the folder and stared hard at another photocopy. It was of her blood group. 'AB-' it read. She had no idea of the significance.

Puzzled, she looked around the small outdoor cafe, noticing people sitting at their tables with iPhones, tablets, a small laptop in one case, all busily tapping away, heads down, oblivious to the noise, bustle, scents and smells of this most iconic place. She tapped her iPhone. Finding a web page with blood groups, she scrolled down and squinted in the bright sunshine to see another page pop up with blood group statistics in neat columns. Scrolling down, she found what she was looking for. 'AB- : 1% of the population' it said. Predominantly seen in the Basque country. Linked to the Tribe of Dan who journeyed to Spain.

Why would they go to Spain? she wondered. And who were the Tribe of Dan? It was all too much to take in, she thought. If she was a descendant of Boudicca, then who was Boudicca a descendant of? She remembered something Commander Taft had said about how the new history was shaking everything up. He didn't understand it. Neither, she admitted to herself, did she.

A wave of anger swept over her. Why had she closed her mind to everything outside of her work? She felt a strange sense of regret and a moment of absolute clarity followed. That was what had driven Robert so hard. Knowledge, understanding, questioning, making sense of a world that had other dimensions, not just the mundane, the repetitive, the logical, the procedural. He had wanted the inner life. She had wanted action. She understood, for a moment at least, why they were destined to be two sides of the very same coin.

Branwen returned laden with striped pink and blue plastic bags, a look of sheer delight on her serene features. "So very cheap!" she exclaimed. "Do you know, Ceris, I've enough roots and spices here to last for ten years."

Ceris raised an unimpressed eyebrow as the waiter hovered, waiting for instructions. Branwen waved him away imperiously as she motioned for Ceris to get up. She wanted to go and she wanted to go now.

Ceris couldn't help but reluctantly admire her. Although around the same age as she was, Branwen had an air about her that oozed unshakeable confidence.

She was the type of person, it seemed to Ceris, who couldn't understand objection or dissension; who ignored what she didn't find relevant and imposed her will because she felt she knew best. It was both frustrating and strangely endearing. She was beginning to see why Steve Waterman held her in such high esteem as she followed the petite young woman out of the open-air café.

"Explain to me, Branwen," Ceris said quietly. "Explain what I have to go through in this … initiation." She swallowed.

"Tonight, you will take the mistletoe. In seven days, the essence will activate. Nothing will happen until that point. When the first phase begins, we will take the boat to the island, the same one Robert took over a year ago now and, in 24 hours, it will be over. Nothing I say, nothing I explain can prepare you for what is to come but you must know that I will be with you, accompanying you on your journey. You will never be alone and nothing bad, nothing awful will happen.

"Your mind, your senses, your spirit and your knowledge of the sacred inside us all will be awakened. When that happens, the core of a person's being is foregrounded for the rest of his or her life.

"For me, it was in the healing arts, for that is where my spirit belongs. For Robert, it was in the druidic arts of learning, understanding and interpretation. He does not have the poetic or prophecy gifts although we had hoped very much that he would prove worthy in that sphere of knowledge. But there it is." She shrugged her shoulders as if it was of no matter.

"So, what do you hope, where do you hope my spirit lies, Branwen?" Ceris couldn't believe she was asking her this question, but she was.

"We believe you to be a true descendant of our last Queen." She bowed her head as if in obeisance. "We believe that your spirit will answer the call of the warrior. But we cannot be sure. Nothing, in this life, is certain, Ceris. We hope and we believe that you will prove worthy.

"Boudicca was a warrior of the first order. She led Britannia against the Romans, winning many battles, decimating several legions. Today, the war is different.

"It is a war of hearts, minds, spirit and soul. We must redeem the land, the people from its bastard inheritance, its focus on masculine power and control, and its reductive capacity to sneer at anything that doesn't celebrate nihilism in all its forms. We have to, if, as a people, we are to survive." She paused, hailing a battered white Nissan taxi as they exited the souk.

Climbing in, its suspension barely lifting off the floor, she instructed the driver to take them to Giza. "I want to see where you took that photograph," she said very quietly so that the taxi driver wouldn't hear.

Ceris looked out of the grubby window at scenes that had played out across that ancient city since time began. Narrow streets filled with people walking, talking, bartering, shopping, and squatting on pavements playing dice. Men in long white thobes, some wearing head coverings, others bare headed. Women, dressed head to foot in black abayas, some with facemasks made of leather, covering the lower face and nose.

Her head swam with half-formed questions and inarticulate fears. The afternoon haze of pollution was yellow as they screeched their way to the plateau. No air-conditioning in the taxi left Ceris feeling uncomfortably hot and sticky. She sighed, her thoughts unaccountably turning to Robert.

What was he doing now? Knowing him, with his head stuck firmly in a book or transcribing one of the thousands of scrolls, parchments and inventories piled high in that old wooden box she'd helped to bring to the island. She rubbed a damp tissue over her neck and forehead, feeling her light cotton blouse clinging to her back uncomfortably. She turned to Branwen, ready to comment on the heat, to find her perfectly composed companion fast asleep, not a bead of sweat to be seen, clutching her striped plastic bags filled to the brim with roots, spices and who knows what else.

CHAPTER *21*

"I want that notebook and I want it now!" Lord Crispin Farndon screamed in the guard's face. "I know he left it here and I know you've taken it. It was on him when he collapsed in the King's Chamber and it's very important!"

"500 Egyptian Pounds," the guard beamed through his startlingly white teeth. "And a bottle of Johnny Walkers."

Farndon relaxed. He could handle corruption, threats and bribes. He counted out 500, added in an extra twenty, telling the smiling Ali that he could buy two bottles at least with the extra money. Ali appeared to be satisfied as he delved into the vast pockets of his grubby dish dash to retrieve a small leather-bound notebook secured by a strip of thick red elastic to keep its innards intact.

"Where did you find it?" Farndon asked the beaming Ali.

"On the floor, next to the sarcophagus," he grinned. "The man he was very ill. He wanted to go and see the bird. He did not want to go to the hospital. The ambulance came and he was taken. Very ill man. Very sad. He die?"

"No," Farndon replied slowly. "He is very ill but he didn't die. He may recover, he may not. He is my friend." Farndon felt an emotion he didn't know he still had: sadness.

"Allah will protect," the friendly Ali advised sagely. "Have faith, Mr Farndon. All will be well. Who is he, your friend?"

"He is, or was, the King of England," Lord Farndon replied sadly. "You have heard what has happened in England?"

"Yes, yes," the eager Ali nodded. "Your country is very interesting to me, Mr Farndon. I would like to visit it one day. Get a visa and maybe a job. Earn enough money so that I can have a wife and a family. This is my dream."

"My friend believed that religious men from your country came to my country, many, many years ago. He believed that England became home to an Egyptian race of people who sailed to my country from yours, four thousand years ago."

"Yes, yes!" Ali nodded vigorously. "We have records that show this. On stela and on papyrus. I can show you. I will need money to show you."

Lord Farndon eyed his new friend up and down for a moment as both of them stopped and stared at the sight of two young women, mid-thirties, one with short fair hair cut in a straight fringed bob, the other, small, petite, with brown curls cascading down her elegant shoulders. They paused at the entrance of the Great Pyramid and handed over two striped plastic bags to the guard. Giving him a small tip for his trouble and a composed thank you, they both entered the vast monolith, disappearing into its depths.

Ali and Lord Farndon turned back to face each other. "Very beautiful ladies," Ali beamed appreciatively.

"Do you know them?" Farndon asked, immediately on the alert.

"Yes, yes! The taller one, with the fair hair, she was here the night your friend was taken ill. She called for the ambulance. I was on duty outside the pyramid as the secret service cars escorted your friend to the hospital. Very sad night." He shook his head mournfully.

"I need to know what they want, them coming back here … it's a bit odd," Lord Farndon muttered. "Follow me, Ali. I need to find out what those two British ladies want."

☥✝☥

Branwen appeared to float up the grand gallery, stopping at intervals to examine the stonework, the grooved indentations and briefly gasping in awe at the elongated archway leading to the great step.

"This is the entrance to the womb of the world," she whispered to Ceris. "Look, see the shape, the outline? This is a birth canal made of stone! I had suspected ... but now I know," she mumbled. Ceris looked askance at her, thinking how very odd her companion could be.

Not remotely interested in anything cultural, historical, or esoteric, Ceris focused on simply getting them into the King's Chamber. Once she had completed this task, she could look forward to an hour or two in the hotel gym, which had one of the new cross trainers she admired. She allowed the happy thought to momentarily distract her as she contemplated the pleasure she would feel after a hard workout by taking a quiet dip in the hotel pool. She paused her power walking while she waited for Branwen to hurry up. Turning to catch a glimpse of her companion down the long, steep shaft of the gallery, she noticed two men loitering at its foot. One was Egyptian wearing a dish dash that had once been white, the other she couldn't see clearly, his dark clothes blending into the gloomy light far down in the distance.

Branwen finally caught up with her, her eyes sparkling, cheeks pink from both exertion and excitement. "There were panels here," Branwen murmured. "You can see the grooves where they would have fixed them. Long, vertical panels. I have read of these. On these panels, the Ancient Ones wrote down an illustrated history of the world. The panels would be covered until the initiate was ready to emerge from the womb; to be reborn, then the covers would be taken away to reveal the sacred truths. This is such a privilege, Ceris," she beamed. "You have no idea how much I've longed to see this monument."

"See those two men behind, at the bottom of the gallery?" Ceris whispered.

"I see them," Branwen replied.

"I have a feeling they're watching us," Ceris murmured softly.

Branwen sniffed. "They are of no account. Come, show me where you took the photograph," she commanded.

†Ť†

"Well, what did she say?" Lord Farndon hissed. Ali shrugged his shoulders as his eyes swept the trickle of tourists leaving the Boat Museum. Farndon pressed another 100 Egyptian Pound note into his hand to be met with a wide, cheerful smile.

"She said it was a bird."

"What do you mean, a bird?" Farndon was becoming exasperated with his new friend, who seemed to take great delight in arranging meetings in very public places.

"Just that," he grinned, obviously enjoying the drama.

"Where was this bird?" Farndon held his temper in an effort to appear calm but he couldn't fool the hardened Egyptian, who could read people as if they were open books.

"Why is this so important?" Ali asked. "I am troubled by this. This is my country. Those are two beautiful ladies. You want to hurt these ladies?"

"No, no. Of course I don't want to hurt them. I don't want to hurt anyone, Ali. I just need to know what it is the tall one saw in the King's Chamber. She took a photograph. I know about that. What I want to know is what is in the photograph. It is very important, Ali. Very important. For me and for my country."

"You tell me it is important." Ali seemed to have grown six inches as he straightened his shoulders and lifted his dark stubbled chin. "You would have me give you the secrets of my country? This is an ancient land, Mr Crispin Farndon, a very ancient land. A land that has secret teachings that go back to a time before time itself was recorded and you want me to give you these secrets? Who are you to demand such things?"

Lord Farndon was totally bemused. He had no experience of dealing with men like Ali, a walking paradox of dodgy dealings and lofty idealism. His usual approach to any direct confrontation was bluster mixed with impeccable manners. That wouldn't serve him here, and he had the sense to acknowledge it. He scratched his thinning head and rubbed his aristocratic nose before finally admitting defeat.

"You're right, of course, Ali," he admitted. "Perhaps I am asking too much of you. I accept that. But, you see, my country is in a desperate state.

"We have this woman who used to be Prime Minister, but who now calls herself Lady Protector. For the past fifteen months she has gradually destroyed my country. Its people are frightened. No one is allowed out after nightfall. Travel is banned."

Ali looked at Farndon and raised an expressive eyebrow.

"I had to get a special dispensation to come here, Ali. Granted to me as my friend King Alfred was taken seriously ill."

Ali stared at the peer impassively.

"As I said, my country is disintegrating, Ali. All because this woman, this Lady Protector, this Angela Astley baggage, has decided that we need to revert back to a pre-Roman time in our history and re-introduce the Community Law, the Brythonic Law, the 'Ancient Law' as she calls it. It means that our world is, bit by bit, being turned upside down, Ali. It's a move backwards, not forwards. But she and her supporters can't see that, of course."

"And you want a revolution?" Ali asked calmly. "You want to put the old world, the world you had before, back in its place?"

"That's exactly what I want to do, Ali. Somehow, I have to find the means to discredit the prevailing order. It's as if everyone's become mesmerised by the new thinking. When it gets to the point that your own King is seriously thinking to abdicate, a line of succession going back millennia, you have to admit that something is radically wrong."

He paused and looked directly at the young Egyptian. "This is why I need to know what she saw in the King's Chamber. If I can discredit it, find a rational explanation, disprove any of the mad theories they're bound to come up with to ensnare the people of my country, then you will be doing me a huge service, Ali. I hope you understand what I'm up against."

Ali looked off into the distance as if contemplating his next words. "There's someone you need to talk to, mister," he said calmly, as a tall, well-dressed man walked up, stopped and shook Ali's hand warmly.

Lord Farndon froze as Commander Taft nodded politely, saying, "We meet again. Shall we walk?"

Ali left them walking back toward the Great Pyramid. He didn't envy old Farndon. Taft was in fine fettle and looked as if he was about to give him a grilling that he knew, having been on the end of one himself some time ago, would be excruciating.

But Taft had every right, Ali thought. Farndon had been allowed to come in place of Prince John who, rumour had it, had yet to recover from touching the cauldron over twelve months ago. Indeed, rumour also had it that he was being permanently medicated for anxiety and insomnia. And it was a well-known fact that Farndon had contacts. The sort of contacts that could make things happen. "Let him loose," Sir Rufus had advised.

He would wait a moment, as instructed, and then change into his business suit before heading back to the embassy.

32, slight of build with model looks and an air of expectation about him, Ali Alalladin was no stranger to the esoteric or to secret intelligence. He was also an enthusiastic member of the Heliopolis Amateur Dramatic Society. It was good to practise his thespian skills from time to time, and he had enjoyed his bit part in the unfolding drama. He sighed and lit a Davidoff, his second of the day. The head rush left him feeling mildly dizzy. He had a report to write, he reminded himself, but that could wait until this evening. There was no immediate deadline to meet.

He wondered what Taft would do with His Lordship. Would he try and turn him?

No, unlikely. If anything, there was considerable sympathy for Farndon's viewpoint as mutterings across the Channel and more recently in Washington had shown. Best to contain the old bugger he thought. He could prove to be useful in the future. Contingency Planning. It was an art form in the secret services and Ali knew more than most that Taft and his boss Sir Rufus were masters of that particular game.

It was time to make a move. He glanced around the plateau, tourists still milling about although not as many as earlier. Carelessly, he headed over to the watchman's hut on the far side of the plateau, which overlooked a side garden belonging to the Mena House Hotel.

The air was cooling down after the thumping heat of the late summer day and, soon, night would fall like a thick dark blanket overlaid with gossamer stars.

As he walked, he could hear music, the passionate, joyful strains of *Habibi* sung by a voice he didn't recognise coming from a tinny transistor radio in one of the multi-storeyed apartment blocks on the edge of the plateau. He could smell cooking: rice flavoured with saffron, minted lamb, fried food. His stomach began to rumble as he sniffed the air once more, salivating at the thought of a decent meal. He hadn't eaten all day. "No matter," he thought, climbing the steep bank to the watchman's hut. There were packets of biscuits, fruit and chocolate in the rusty old fridge. It would do.

†‡†

Branwen stood at the window of Ceris' hotel room, looking out onto a thin strip of garden, its velvet grass cool and inviting in the hot, sticky oppression of the late afternoon. Half hidden behind the fussy drapes, she watched, cat-like, as Ali unlocked the grey metal door of the watchman's hut and silently let himself in. Ceris was busy honing her fitness on some cross trainer that she had enthused about on the short walk from the plateau to the hotel earlier, Branwen mused. She had time enough if she was quick.

Slipping on a pair of open-toed flats, she nimbly climbed down from the first floor balcony, landing neatly on a gravelled patch of flowerbed below. She edged toward the perimeter fence, entering a small gap used as a short cut by hotel personnel.

Climbing the steep incline leading directly to the plateau, the dusty track to the watchman's hut wound up and around in a spiral formation. The ground was hard, chalk white in places that she recognised as limestone, the soft, porous rock that the plateau was built upon. Finally, she heaved herself up the last steep incline, pulled the heavy grey metal door ajar and entered the grubby small square room furnished with a rusting metal fridge in one corner and a sagging discoloured armchair in another.

"Well?" she challenged. "Do you have it, Ali?"

Ali offered her an apple from a paper bag resting on his lap. "Do I have what, Branwen?" he grinned, his handsome face alight at the sight of her.

She threw him a look of contempt. "Don't play games with me! You know exactly what I mean."

"Is it tonight?" he asked, suddenly serious.

"It begins tonight, yes," she responded, her eyes narrowing as she flicked her long brown curls in a gesture of disapproval at his temerity.

He eased himself out of the rapidly disintegrating old chair, attempted to sweep it clean in a gallant, one-handed gesture and invited her to sit. She regally marched over, emitting a defiant, proud, uncompromising air as she archly raised her left hand, swinging it strongly against the right hand side of Ali's shocked and surprised face. The hard slap brought tears to his eyes as he quickly swallowed his pride and squeezed back the moisture threatening to escape. She pushed him, with one hand flat against his muscular chest so that he fell hard into the soft sagging chair.

"It's over there," he said, avoiding her blazing eyes and pointing toward the slim metal floor-length locker standing next to the dilapidated fridge, now humming noisily as if in protest at what it had just witnessed. Striding over without a word, she opened its loose flapping door with one finger and extracted an object wrapped in a gaudy red cloth, a cheap fabric, unpleasant to the touch, smelling of dust and sand and ambergris. Tucking it under her arm she turned to Ali, her haughty look speaking volumes.

"Never, ever, think that you can speak to me with disdain," she spat. "You know who I am. You and your ancestors swore an oath many, many years ago and that oath cannot be broken. You see me as just another young woman. Someone to play with. Someone to flirt with. I am none of these things and you would do well to remember that. I will not issue threats, nor will I seek vengeance for so rude an attitude from one sworn to defend and obey without question. But I will, if pressed, make sure that it is known that your clan, your family, has insulted the High Priestess of Prydain. That could prove fatal, Ali."

CHAPTER 22

Commander Taft disliked hospitals with an intensity that surprised him each time he had to venture into one. Not that he was a frequent visitor to medical facilities. He enjoyed robust good health though of late he had become fleetingly aware that his energy levels were not as they had been ten years ago. He found that he really did need his eight hours each night and that burning the candle at both ends was something best left to those younger, those more inclined to get by on just a few hours. With age came experience. Yet hospitals, he admitted to himself, still left him trying to stem the sense of panic residing just below the surface.

The King was sitting up in bed. His small, slight physique outlined beneath a white starched sheet folded over a pale green comforter. He was holding a hard-backed book with his good hand, the other lay stiffly to his side. He looked startled as Taft pulled up a straight-backed chair and folded his tall body into its rigid structure. He looked out of place, as if this was the last place on earth he wanted to be.

"Good evening, sir." Taft's tone was abrupt. "I'd like you to explain this." Reaching into his inside jacket pocket he removed, in one swift gesture, a small black leather-covered notebook, its red elastic strap smudged with traces of dirt and dust. They looked hard at each other. Taft clenched his jaw as the aroma of pine disinfectant wafted in from the corridor outside.

The King smiled weakly. "So much trouble I've put everyone to," he whispered. "So much still left to understand. I feel very stupid, Commander. Very stupid indeed."

Taft shifted his rigid frame in the straight-backed chair, noting the pallor on the King's thin features. The doctor had advised that he needed to stay for further tests over the next few days then a gradual rehabilitation programme could be implemented once he was home in his own country.

"Tell me what happened," Taft said firmly. "Why the Great Pyramid?"

"Is Lord Farndon here?" the King mumbled. "He came to see me earlier today. Something about my brother? Where is John? Farndon said something about him being held in psychiatric care? Is this true?"

"Prince John is still in Glastonbury and, yes, it appears he has suffered extreme anxiety since you last saw him. But you mustn't concern yourself, sir. He is receiving the best of care and Archbishop Odo is making sure that he has everything he needs. As for Lord Farndon, we've had some serious misgivings regarding his recent interactions. No matter. He's here, under supervision at the embassy.

"They're flying him home later today, under guard. He'll be escorted back with two of their finest. I've arranged for one of my men to interrogate him once he's on British soil. He's a slippery character and it's incredibly frustrating. We can't get to the bottom of it with him. He's hiding something, yet every enquiry we've made leads to a dead end. Either he, or someone very powerful, is watching his back, and whoever that person is, they have unlimited resources at their disposal. We have a handful of leads not yet explored so I'm hopeful.

"Now, tell me, what's the connection here? Why Egypt? And why, specifically, the Great Pyramid? Your notebook shows particular interest in the sarcophagus and I need you to explain why that is."

The King closed his eyes wearily as he exhaled a tired sigh. He slowly opened small cloudy orbs that seemed to Taft to be full of knowledge and hard-won wisdom. The King watched silently as Commander Taft shifted his weight on the hard chair.

"That's something I will come to, but you need to understand context, Commander. Context is everything when dealing with artefacts, manuscripts, even secondary sources from the pre-antiquity era. If you look back to the relevant primary sources," he began, "you will find references, in both Greek and Roman records earlier than 45 BC, to the fact that some of the finest universities existed in Celtic lands.

"One account records sixty universities catering for up to 60,000 students across the known Celtic world. Ancient Britain catered for one third of that population. There were two particularly important places of learning, the Oxford and Cambridge of their day. One was situated in Bangor on Dee on what is now the border between England and Wales and the other on Ynys Mon, or Anglesey.

"Both were Druidic Colleges where initiates were selected by oral competition, the root incidentally for present day viva voce examinations in universities of the modern era.

"There were others, of course. Most notably in Ireland. Founded by the great wave of exiles from both Syria and what we know as Egypt today.

"The daughter of a pharaoh fleeing the insurgencies of Upper Egypt after the death of her father brought the disintegrating court, complete with its scribes, master builders, craftsmen and women and most importantly, its priests, to the Emerald Isle.

"They also brought the *Book of Thoth* as transcribed by Hermes Trismegistus. This became known as *The Emerald Tablet*, because of its associations with Ireland. As an aside, legend has it that the original *Book of Thoth* that *The Emerald Tablet* is based upon, resides in a secret place within the Great Pyramid."

His thin face began to look more animated as some colour entered his cheeks. In his small cloudy eyes the hint of a sparkle was beginning to form. Taft suppressed a smile. The King was well known for only engaging on any meaningful level when on the subject of religious and philosophical belief systems. His studies of ancient religions had earned him both an international reputation and the despair of his household and staff. He was utterly disinterested in anything else.

"And so we know, from a variety of sources, that several thriving communities of learned men and women -"

"Women?" Commander Taft said, shocked. "Were women involved in education? I always assumed that it was only in recent times that they were allowed ..." He broke off, embarrassed at how sexist his comments made him sound.

The King looked delighted, more colour entering his pale cheeks, eyes now sparkling at the chance of a debate. "Ah, Commander. I see you're shocked. Would it shock you further to know that women were treated like goddesses? They were revered, Commander, totally revered. So much so, that *Meritaten*, on arrival in Ireland, was given a new name, as was the custom of the age. Henceforth, she was known as *Scota* and she became the tribal chief, the new *Pharaoh* if you like, of what scholars call *The Other Exodus*.

"They believed that a new life had to have a new name. A bit like a rebirth if you see what I mean. Well, after some rest and recuperation, *Meritaten/Scota*, her husband *Gaythelos*, and the rest of her court travelled across the water to Scotland. Named for *Scota*, it was a scarcely populated land that turned out to be easy to subdue with the technology that they had brought.

"Incidentally, did you know that the bagpipes originated in Egypt? As did the kilt. In fact, there are many depictions illustrated on stela, tomb walls in the Valley of the Kings and on pylons and obelisks, showing men wearing the kilt and playing an early iteration of the bagpipes. Fascinating, isn't it?

"Anyway, to continue. The historian *Manetheo*, writing in 300 BC tells us also that *Meritaten/Scota's* father was *Cingris*, a contemporary of Moses. Others say that he took a new name, the name Akhenaten. We know from written sources that it was from their capital of Memphis, near present day Cairo, that the priestly class fled. The royal party sailed first to Spain, then to Ireland and finally to Scotland, the priestly class becoming what we know of as the druids of Celtic history. Their territory spanned the west of Britain, from Scotland, through Lancashire, down to Wales and Cornwall.

"Why did they flee Egypt? It's complicated and to explain thoroughly you would need to have some background in the subject. However, in layperson's terms, it comes down to the age-old matter of belief and of a rising power-base using its resources to dominate and destroy the indigenous culture. Sound familiar?

"Let me tell you why. You see, it was common knowledge that the great Celtic Colleges, particularly those in Dublin, Edinburgh, Bangor and Anglesey could trace their founding to the great exodus from Egypt. There were a group of people who didn't want to follow Moses to his version of the Promised Land. They believed in a different theology based on the power of the transcendent, the power of nature and the belief that this world was a school for learning. Until the lessons were learned, the soul, or the Ka as they called it, would keep returning."

"They believed in reincarnation?" Taft asked, incredulously.

"They believed in reincarnation," King Alfred repeated, his face becoming animated as he continued. "The tribes moving off to the Promised Land believed in the Abrahamic God, the god of retribution, whereas the Druidic Tribe of Dan, or the *Tuatha De Danaan*, believed in reincarnation. They brought four magical treasures with them to Ireland. The Dagda Cauldron, The Spear of Lugh, The Stone of Fai and The Sword of Light."

"The Dagda Cauldron?" Taft was visibly astonished at this disclosure. "Is this the same ..."

King Alfred looked at a point in the distance as his eyes grew misty with thought. "Yes, Commander, it is the cauldron, the very same. It was added to, on arrival in Wales, as was the custom. You see, these artefacts acted as both magical instruments and historical documents. Bran as Arch Druid re-named it, as was the tradition, adding druidic embellishments particularly relevant to nature. Hence we see Celtic swirls, representations of fruit, trees, animals and, of course, the famous handle made from plaited silver twisted in the shape of mistletoe.

"All belief systems, Commander, are heirs of their ancestors. Druidism was the heir of the ancient pharaonic religion that manifested itself many, many, thousands of years ago. We are told by the so-called 'experts' that the pyramids are four thousand years old, are we not? Yet any geologist worth his or her salt will explain to you that both the pyramid and the sphinx show evidence of submersion in water. That water, Commander, can only have come from either a massive flood or the melting of the ice caps.

"However, to continue with your education. The schism created a massive vacuum in Egypt as the great and the good, tired of the increasingly despotic actions of its new Pharaoh, came to Prydain, or Britain, at the invitation of the Colleges. The Arch Druid himself had been trained in Giza, you see, and at Heliopolis.

"Prydain was revered by the ancients, Commander. Not that you'll find any of this in the official histories, of course. Most of this information was aggressively suppressed. But it is there, in the archives, most particularly the early archives, which tell of the Tribe of Dan sailing to Ireland.

"While some stayed and settled there, many more, including Scota, sailed on to found Scotland and play a massive role in the shaping of a nation that, at the time, was without borders.

"If you look closely at the shape of our island, what does it remind you of?"

Commander Taft looked blankly at him whilst trying to visualise. "A triangle?" he offered helplessly.

The King nodded encouragingly, waiting for Taft to make the next, obvious, connection.

"A pyramid!" he finally barked as the King slapped his good hand on his crisp white sheet.

"Exactly!" The King tried to smile, but one half of his face had suffered a grand mal, drooping noticeably, leaving his features distorted. Taft felt a wave of warmth toward him. He had the reputation of being a cold fish, disinterested in anything outside of his research, a loner who had avoided close relationships throughout his adult life. Still single, he had, it was said, heaved a sigh of relief at the social changes introduced by Astley.

"My assistant, Pendragon, mentioned something about a bird? A raven and an ibis as I recall. You were insisting that they had to be found. Do you recall any of this?" Taft looked keenly at his reaction, which was calm, measured even.

"Yes. I do recall, Commander. Although I've had a severe stroke, my memory is remarkably clear." Taft felt as if he'd been told off.

"There's a secret passage in the Great Pyramid, Taft. When the Tribe of Dan began their exodus, this entrance to a secret chamber was resealed, its marker removed and a new marker put in place that would reflect the new covenant, inscribed in a manner that would only be visible to the rightful heirs. The initiated, if you like."

"Is this true?" Commander Taft looked shocked. He had never heard of such a thing. Wasn't the history of the Great Pyramid thoroughly documented? How could there be anything left unknown about the monument?

The King looked amused. "What you have to understand, Commander, is that history is always written by the victors. It is their version of events that enters the collective. Through education, social policy and such-like, eventually morphing into a supra collective or culture.

"Our history – our real history – is very different, particularly the years spanning 500 BC to 500 AD. Indeed, by rights, my family should never have ruled had the real heirs to the kingdom had their collective story told."

He smoothed down his sheet with his good hand, momentarily revealing a tiny tattoo on the underside of his wrist in the shape of a bird in profile. Delicately executed, it was perfect in its proportions. Taft narrowed his eyes, registering the strange embellishment as the monarch settled himself on the pillows, a sigh escaping as he closed his eyes.

"I'm very tired, Commander," he said quietly. "You will have to excuse me."

Commander Taft sat there, unmoving, his mind racing with this new information and what it meant. He waited for a few minutes, his eyes never leaving the sleeping face of the monarch, hoping that the conversation would re-start once he had napped. It was obvious after a minute or two that he was sleeping heavily. Taft shifted his tall frame, rubbing his long legs to restore circulation. As he stood up stiffly, he realised that he had been sitting completely still for over an hour.

Closing the door quietly, Taft walked down the long, cream-painted corridor. The smell of antiseptic, disinfectant and that peculiar aroma of laundered sheets that permeated the very air of a hospital sent his faculties into panic mode. "Breathe," he muttered to himself, repeating the words like a mantra as he made his way toward the main door and exited into the blindingly hot early evening.

"Did you monitor the package?" he snapped at his driver.

"The package has been collected," the driver replied.

"Switch on the tracker," Taft barked, his eyes a steely grey in the half-light as the driver flicked a switch next to the satnav console in his Jaguar XF.

"You're late!" Commander Taft fumed as an immaculately suited and booted Ali Alalladin hopped into the front passenger seat, his face a picture of frozen mortification.

"Where did he go?" Commander Taft demanded.

"We dropped him at the airport, sir, as ordered. Security peeled away as instructed. He left, jumped into a taxi and was spotted heading back toward Giza. We have surveillance. We have it covered."

"I hope so, Alalladin." The security chief narrowed his steely eyes menacingly. "Because if this goes pear-shaped we're talking Armageddon. And don't think I'm exaggerating because I most certainly am not!"

"Indeed, sir," Ali acknowledged, gripping his right knee with both hands to stop it shaking.

CHAPTER 23

Steve Waterman locked up the isolated manor house, battling with his keys as a force five wind blasted the overhanging yew tree, knocking a branch into the upstairs window with a thunderous bang. He stopped, glancing up at the darkening roofline. It was all right, the glass was triple-glazed, and, anyway, he didn't have time to run back in and check any damage that may have occurred. He took a deep breath, suppressing the instinct to run back in and find out.

The wind was howling as he pulled his wax jacket closer, zipping it up firmly against the driving rain. His old wellington boots squelched in the puddles of mud rapidly forming in the pock-marked driveway, its uneven surface making him take extra care with his footing as he wrestled with the large wooden cross-bar gate, looping the circle of rope back over its post to secure it against the darkening elements.

He tramped down the high-hedged lane, hands shoved deep in pockets, a small torch throwing a thin beam of light on the narrow road ahead. He was almost there, another mile and then a left turn across wide-open fields.

Why they had to meet at the standing stones, he didn't know. He felt in his inside pocket for his security pass. It was curfew now. To be out and about and seen to be so could result in a swift internment in the detention facility nearby. He gripped it hard. Like a talisman, the small piece of hard ink and plastic was his get out of jail card should he need it tonight.

"Waterman?" A disembodied voice arose out of the darkness as he stumbled then recovered himself, feeling the outline of a car bumper against his leg.

"Robert?" Steve Waterman asked, a note of puzzlement in his deep cockney voice. "What are you doing here?"

"Waiting for you," Robert Bailey replied quietly. "Get in." Robert opened the door of his Mercedes A Class as Steve reached out to grab the passenger door handle.

"What's going on, Robert?" Steve asked carefully. There was a manic look in Bailey's eyes that Steve wasn't happy about at all.

"Why are you going to the standing stones, Steve?" Bailey fired at him. "Do you know what's there?"

"Look, Robert. I do know why, and, yes, I do know what's there. It's orders, that's all. And you shouldn't get involved."

"Orders? Whose orders?" Bailey shouted.

Steve Waterman pressed his mouth shut. He shouldn't be having this conversation.

"I know what's going on, Steve. It's Branwen, isn't it? She's got Ceris, hasn't she? Is it tonight? Are they going to do it tonight? I have to know, Steve! I have to try and stop it!"

"Why?" Steve Waterman turned on him. "Ceris has agreed to it. She is prepared for it. Who are you to say what she can and can't do? She is her own person, Robert. She can make her own decisions."

Robert Bailey slammed the car into gear, gunning the engine as the tyres screeched their way up the narrow lane, around a hairpin bend, up a steep hill and out onto the flat lands where a hint of grey sparkle in the distance revealed the hard edged boundaries of land and sky. He was heading for the standing stones.

Steve Waterman covered his face with his ham-like hand. This was not going to end well.

"Robert! Just stop. Stop! You can't barge in like this. You'll get arrested. This is madness, Robert. You have to stop this. Stop it now!"

Robert Bailey, his face a picture of focused determination, ignored him. As the Mercedes approached the rusted metal gate leading to the field of the standing stones, four security guards blocked the entrance. Bailey's Mercedes screeched to a halt. The four armed security guards surrounded the vehicle, RS 77's pointing ominously in their direction. Red laser lights choreographed a dreadful dance of death as the deadly beams criss-crossed each other, pointing all the while at the two occupants in the car.

Steve remained immobile. He knew from experience that to make a false move would probably result in any trigger-happy rookie blasting them into oblivion.

"Keep still," he hissed menacingly to Robert. "Don't move. Leave this to me."

Robert Bailey's hands gripped the steering wheel, his knuckles white in the glare from the red laser lights now fixed, one each, on their chests. Both doors were thrown open as in a single sweep both men were pulled to the ground, wrists locked behind with plastic tags as they were dragged and pushed through the open gate and into the silent field.

No one spoke. Laser beams continued to dance against the black of a moonless, starless sky. Robert crawled to his knees and tried to stand up, only to be kicked back into the muddy grass by a black-suited guard, his face obscured by a full-visored helmet.

Steve pulled himself up to his knees and whispered, "Just stay calm, Robert. Don't antagonise. Don't lose it, mate."

Robert Bailey growled something back but Steve couldn't make out what he had said. He was angry. Dangerously so.

"Untie him," a familiar disembodied voice announced as two guards sliced through Waterman's plastic restraint, pulling him to his feet. "Take him to the island. He's needed there. He should have been there twenty minutes ago."

Steve Waterman let out a gasp of relief as he was roughly frogmarched to the edge of the small lake just visible in the centre of the field. The standing stones surrounding it looked darkly ominous as his eyes adjusted to the low light. A half moon appeared fleetingly in the heavy darkness just as the mournful sound of bagpipes playing a haunting lament wafted dreamily over from the distant water.

☥☥☥

Robert Bailey heard the sonorous sound and held his breath.

So, there was a connection, he thought to himself, one that he'd sniffily dismissed as being outside the accepted canon of knowledge. He recalled that his initiation had involved the soaring music of the angelic harp. Why, then, the dissonant tones of the bagpipes for Ceris?

He forgot his simmering anger as he began to ask himself questions he'd avoided for fear of being seen as unacademic, unorthodox even. He realised, with a jolt of visceral recognition, that he had allowed his preconceived notions, his academic training, to discount some of the chronologies, some of the commentaries, some of the lesser histories penned by the Alexandrians rather than the more orthodox Romans. Why? Because it was establishment policy to do so. And he was an establishment man.

The King had been right. He shook his head, marvelling at his weakness when faced with the alternative history the monarch had presented him with. He had been right.

Yes, he had been intrigued when faced with those first century documents telling of an ancient migration four thousand years ago. First to Ireland ... had it really been called I-RA-LAND? It was possible, he surmised ... Hadn't Prydain morphed into Brydain and then into Britain? The etymologists had proven the latter unequivocally. It was possible! If so, then the music he could hear drifting across from the small lake made sense ... He had to get to the island. He had to see for himself. He closed his eyes, willing himself to find the inner power he knew he possessed but feared to explore.

What was the matter with him? Why was he constantly hiding behind his books, his position, the great Archbishop Odo? Always hiding himself away from others. Always immersed in translations, commentaries, manuscripts. Leading a life more reminiscent of an anchorite than a 21st Century full-blooded male.

Was he always destined to live in fear? Was he always destined to live a half-life hiding away in a world that couldn't hurt him? Couldn't abandon him because that world had passed and could never be again. A safe world. His world.

The thought exploded in his head like shooting stars as he let out a mighty roar, filling the field, the spaces between the standing stones, the lake, the island with an echoing thunderous force. A thin crack appeared in the heavy darkness. A fragrant light bathed him in shimmering purple, red, green and blue.

He rose to his feet. Four security guards surrounded him, rifles aimed at his head, chest, legs, and face. He stood still. Lifting his hands, he touched the wind as it caressed his face.

He heard the sound of birds scrabbling in their nests, he tasted salt and breathed in the pure island air before turning toward the sound of the bagpipes, their mournful, sorrowful tones filling every fibre of his being with a dawning acceptance.

He stood, rigid, as the owner of the disembodied voice gradually began to materialise in front of him. "Leave him!" it commanded. The security guards slowly moved to one side, allowing her through.

"You want to rescue her, don't you?" she said smoothly. "You want to stop it all. You think you can?" she laughed, a deep-throated, mocking laugh that left him feeling strangely detached.

"Take him!" she commanded. Guards surrounded him as he was bundled into a blacked-out SUV. He felt the prick of a needle in his neck as he slumped, unconscious, on the grey leather seat. She nodded to the guards, giving silent permission for them to take him to the containment facility. It was simple really; he could be charged with breaking the curfew and held for a week while they decided what to do with him.

Bev Jennings, newly appointed Foreign Secretary, flipped her iPhone open and answered the incoming call. "Yes, it's all under control. He came close to disrupting the ceremony but we managed to contain him. Tell me. How did you know he'd go off on one?"

"Oh, we've had several warning signs, Bev. Most recently he's been lording it over the teams of scholars. They're a feisty bunch – and didn't appreciate his high-handedness. It's a real pity, Bev ... but we can't afford arrogance and egos to get in the way. Wrong constructs lead to rotten cultures ... though how we're going to plug the gap I honestly don't know."

"Will you tell Odo, or shall I?" Bev Jennings sounded impatient, dismissive even.

Angela Astley frowned. "He's with me now, Bev. I'll tell him. What do you plan to do with Robert Bailey?"

Bev Jennings moved over to the rusted gate and leaned on it. She was tired, exhausted with the constant travelling up and down and across the country. On an almost daily basis it had seemed of late. Fire fighting dissidents hadn't been in the job description, she told herself ruefully. Neither had an interregnum. She was tired of it all.

Her promotion to Foreign Secretary had been a dream come true, she thought sadly. Except there was no foreign policy in this new administration. She was tasked with monitoring statistics on border controls, coastline surveillance, attending meetings on barrier insertions in each of the Cinque Ports. To say nothing of organising the almost medieval insistence on reclaiming the beacon sites all over the coastline. And organising twenty-four hour manned watch shifts for her civil servants to squabble about. She was not hugely impressed. In fact, she was angry. She bit back an overwhelming desire to say something hurtful.

"What do we want from him, Angela?" she asked carefully.

"What we've wanted all along, Bev. We want to be able to slot Bailey into position as the first Arch Druid of the New Covenant. Without him, we have only the secular aspects of the state under control. We have to have a figurehead who represents the spiritual. Someone versed in the ancient disciplines of the old laws. Someone who commands the respect and, if possible, the affection of the nation. A defender and a protector of the community law and the community spirit. Someone who can access the old magic."

Angela looked at the Archbishop sitting opposite, nursing a rather good Chablis as he generously helped himself from a plate of finger rolls laden with fillet of salmon and cream cheese. He raised his bushy eyebrows and pointed to the newly confiscated painting of Castle Dinas Bran hanging above his stone mullioned fireplace. Angela Astley cut the conversation short.

"I'll be in touch, Bev. Just keep him under supervision for the next few days while I work something out. While *we* work something out. The Archbishop has to have a final say and we need to discuss it fully. I'll contact you tomorrow. Are you staying on the island? Good. Speak then."

"Well?" She raised her perfect eyebrows in concert with his.

"It all depends, my dear. It all depends on whether or not he's had the awakening. If he has, then we could be in for quite a bit of trouble. You see, the awakening means he's accessed the secret codes, the druidic magic if you like.

"If so, then he will have a certain power that you or I can only dream of. But it has to be used for good, my dear. That too is part of the ancient code. If he's tempted to use it for ill – which I doubt very much indeed – then it will consume him."

"But what do we see as his role, Odo?" Angela Astley prodded, determined to find out what he thought.

"Well, my dear, we should see his role as my replacement. Instead of Archbishop, Arch Druid of Canterbury. But you appear to have serious doubts, I think?"

"I'll be honest with you, Odo. I thought that it would be easy, yet it's proved to be anything but. You've groomed him for this role since he was a young boy. You sent him to Westbury Park, guided him to study comparative religions at Cambridge, ensured he kept up with his studies in ancient languages, and gave him his first job in your library. You more than anyone know what makes him tick. So why is he giving us problems? And why the desperate, ridiculous attempt to save young Pendragon? What is going on?"

"He's confused, Angela. He hasn't been able to separate his feelings for Ceris from his druidic destiny. Then there's the free will aspect. We've steered him in this direction – more particularly, I've steered him in this direction since I found him abandoned on the steps of my church in Somerset. It will work out. I have every faith that it will and you must have faith too.

"Robert is an extraordinary individual but he is still a young man and, like most young men, feels the need to rebel from time to time. We must allow him this small rebellion, my dear."

"What about Branwen, though? She appears to have little regard for him and his many talents?"

"Ah, Branwen," the Archbishop beamed. "The heir to Taliesin. If all else fails, then Branwen will succeed me, Angela. She, more than Robert, is the natural heir to the Brythonic. But she doesn't have the theology. She lacks the academic rigour that Robert possesses. It's a pity. If she had been given a similar education then there would be no contest. As it is, we have to maintain a certain standard of both the old and the new knowledge and Robert more than most meets that criterion."

The Protector sighed heavily. Disappointed, she shifted her position on the deeply cushioned sofa and looked directly at her old friend's heavily jowled features. His clouded eyes looked fondly back at her.

"Don't worry," he smiled. "Robert Bailey will surprise us all. Let him loose, Angela. Watch and wait. He is in the first phase, now, of throwing off the mantle of the material world. Remnants of that world remain in the unrequited feelings he has for Ceris, the anger he feels towards Branwen, the annoyance he feels towards Steve Waterman, the awe he feels towards Commander Taft and the deep respect, maybe even filial love, he has toward me.

"He is like a small child, finding his way, throwing off the caul of a different kind of birth. One whose midwife is a woman he fears because he knows that she has the power: Branwen.

"Robert doesn't trust her, doesn't like her, yet he is drawn to her. She knows this and it amuses her. And he doesn't know how to respond, lost as he still is in the conventions of male/female stereotypes. He cannot understand that she, and after tonight, Ceris, no longer fit into that archetype. It will be difficult. We have to be patient."

Angela Astley shook her head in disbelief. "Patience? Do you have any idea of how close we are to losing the initiative? How close we are to failing? We did not, when planning this campaign, take into account the size, the current size, of the population, Odo. We have 67 million people living in this country. Not the few thousands of the pre-Christian era, the Celtic era. It's quite, quite different!"

"Of course it is, my dear. You're quite right, of course. Add to that the fact of secularism, materialism and the sheer awful ignorance choking the life out of the populace and what we aim to create in this land is nothing short of revolution. Or, perhaps, counter-revolution. The original revolution took place, as you know, with the Roman invasion. More particularly in the horrific events that took place in the 1st Century AD.

"We may not see the fruits of our labours within our lifetimes, Angela.

"But we will go down in history as having cut out that cancerous mind-set and replaced it with something more human, more fitting, more spiritually satisfying than the excesses of capitalism, communism, socialism or liberalism.

"To enter the next phase, we need to have a leader. Someone who can take on the intellectual mantle while you retain the political. I remain convinced that Robert is the right person for this. He needs help, I grant you. He needs guidance, which I can give him. He also needs to challenge himself and this is where Branwen comes in. Her powers are extraordinary, my dear, but she will not accept him unless and until he proves himself. And this is where the patience I mentioned a moment ago also comes in.

"We have to arrange matters in such a way that Robert earns the right to be both seen and accepted as the first Arch Druid of the modern era."

"And how do we do that?" Astley asked, throwing her old friend a look that was both amused and unconvinced.

"We let him loose, my dear. We let him follow his instincts, exercise his free will, allow him to find himself. And we take him away from his books, remove the crutches he has leaned on all of his life and provide him with Teachers."

"Teachers?" she laughed.

"Just so," he responded. "Robert must spend a period of time in Ireland, Scotland, Egypt and Istanbul. Six months in each place should do it. With your permission, I will arrange it."

"Two years?"

"Yes. Two years, my dear. We have to be patient."

"And what do we do in the interim?" she asked.

"We prepare, of course. And when we are fully prepared, we reveal the secret of the cauldron."

"Does anyone know we have it?" she asked, a cloud of concern hovering over her pale features.

"No one knows, Angela. Except the two of us," he replied.

They both looked intently at the brooding landscape in the oil painting, resting their eyes for a moment on the ruined arch sharply foregrounded and bathed in an otherworldly, golden light.

"When will you conduct the immersion, old friend?" she asked.

"Soon," he replied enigmatically. "Patience, my dear. Let Robert finish his education. In two years' time when he returns from his travels, his 'grand tour' if you like, he will be ready for the final ceremony. I want to raise Branwen's profile in the interim, whilst he is away. She deserves more recognition than she's had to date."

"Why?" she asked, puzzled at this new announcement. "I thought Branwen, while talented of course, wasn't in the same league."

"It's the way she handled young Ceris, my dear. Branwen was determined that Pendragon should access the first level of initiation. It's worked too. She's stronger, swifter, less repressed. Branwen worked her magic in Egypt, to reduce the levels of emotional repression deep inside the girl. She wants Ceris to succeed, has respect for her and sees her as the natural heir to her great ancestor."

"Boudicca?"

"Yes, Boudicca. Now, this tells me that Branwen has the sight."

"The sight?"

"It's hard to explain, my dear, but a few, a very few people of the Brythonic have what is known as 'The Seeing'. Personally, I haven't come across it in all my years in the church but I know it's a fact, a recorded fact, in two of the Glastonbury documents. It is stated that in every Brythonic generation, a seer would be born. He or she would be known by their deeds. Known by their ability to prophesy. Branwen met the first criteria but not the last. Until yesterday.

"Look at this," he said, handing her a folded sheet of blue writing paper tucked into a matching blue envelope. "Look at the postmark." He pointed to the right hand corner of the envelope at the black circular mark imprinted across a first class stamp. "What does it say?"

"It's dated twelve months ago," she said, not comprehending.

"When did the King have his stroke?"

"A couple of months ago."

"Now read it."

Angela Astley unfolded the blue paper and scanned the contents of the letter. Short, sharp, three paragraphs, signed and dated by Branwen. "So, she knew?"

"Why do you think the ambulance arrived within a few minutes? Yes, she knew and she wrote to warn me in advance. Nine months in advance. I told Sir Rufus, who told Commander Taft, and he arranged for a private ambulance to be put on standby near to the plateau. Evidently, according to Taft, the doctors at the hospital told him that if there had been a delay of more than twenty minutes, he wouldn't have made it."

Angela Astley looked at her old friend in astonishment. "I had no idea," she whispered.

He shrugged his round shoulders and nodded in agreement. "None of us did," he whispered back. "But do you see what this means?"

"Yes, yes I do, Odo. How did we miss that?"

"We didn't pay attention, my dear."

CHAPTER 24

Ali Alalladin had been recalled to London.

"There have been developments," Commander Taft explained. "Protector and Archbishop Odo want you to assist Branwen. It looks like she has too much on her plate at the moment what with recent developments."

"Do you mean Robert Bailey?" Ali enquired respectfully.

"Yes, I do. He's on secondment. Scotland, I believe, and Branwen needs someone to help out on the lecturing side. Bailey was teaching a class in ancient classical literary interpretation that we can't fill. Appears you're a bit of an expert?" Ali's coffee-coloured complexion blanched at the prospect but he said nothing.

Commander Taft winced. Branwen had quite the reputation for unnerving young men he thought. "So, Alalladin, what's your response?"

Ali swallowed hard before replying. "Sir," he mumbled unhappily. "I'm sure there are those better qualified than me. And I am very rusty, haven't done anything except a little reading on the subject for the past ten years."

Commander Taft pointed to the upright chair opposite his desk. "Sit Ali," he said quietly.

He had never used Ali's first name before and it came as a pleasant shock for the young man to hear it out loud.

"There's more to it. The Interregnum is at an impasse of sorts and it's imperative that we have good people in situ to see us through this short-term tricky patch. Moreover, we need you to work with Branwen and possibly Ceris, too, very shortly. We have many enemies."

Ali looked into the Commander's eyes, recognising the troubled concern and deep division within.

He could see that the Commander was having a hard time in accepting the new society beginning to emerge. He was deeply disturbed and torn between his duty and his conscience.

"I'm not sure I can work with her, sir," he said miserably. "Branwen, I mean, sir. She is dictatorial, impossible, lacks humour and makes me feel stupid sir."

"So you're saying you won't work with her?" Commander Taft frowned.

"No, I'm not saying I won't, sir. What I am saying is I don't really see how it can work. She is completely, totally impossible, sir. Isn't there anyone else?"

Commander Taft tapped his teeth with his pen and thought. "I don't know the answer to that. I will find out. I'll speak to some people a bit further up the food chain and see what I can do. Don't get your hopes up. This request has come from Sir Rufus himself. I must say, however, we really do need you here, Alalladin, keeping an eye on Lord Farndon. He's still here, I assume?"

"He is, sir. We're waiting for him to make contact with his handlers. He has been very clever thus far. No leads as yet. Looks like he's buying cheap mobiles, using them once and disposing them. We've operatives going through the rubbish bins looking for discarded phones, though I fear that anyone seeing him throw one away will retrieve it to use. As you know, there's plenty of poverty here in Cairo."

"What do we know so far?" Commander Taft leaned back in his leather executive chair expectantly.

Ali relaxed. Just maybe he was being let off this secondment to the dreaded Branwen. He fervently hoped so. "Well, sir, we know that Lord Farndon is a loner. No friends apart from Prince John. He has tried, through his friendship with the prince, to ingratiate himself with the King. The King tolerates him but doesn't socialise or personally invite him anywhere. He appears to have little interest in him really.

"We also know that Farndon is deeply old school. Eton, Cambridge, The Guards, various boards including the British Museum and a seat in the House of Lords as an independent Conservative. Very right wing in his views, very establishment in his outlook. Never married, but carried a torch at one point for Angela Astley. It's said that he's never forgiven her for turning him down when they were at university together. Seems he carries a grudge.

"An interesting point is that, a year or so ago, he converted from High Anglican to Roman Catholicism, is a regular church goer and has been known to attend the Templar Church on occasion for special, dedicatory services.

"No known issue but has a younger sister and three nieces. Also, sir, and this is interesting, he scored in the top one thousand in the national assessments."

"Meaning?" Commander Taft was testing his subordinate.

"Meaning, sir, that Farndon is of Brythonic stock. He has no Saxon, Roman, Norman, Scandinavian blood in his veins. He is pure Celt and truly of the Brythonic."

"Does he know this, I wonder, Ali? Were they told this when they were assessed?"

"I've heard that they were not, sir. Reason being it could unleash all sorts of racist nonsense. You see, sir, what the national assessments wanted to do was to identify those who had the potential for druidic conversion, not create divisions that could never be healed."

"Are you Brythonic, Ali?" Taft couldn't help but ask, his curiosity overwhelming him.

"One of the exiles, sir," he said simply. "My people were part of *The Other Exodus*. The ones who left Memphis, Giza and Amarna too, over four thousand years ago with Queen Scota and Pharaoh Gaythelos.

"Moses left for the Promised Land and we left for the Sacred Land – home of the Hyperborean Wind, or sacred Western Isles of ancient myth and legend.

"My people settled first in Iraland, or Ireland as it became known. Moses' people settled in what became known as Israel. Isis and Ra. The sacred female and the sacred light.

"As in antiquity, we moved east, to Scota's Land, taking our sacred music, the music of the wind, with us in the form of the bagpipes. Our early priests and priestesses built Stonehenge, Silbury and Avebury. We became the administrators, lawgivers, judges, doctors, poets, magicians and teachers. Building magnificent colleges in sacred spaces: Iona, Glastonbury, Anglesey, to name just a few.

"My people wanted to live in peace. They didn't want to have to fight any more wars, or feed a growing class of administrators who had the power of life or death if you wouldn't do as they wished. And so, like Moses, they chose freedom.

"Except that Moses' people repeated the mistakes of their forefathers, creating more wars, more dissent, more suffering.

"My people eradicated conflict through the Community Rule. Later, early Christian monasteries adopted our template. Instead of constant conflict, or rampant materialism through creating back-breaking industries in food and consumer goods – its surplus to be sold to the highest bidder – we turned instead to knowledge, law giving, community, healing, poetry and, yes, magic.

"Life is about harmony, not discord, Commander, and it is the discordant, resonant notes of the bagpipes that remind us of this. It is this harmonic destiny that we fight for now, in Britain, Commander. Once again, we have to meet our fate. And I am ready for that. Perhaps it too is my destiny."

Commander Taft said nothing. He was intrigued with Ali Alalladin's monologue, recognising in himself that he needed to make sense of things before they threatened to overwhelm him. He shook himself, shuffling the loose papers from Ali Alalladin's file into a neat pile.

"Sir?" Ali frowned at his cell phone as it buzzed discreetly.

"Go ahead," Commander Taft said as he swept a stray paper back into the pile.

"He's just entered the Great Pyramid, sir," Ali said excitedly.

Commander Taft smiled. He remembered well the excitement of staking out the target. "I want that mobile phone, Alalladin." The Commander frowned.

"I'll do my best, sir," Ali replied as he dashed out of the cool air-conditioned office and into a revved-up car waiting impatiently outside.

Lord Crispin Farndon paced up and down the King's Chamber, his Maglite torch sweeping up and over each severe granite slab. The small room was oppressive, stark, and bare of decoration save for the jagged-edged sarcophagus strangely angled, appearing to the uninitiated to serve no real purpose in the massive ancient monolith.

Unusually, the chamber was empty. Farndon had monitored footfall, noticing that from four in the afternoon, the tourist numbers shrank to single figures. Darkness fell swiftly in Egypt and most still indulged in afternoon siestas.

He consulted his notebook, the red elastic strap now ragged, its elasticity barely holding the outer covers together. What had the King written? Something about the golden mean. He had had assurances that these notes were authentic. There were people at the embassy, unbeknown to Taft and company, who were, he knew, on his side.

If he could just discover what they wanted then he had the highest assurances that his reward would be bountiful: militarily, financially, historically. The only way, he knew, to stop what was unfolding had passed the point of talk and negotiation. There was no memorandum of understanding that could solve the problems Astley was creating with such fervour. No, war was the solution as it had always been in these islands. Invasion, subjugation and occupation.

Just as his ancestors had done before.

He swept his lightweight torch once more over the flat stoned ceiling, angling the beam at every pockmark he could see. Nothing. He sighed, walked over to the huge granite box and rested his hand on its edge, the beam from his torch creating distorted shadows as he shifted his weight. Suddenly, the torch slipped from his hand into the strange granite box, its metal and rubber casing striking the stone, setting off a loud reverberating sound. F sharp. Where had he read that the world hums to the rhythm of F sharp? The strange resonance entered him, its note beating in time with the sound of his thumping heart.

What was that? He shifted his weight again, throwing the beam further up into the corner of the roof. Grabbing his camera phone he clicked several times, unsure of what he had seen, unsure whether or not it was just a trick of the light, a trick of the mind. Perhaps he was seeing what he wanted to see?

Still unsure, he made his way out to the low exit tunnel, scrambled down the great step and into the grand gallery, an almost sonic sound still echoing off the giant granite slabs.

Desperate to remove himself from the hot, oppressive atmosphere of the pyramid he exhaled a sigh of relief as he felt the hard limestone dust of the plateau under his feet and breathed. He needed to sit. He was feeling strangely out of sorts as he clenched his fists to stop his hands from shaking, his legs from giving way as he felt the reverberating rhythm seep deeply into his very bones.

He was unsteady, he felt oddly unco-ordinated. Entering a ramshackle cafe at the foot of the plateau he gratefully found a secluded spot away from door and windows, away from prying eyes. He looked around carefully, sliding his cell phone silently onto the small white plastic table. He ordered coffee. Dark, bitter Arabic coffee sweet and energising. Taking a scalding sip his breathing relaxed, slowly returning to normal as he carefully surveyed the half dozen pictures just taken.

"Yes," he mouthed. There it was, the faded outline of a bird, a composite picture in profile, in relief, of a raven/crow merged with an ibis. He had been right. This was it!

He chose the best image, attached it to an email and pressed send. There, it was done. If they found him now it didn't matter. They could arrest him for all he cared. He allowed his anger, never far from the surface, to rise up.

He would show that stupid woman Astley. He would make both Alfred and John suffer for their abandonment of all that had been held dear. Almost 2000 years of history, of kings and queens, wars and settlements, family fortunes, great houses and great men. All to be torn asunder by that woman and her snivelling acolytes.

She would rue the day she was born, he muttered to himself, indulging for a moment in a fantasy of him throwing her carelessly into a dungeon, shackled in chains, begging for mercy, tears streaming from her lovely eyes. He would ignore her pleas for mercy. He would stand tall and proud, mocking her desperate cries for help.

Her hysterical declarations of love and desire would leave him cold. He would wait for her to apologise. Yes, she needed to apologise. She had caused him so much anguish over the years. They could have had such a wonderful life together if she had just behaved.

His phone pinged, startling him from his reverie. 'Benedictus' the message said. 'Rome wasn't built in a day.' Farndon allowed himself a small smile. It was good to have friends in high places.

And it didn't get much higher than the Vatican.

CHAPTER 25

Commander Taft walked her through Departures toward the Air Italia desk as he handed over her new passport emblazoned with the Special Services silver-embossed logo on a midnight blue background.

"Remember, you now have diplomatic immunity. You may need it," was his cryptic aside.

She glanced at him, a half amused smile playing on her lips. "I see, sir. You think matters could get messy?"

"I sincerely hope so," was his enigmatic response. She laughed, a full-throated, delighted laugh without inhibition.

He laughed too, their collective confidence palpable. Check in completed, they turned toward an empty Costa where a frantically waving Ali Alalladin had saved three discreet seats in its spacious interior.

"One latte, one cappuccino and ..." Ali hesitated. "Still water?"

Ceris helped him out. "Thanks," she smiled. "It's all I drink these days."

Ali looked interested. "You used to drink coffee?"

"Oh yes, gallons of the stuff," she said brightly.

"What happened?" He was genuinely interested.

She looked at him carefully, glancing for a second at Commander Taft, who nodded as if to give her permission.

"He's one of us, Pendragon," Taft said quietly.

"Of course, sir." She smiled directly at the fidgeting Ali who was beginning to look charmingly embarrassed.

"Well, long story short, I recently agreed to take part in a ... ceremony, I expect you could call it. An initiation ceremony on a tiny island in the middle of a small lake. The whole area was surrounded by ancient standing stones.

"They looked menacing and forbidding in the daylight, yet at night-time, the time we were on the island, they seemed to emanate a protective air. Almost as if they could leap out of the earth and defend you from attackers. Strange, yet somehow reassuring.

"Anyway, the potion began to work as I had been told. Seven days and seven nights after taking the draught, the concoction would act. And it did. It was the most amazing experience of my life, Ali. I met the Ancestors. I received the Code. I was accepted and protected and told that anything caffeine or cocoa based would dilute the new powers received.

"And so, I had to give up my two favourite things in the world: coffee and chocolate!"

Ali smiled in relief. He had thought the story would turn out to be a dark, miserable tale and his face showed signs of released tension, which Taft found highly amusing.

"Tell him who supervised it all," Taft commanded.

Ceris turned towards him, equally amused. "Do you think that's wise, sir?"

"Oh he's man enough to deal with the information. Aren't you, Alalladin?"

"Sir?" A confused Ali looked from one to the other, pausing as if one or both would offer a clue.

Ceris fixed him with a hard stare reminiscent of …

He took a deep breath. "It wasn't her, was it?" he asked, overawed and very nervous. "Tell me it wasn't her, was it? If it was, I don't think I can bear it. She might want to do the same to me. Oh no, sir, I don't have to do the same do I?"

"Do you mean Branwen?" Ceris asked innocently. She covered her face with her hand as both she and Taft looked away from each other to stifle the hilarity.

"Right, enough." Commander Taft wiped a tear from his eye as Ceris blew her nose to cover her amusement.

Ali sat looking first at one, then the other, his panic melting into an easy humour, a slow smile crinkling his eyes as he held his hands up in supplication. "I know, I know," he relented. "I find it amusing too. No one bothers me as a rule, Commander, but for some odd reason she terrifies me. It's as if she sees through you. You can't second guess or manipulate her like you can with most …"

"Women?" Ceris finished off for him, her eyes like steel as she held his gaze fearlessly.

Ali looked away.

"Oh, she's fine!" Ceris said brusquely. "She's just incredibly direct, has strong, almost medieval standards for manners, decorum, politeness etc. and behaves as if she's a queen. Which she is actually, if you think about it. You'll be all right providing you don't upset her.

"I would not like to be on the receiving end of upsetting her, Ali. Seriously, she can be both furious and dangerous. Treat her with total, unconditional respect and she'll be reasonable with you. Just don't expect her to want to be your friend.

"Branwen doesn't do friends. And if she gets any idea that you have, let's say … any carnal desires … then your number's up, mate. She doesn't do anything that's not for a higher purpose. You'd best understand that if you find yourself working with her at some point."

"I see, he mumbled, not convinced. "You received the Code?" he asked Ceris in wonder.

"I did," she murmured, closing her eyes for a moment as if relishing the memory. "And I am both grateful to Branwen and honoured that she thought me worthy."

"To business." Commander Taft looked at his watch. They had exactly thirty minutes until Ceris had to leave for the executive departures lounge. Maybe longer, as business class always embarked last, along with first class passengers.

The airport was very quiet these days, he thought. No more hustle and bustle, manic passengers and staff careering through duty free, up and down escalators with cabin bags stuffed to the gills.

The Interregnum had stopped all that. These days, people travelled only for business, and that business had to be approved by the authorities. He sighed. He still wasn't used to all the changes the Interregnum had brought. Maybe he was getting too old for any more change in his life, he thought morosely.

"To business," he repeated. "Ceris, you know what your remit is?"

"I do, sir," she acknowledged assertively. "I have to find Farndon's handler. We have clear evidence from the retrieved cell phone that there's a Vatican connection. What little information we have comes directly from Farndon himself and that is limited. It's not that he's hiding anything, it's more that he has only been given information on a 'need to know' basis, we think. All we've managed to get out of him is a name and it's not a name that is on any list, register, directory, meeting or minute schedule that we can access. All we have is this name."

"And what is this name?" Ali Alalladin asked.

Ceris looked him straight in the eye as she leaned forward, moving the two coffee cups that were creating a barrier between them. "Aristobulus," she said quietly.

Ali blanched as he searched their faces for understanding of the implications.

"Do you know what that name means?" he asked. "Do you know who he was, Commander?"

Ceris turned to her boss, raising an eyebrow as Commander Taft glanced again at his watch and frowned. "Go on Ali, tell us what you know," he said evenly.

Ali gazed off into the distance as he began to recount the recent information retrieved from King Alfred's notebook. Combined with his formidable understanding of Egyptian and European History, he held them both silently spellbound as he explained.

"There were two separate and distinct cradles of early Christianity in Britain. The mission of Joseph of Arimathea at Glastonbury around 34 to 38 AD, and the mission of Aristobulus at Llanilid, just a couple of years later. Both missions were protected. The former by Arviragus, the latter by Caradoc, his cousin and Bran's son. Like Bran, both these men were Brythonic Kings, Warriors and Druids.

"Joseph came from Jerusalem, he was regarded with favour by the elite of the time. Aristobulus, however, came from Rome, from the national enemy and that did not sit well with the Brythonic given Rome's history of invasion.

"Two terrible events now conspired to raise the level of hatred for the Romans to a new height. Both of these events led the ancient belief system we call Druidism to identify its sufferings with the sufferings of early Christianity. These momentous events became known as the Boudicca Outrage and the Menai Massacre.

"Orders were issued from Rome to Suetonius Paulinus to destroy, at any cost, the chief seat of Druidic learning held by the western Britons.

"At the same time, Seneca, Nero's adviser, celebrity philosopher and a ruthless moneylender, demanded immediate repayment of an enormous loan he had made to the Iceni. When Prasutagus, King of the Iceni Tribe in Prydain, couldn't or wouldn't pay up, the Roman prefect in Lincolnshire was instructed to take control of all the lands, holdings, castles, palaces, treasure and domestic goods owned by the chief.

"War erupted: Prasutagus was killed and his queen, Boudicca, took over. Some sources say upwards of 200,000 Britons waged ferocious battle against the Romans and, for a time, they won some of the bloodiest battles this land has ever seen.

"As we know, the Roman legions were too powerful, too organised and too disciplined in the art of warfare. The Iceni lost. And Prydain was never the same.

"As for Aristobulus, he was killed, martyred. He was also the first Bishop of Britain, consecrated by St Paul himself."

"So, what, if any, is the connection, Ali?" Ceris asked.

Ali rubbed his nose thoughtfully as he pondered his reply. "I think the connection lies in the choice of the name itself: Aristobulus. He is deeply associated with St Paul's mission, Ceris. And it was this second mission – the first mission was that of Joseph of Arimathea, of course – that set the stage for the eventual Roman domination of both spiritual and temporal, government and church!

"You see, if you have an administration run by an elite bunch of foreigners who are trying to manage a population who have no regard for either their laws or their spiritual values, then you have problems. By merging both the material world with the spiritual one, you subdue a population."

"And Aristobulus did that?" Ceris asked wide-eyed.

"He began the process, yes," Ali replied. "You see, the first mission to Prydain or Britain was the Joseph mission. Sanctioned by James the Just, brother of Jesus. Significantly, it was founded on the words and works of Christ himself. The original gospel if you like – which was quite different from the Pauline version emerging at the same time.

"Here in Britain, that original, James the Just / Joseph of Arimathea sacred belief system melded with the indigenous belief system of Druidism. As we know, Druidism itself was based on the teachings coming out of Egypt after *The Other Exodus*.

"Both had very similar philosophies, both had very similar sacred observances and both had access to the workings of miracles through harnessing the powers of the natural and the supernatural worlds.

"By contrast, Aristobulus was a devotee of Saul of Tarsus who, after his conversion on the Road to Damascus, became Paul of Tarsus – note the name change!

"Paul developed an opposing school of thought to James the Just that became known as the Roman School. In this school he decried the role of women, especially, and that hatred of women became a founding principle of the new church. It empowered his followers to lay the exclusively male foundations for what became the Roman Catholic Church.

"You see, James the Just and his followers believed in equality, and one of the greatest of their number was Mary Magdalene, Jesus' beloved, whom Paul hated with a terrible passion.

"That's an edited explanation, I grant you, but in summary, that is exactly what happened."

"So, Aristobulus came to Britain with a Roman remit?" Ceris asked.

"Yes, that's exactly what he did. He was well regarded, according to contemporary commentaries, purely as a religious man. But the remit remained, of course. His job was to convert Prydain/Brydain/Britain, to St Paul's interpretation of the Holy Word, not Joseph of Arimathea's.

"In Merton College, Oxford, there is a manuscript which contains a series of letters written between St Paul and our old friend Seneca."

"The same Seneca who lent huge amounts of money to Boudicca's husband, Prasutagus?" Ceris asked.

"The very same," Ali responded darkly. "And we know from that correspondence that Paul was determined to conquer the Britons with his version of 'The Word', using Seneca's influence with Nero to order the Menai Massacre and the Iceni genocide.

"It was the calling-in of loans, Miss Pendragon, that caused these dreadful events. Just as in 1933, the American Congress voted into law the Emergency Banking Act that declared the States bankrupt. The Federal Reserve was set up as a private bank and the American people lost their sovereign status, becoming vassals, not freemen, under the new law.

"So you see, in Britain in the 1st Century, and in America in the 20th Century, the Roman rule of law took from the many, the people, and gave it all to the few, a small number of despots. I think this is what we're all trying to overturn. We desperately need to get back to the Community Rule somehow."

Commander Taft tapped his watch meaningfully. "Time to go."

Ceris sighed as she took a final sip of her glass of still water.

"Sir Rufus will meet you personally," Commander Taft said quietly.

Ali's eyes widened. This was an important job, he thought, wishing fervently that he could be part of it instead of being here, on secondment, with the prospect of having to work with Branwen looming over him like a massive black cloud full of despair.

Ceris gathered her coat, bag, passport, ticket and laptop in one sweeping movement. As she headed toward the departures gate she was lost in thought, thinking hard on what Ali had said just moments before, still unsure of what it all meant. Yet strangely, ominously, something deep inside her had begun to stir.

Something ancient, primeval and very deadly.

"Did you know St Paul is reviled by some influential religious groups?" Ali Alalladin suddenly asked Commander Taft as they sat in companionable silence watching Ceris head for her plane.

"Explain," Commander Taft said.

"The Ebionites believed Paul to be a false prophet whose task was not to convert Romans to Christians but Christians to Romans and, significantly, one of the Hadiths of Islam cites Paul as an imposter who took the message of the Prophet Jesus and used it for his own ends. This belief stretches into more recent history, sir, as it is on record that Benjamin Franklin, Voltaire, Walt Whitman and several literary lights of the 19th and 20th Centuries felt the same! Interesting isn't it, sir?"

"What do we know of this Aristobulus, Alalladin? Not your historical first Bishop of Britain, I'm more interested in this most recent incarnation. Why sign off that message to Farndon with that name?"

Ali swept back his glossy jet-black hair, his handsome face Pharaonic in the bright lights of the empty Costa. He adjusted his Hermes tie. Pulling the snowy white cuffs of his pristine shirt, he leaned forward across the small table, his features intense in the charged atmosphere pervading their discreet alcove.

"There has to be a connection," Ali muttered, his mind whirling with the endless possibilities. "Aristobulus was in Rome with St Paul. Bran the Blessed was in Rome to bring back Caradoc, his son, who had been taken as hostage. Both Bran and Aristobulus travelled back to Prydain, with the newly released Caradoc. So, we have a connection with Aristobulus and Bran.

"Now, Joseph of Arimathea was sent to Prydain by James the Just, brother of Jesus. Joseph dies, his replacement is brought in by his son-in-law, Bran the Blessed.

"The replacement of course is Aristobulus. And Caradoc was released from hostage in Rome in payment for Bran agreeing to the replacement.

"Yet Bran's wife, Joseph of Arimathea's daughter, Anna, was in a terrible dilemma at this decision. Of course, she wanted her son Caradoc home, she knew exactly what could happen to the hostages in Rome but she also knew, better than any of them, how Paul operated. She had been a small child at the knee of her aunts when Paul had berated the women for daring to speak in his presence. She knew that the future would be dark if her father's legacy, the legacy of Joseph of Arimathea, were to be supplanted with the doctrine of Paul.

"Now, Bran was the Royal Arch Druid of Prydain and he was clever, very clever indeed. He felt that he could manage the situation once on his own soil so he agreed to the appointment of Aristobulus. However, dissent was deliberately created when Aristobulus was created Bishop of Britain by St Paul ... so we have two distinct, separate leaders of religion for the first time in the country's history. And this was unprecedented in the history of Prydain.

"Legend has it that Anna died of a broken heart not long after these events unfolded, leaving Bran the Blessed totally bereft, for she had truly been his soul mate. He recognised that her fears, the dire warnings and predictions she had made about allowing Paul's doctrine into the sacred land of Prydain, had been accurate. Bran then took unprecedented action.

"Bran travelled to Anglesey and, according to legend, had a vision on the banks of the Menai Straits as he was preparing to cross over to the island. It was this vision that motivated him to secure the future through writing down druidic laws and histories, assisted by the great colleges of Anglesey, Iona, Dublin and Bangor."

Ali paused to take a sip of his cold coffee. His eyes had a far-away look that spoke of deep sadness.

"You have a very thorough understanding of all this, Alalladin," Commander Taft said approvingly.

"Years of post-grad study, sir," Ali replied, his thoughts elsewhere.

"So. Why, in your obviously knowledgeable opinion, the cryptic comment on Farndon's cell phone, 'Benedictus, Rome wasn't built in a day'?" Commander Taft probed.

"Well, 'Benedictus' just means blessings."

"Could it also be a reference to Bran? Bran the Blessed?" Taft barked.

"Possibly, Commander. Yes, it is possible," Ali said thoughtfully.

"And what about the 'Rome wasn't built in a day'?" Taft enquired, his eyes narrowing as if he already knew the answer.

"Has to be a reference to the Paul doctrine overwhelming the James the Just doctrine with Rome as the symbol for Britain. A battle for supremacy, perhaps? Between Paul /Aristobulus for the Romans, and James / Bran the Blessed for the Brits?"

"Are you saying that there was a counter-revolution taking place after the two massacres?" Commander Taft could be relentless.

Ali found himself perspiring heavily as he tried to formulate his responses to Taft's increasingly tough questions.

"Yes, I think that's exactly what happened, sir. I think Bran realised that he'd been had by Paul and Paul's emissary, Aristobulus.

"Bran was between a rock and a hard place. He had to get Caradoc out of Rome, Caradoc was family and you didn't abandon family, then or now. Hostages lived on a knife-edge and on a whim could be executed by those in power. The price he paid for getting Caradoc out was agreeing to have Paul's choice instead of James the Just's choice as the first official Bishop of Britain. It's a decision he lived to regret.

"Who is the Bishop of Britain sir?" he asked.

"Do you mean Aristobulus, the first Bishop of Britain?" Commander Taft asked.

"No, the current one, Commander. Is there a current Bishop of Britain? I thought the office had become redundant after Augustus?"

"Are you sure you mean the current one?"

"I do, yes."

"Isn't it Archbishop Odo?" Commander Taft said carefully.

Ali Alalladin's eyes widened in astonishment. "Could he be Farndon's Aristobulus?"

"It's possible." Commander Taft looked seriously at the young man. "In this game, Alalladin, anything is possible."

✝✝✝

Armed with an old map of the catacombs, Ceris slid unseen through a gap at the rear of the underground chambers of the Coliseum. The tourist party she had tagged along with continued its chattering as the guide pointed out some of the more gory details of its awful history.

She shivered, as she caught the thin vibration permeating the air surrounding them, one of death, pain, anguish, and horror.

Grey stone walls sweating with the tears of centuries, stagnant water pooling in thick puddles on the worn flagstones and cobbled walkways, the smell of fear in the still air after all this time, and the graffiti, barely visible, spelling out the names of those who had once walked these dank tunnels to their terrifying deaths.

A tree was growing out of one of the walls leading off from the central tunnel. She stopped, her eyes widening at its symbolism. There it was! Commander Taft had told her to look hard for it and she had asked the Ancient Ones for assistance in the quest. It was the first time she had done so and there it was. 'Stagnant water, upside down tree.' The roots of the thing growing out of the curved stone roof, its thin branches, gnarled, leafless, spreading downwards onto the cracked stones beneath.

He had said it would be a Yew tree. She didn't know. He had said that the Yew tree held sacred significance to the Druids. It was able, even when 5000 years old, to grow new shoots. It had, according to the Sacred Book of Bran, magical powers, too, releasing a gas we now called taxine, which could cause hallucinations.

Hadn't there been a grove of Yew trees on the small island in the lake?

All she did know was that it was exactly as he had said, here, in the underground chambers of the mighty Coliseum.

How had he known these things? Commander Taft was becoming an enigma, she thought to herself, as she remembered the many times he had forewarned her of coming events. How did he know? He wasn't, as far as she was aware, privy to all the esoteric insights that Branwen, Robert and Ali were. She must talk to him.

She paused, scrabbling in her backpack for her penknife. If he was right, then the entrance to the secret archives should be close. She looked around, there was no one about. The tourist party could be heard further up the long walkway, a distant sound now.

She was on her own. She breathed a sigh of relief. This would take time and would be best left until darkness fell. She slipped into a nearby alcove, dark, damp, uninviting. Checking her backpack for necessary supplies, she breathed deeply, inviting the veil of the other, the trance-like state she could now enter at will, to sustain her and protect her from the darkness both physical and spiritual slowly surrounding her.

Her heartbeat steadied and her temperature dropped as she slid into that other place known only to Warriors, Ovates and Druids. And waited.

CHAPTER 26

"So, this is it?"

Branwen unwrapped the small package folded carefully in its faded cloth. The smell of ambergris gently wafted up as she placed the small scrolls next to each other on the wide library table.

"It is," she said, staring at him until he looked the other way.

"What are we supposed to do with them?" he asked nervously.

"What do you think?" she said, glaring at him still as if he were stupid.

"I suppose we're expected to translate them?"

"Wrong!" she said, triumphantly. "Robert Bailey has already completed the translation. Your task, O Clever One, is to make connections. Here, read the commentary as well as the translation. What does it mean? We need you to connect this with the others. This is what you're supposed to do with it, as you so inelegantly state."

Branwen turned away from him, her nose firmly in the air, a look of utter disdain on her fine, beautiful features.

Ali Alalladin clenched his fists tight. He wasn't used to being treated like this. Most women, once they were introduced to him, flattered him, made eyes at him, smiled and laughed at his jokes, his observations, flirted with him even. Not Branwen though. It was obvious that she had absolutely no time for him. And that hurt his male pride. He sighed, hoping to garner some sympathy.

Branwen laughed "Ha!" she said. "You are transparent, Alalladin. Like a cheap pane of glass. Be careful you do not crack."

Angrily, he barrelled over to the far end of the vast library table and sat there furiously looking at his cell phone. Silently, she moved the scrolls and commentaries over to him with an arch frown.

"Don't play games with me," she said forcefully. "Games are for children. You may be a child but I am not. I will be back in an hour. I expect some progress to have been made."

Ali nodded miserably. He had dreaded this day, much to Commander Taft's amusement. And now here he was, seconded to the Dissonance Office until further notice, courtesy of Sir Rufus. They could manage for a while without him in Cairo it seemed, especially since the successful nabbing of Lord Farndon's elusive cell phone with its cryptic texts.

Why they'd sent Farndon for training with the Initiates he had yet to work out. In his book, if you were found guilty of a crime against the state you swung for it. Commander Taft had shaken his head and said no, damage limitation took precedence; he would be given another chance. Madness.

As Ali's eyes skimmed over the translations and commentaries expertly compiled by Robert Bailey, he found himself admiring the absent academic for his clarity of expression, the simplicity of his prose, his thorough understanding of some complex encryptions in the original texts.

This was a man who knew what he was doing, he thought. This was a scholar who knew his subject like the back of his hand. He was fascinated, and easily absorbed himself in making quick notes as he read. Time passed swiftly. He was beginning to feel chilled as the temperature noticeably dropped. His stomach felt uncomfortable. He realised he was hungry but there was no one about to ask for refreshment so he sighed sorrowfully and picked up his pen once more.

The door opened, letting in a blast of icy air. Ali looked up from his writing to see fine slivers of snow falling silently on the long narrow Georgian window across from the library table. The air was charged with electricity as he feasted his eyes on the lovely Branwen, wrapped up in a thick woollen cloak, its fur lining visible as she threw it across a chair in an easy gesture. She stood by the window, silently looking at the falling flakes.

"A mighty storm is brewing," she said, still with her back to him. "The island will sleep for two days while the storm rages and then subsides. The lane will be blocked by the morning with six feet drifts."

"How do you know this?" he asked, intrigued.

"How do I know this? I am a Seer, of course! How else would I know?"

Ali bent his head to his writing again, determined not to let her get the better of him. He remembered what Ceris had said at the airport. What was it? Ah yes, treat her with respect, she could be dangerous. He felt a frisson of both pleasure and fear, which startled him. Was he beginning to fall for her? Ceris had warned him about that too.

Silently, he continued his note taking, not daring to look up, conscious of her presence, nervous of what she would say next.

She swivelled on her heel, arms folded and took a seat at the opposite end of the huge library table in a swift, feline movement. "Read to me what you have discovered," she commanded imperiously. "And then write me a summary of it."

Ali swallowed. "I've only just started Branwen, there's not very much to tell you yet. Perhaps in a couple of hours?"

"Now," she said decisively. He shuffled his feet, gathering a handful of scribbled notes written on yellow legal pad paper. Clearing his throat he began, glancing at Branwen nervously as she stared straight at him. Her face was an alabaster mask.

"The first scroll has a reference to Exodus Chapter Seven, Verse Two, in the Old Testament," he began.

"Ye shall speak all that I command you and your brother Aaron shall speak to Pharaoh that he let the sons of Israel go out of his land.

"This is a direct reference to the original Exodus, of course, when Moses led his people to the Promised Land. For forty years they wandered the Sinai until finally reaching Mount Nebo in what is now Jordan. Moses died and leadership passed to Joshua who completed the journey by waging war on the Canaanites then settling his people on the west bank of the River Jordan."

"The West Bank?" Branwen sniffed, mildly intrigued.

"Yes," Ali replied, energised, forgetting his nervousness in her presence.

"What is the significance of this?" she sniffed again.

"Well, according to Egyptian tradition, the west was where the sun went down, where the sun physically set. Throughout the various kingdoms: old, intermediate, and others, Egyptians made their homes on the east bank of the Nile, not the west bank.

"You see, the west bank of the Nile was reserved for burials. The going down of the sun in the west meant death. Its arrival in the morning in the east meant birth, renewal and life of course.

"It was considered strange to want to live on the west bank of a river, to deliberately make your home on the west bank when there were other, more easterly choices. A sign that you were working for death rather than life.

"What we have to remember is that Moses and later Joshua were establishing a new religion. They had discarded the Egyptian belief system which focused on the rising of the sun in the east equating with life and its setting in the west equating with death.

Although, there are some who would challenge that opinion."

"Meaning?" she asked, one eyebrow arched sceptically.

"Meaning," he repeated, "there are those who believed that the new religion, the religion of Moses and Joshua deliberately focused on death rather than life.

"Their god was a vengeful god, a jealous god, a god who demanded retribution. Who operated the first recorded example of engineered genocide on the fields of Canaan whilst simultaneously supporting an early form of apartheid. His people were special, you see. They and they alone were the 'Chosen Ones'.

"I think it's fair to say that this was a historical, not a contemporary mind-set. Modern Jews have a much more enlightened view of the world. Well, the ones I've studied with at least.

"Just maybe, by choosing to settle on the west bank of the Jordan, the people of the Exodus were making a strong statement of intent. Certain scholars have entertained this view. Those of a more revisionist persuasion mostly."

"You said this was the first Exodus?" Branwen leaned forward, her eyes sparkling with interest, her voice softening very slightly as she noticed Ali's hand shakily pick up another sheet of his yellow legal pad and place it carefully on top of his notes.

"Indeed, this was the first. The second Exodus or, as it has become known, *The Other Exodus*, emerged from Amarna approximately two years after the first."

"Tell me about this *Other Exodus*," Branwen said, as she rose from the library table to stand once more at the window. Swirls of snow could be seen. A menacing wind could also be heard.

"You know of this," Ali said. "Don't you?"

She said nothing.

He continued. "Huge changes were introduced by Pharaoh Akhenaten around 2500 BC when he declared that the old religion of multiple gods, goddesses, rituals and religious laws were wrong. He announced that there was only one God and that god he called the Aten. He took his King name from the name of the god as it was believed that the Pharaoh was the living incarnation of the supreme deity.

"Akhenaten moved the entire royal court, its administration, judiciary and executive to Amarna, leaving the ancient temples and monuments of Karnak and Memphis for a strip of land that had nothing except access to the River Nile. Interestingly, Akhenaten built his new city on the east bank of the Nile. This is a connection we need to explore I think. Anyway, he built a city, dismissed his priestly class, fathered five daughters with Queen Nefertiti and created huge dissent. Massive upset.

"The people wanted the old gods back, the priests were desperate to regain power. He was, himself, a weak king who had strange ideas about the meaning of life according to the received wisdom of the time. Inevitably, civil dissent and strife broke out and Akhenaten, Nefertiti and four of his five daughters disappear from the record ... but one of his daughter's does not."

"Meritaten?" Branwen asked.

"The very same," he replied. "Meritaten/Scota, with her husband Gaythelos, journey to Ireland, then Scotland, with their entourage. There is evidence that suggests they stopped off first in Spain before travelling to Ireland. We know that through the predominant blood groups: AB- is the predominant blood group of *The Other Exodus*. It is my blood group too."

"Which includes the Priestly class or Magi," she said seriously.

"Indeed," Ali replied, wondering where she was going with this.

"I want to know what you have learned from the documents," she said haughtily. "You have scanned Robert Bailey's commentary on this?"

"Briefly," he replied sulkily.

"Then tell me what you have concluded," she demanded, her tone one of mild exasperation.

Ali sighed once more and continued. "Robert Bailey writes of an Irish version of the Gospel of Matthew which he discovered in the Windsor archive, 'The Great Box Archive' as he calls it."

"Yes, Ceris brought it from the castle, under guard. 'The Great Box', as you call it, had lain in a small turret room in the oldest part of the castle undisturbed since the 1100's." Branwen's perfect eyebrow lifted a degree as she waited for him to continue.

"Well, in this version of the gospel, which is dated to the 9th Century AD, the phrase '...there came wise men from the East', is rendered, 'The Druids came from the East'. Now, we know from a parallel source, in the Scroll of the Temple of the Aten, that historically, their senior priests had set off on arduous journeys across the known world to study significant astronomical events, particularly those related to the precession of the equinoxes. Solar eclipses and planetary alignments.

"One temple panel shows three priestly figures journeying by Egyptian barque through what looks like the Gulf of Aqaba, taking the desert route through Wadi Rum to Petra and on to Amman. Crossing the Dead Sea from the eastern shore, they would find their way onto the road to Jerusalem and Bethlehem. This is evidence that the route to the land of Canaan was well known.

"There is further evidence, circumstantial evidence I grant you, to suggest that it was indeed Druids who made that journey to see the Christ child, later on, in the 1st Century AD. The star of Bethlehem being the marker in the sky that led them there. Some commentators suggest that they also became his Teachers, bringing him to Egypt to train in the great temples of Memphis and Giza. It would account for the so-called 'Lost Years', but we need primary source corroboration to be more certain.

"If you also look at the Book of Kells, which is 7th Century AD, the illustrations are all Egyptian in character, resembling either Assyrian or Egyptian brush work. Moreover, the Celtic ornamentation in the Celtic cross, Triskell and other circular symbols bears strong similarity with the ornamentation found on clay tablets discovered in Amarna.

"Most pronounced is the representation of birds. Their delineation matches those found on Egyptian fresco painting. But what is truly astonishing is this." Ali flicked his pages of notes over.

"As early as 2000 BC, a canal linked the Pelusiac branch of the Nile, via the Wadi Tumilat, with the Bitter Lakes where a channel was dug to connect it directly to the Red Sea. Now, this fits in with the route taken from Amarna by Scota and Gaythelos according to the Glastonbury Archive, as Robert Bailey calls it."

"Robert is still processing that archive," Branwen said carefully. "He has added to it in recent weeks after his studies in Iona and Dublin. It is not yet complete." She was now stood motionless by the snow-covered window again.

"What are your thoughts on the Amen?" she asked, her back to him, her face firmly turned to the thick snowflakes tumbling relentlessly outside the twelve-paned window. She held a small remote in her left hand, pointing it deliberately at the thermostat on the wall beside the hinged shutters. He heard three clicks then the newly refurbished central heating radiators kicked in with a low rumble. Immediately, the temperature in the room rose to a more than comfortable 22 degrees.

"Thank you," he said humbly. "I was about to reach for my jacket."

"I know," she said simply. "And dinner will be served in exactly an hour and a half."

He looked back at his yellow notes, his hands shaking just a little. He cleared his throat and continued.

"Robert includes the King's notes at this point," he began, his face flushed with uncharacteristic embarrassment, mixed with a deep scholarly appreciation of the research undertaken to arrive at the monarch's findings. "These notes are taken from his brief study of the Sacred Cauldron of Bran; the interior section of which has definite Egyptian inscriptions.

"We know that the hieroglyphic for Amen was a straight vertical pole, like the capital letter 'I', topped with a sun disk with rays. This hieroglyph was known as 'men', meaning mountain, monument or even a block of stone. The image of the sun rising above a tall, ithyphallic stone has to represent something. The 'A' would be a prefix, presumably used to denote either a definite or indefinite article in grammatical terms. Therefore, we have either 'The Monument' or 'A Monument'. Either way, by saying the word out loud, 'Amen', one is giving praise to the giver of life, rendered through the medium of stone.

"We do know from traditional sources that they were in fact simply giving praise to the sun or Aten as it was called."

"Or simply, they were praising a monument?" Branwen said rhetorically. "Perhaps these monuments were symbolic representations. Either way, they had meaning, form and content. Books in stone," she continued, looking directly at him, holding his gaze in a vice-like grip.

"Which monuments were there, approximately 4000 years ago, that could be praised, or had what we might call an iconic status at the time? Think here in Britain and further afield in Egypt," she said.

Ali thought carefully before replying. He felt as if he was being interrogated and that always made him break out in a clammy sweat. He wiped his brow. Branwen didn't flinch but held her steady gaze.

"Avebury, Stonehenge, the Pyramids, Dendara, Memphis, Thebes, Luxor, Valley of the Kings …" he replied.

"And which of these monuments had iconography? And which did not?" she asked.

"Avebury and Stonehenge had no iconography, Branwen. All the others did."

"All?" she asked, stony-faced.

She held his gaze until the door opened, announcing the entrance of Steve Waterman armed with a basket of logs, a scrunched-up newspaper and a large box of matches tucked under his chin.

"Looks like we're here for the next twenty-four hours at least," he said cheerily. "Dinner in ten and then coffee in here. I expect you'll want to carry on this evening?" he said, looking bashfully at Branwen.

"I expect so too," she said in reply, not looking at him.

A look of amazement drifted gradually over Ali's pharaonic features as he glanced first at Steve and then at her. "I am so stupid!" he gasped. "The Great Pyramid has no iconography."

"Yes," she said serenely. "It hasn't. And you are. Yet there is one small point which may prove important to the discussion and it is this."

Branwen passed him a faded green folder. "Look," she said, as he extracted a handful of photographs, some blurred, some out of focus.

"What am I looking for?" he asked, puzzled and unsure.

"Here." She selected one of the clearer images. "What do you think it is?"

He focused on the image, its outline blurred but vaguely discernible. "It looks like the profile of a bird," he said slowly. "It looks like the head and body of a raven or a crow perhaps? There's another image there too … It looks to me like an ibis, the sacred Egyptian ibis."

Branwen spoke. "It was found in the King's Chamber, high up in a corner of the ceiling on a diagonal above the sarcophagus. Robert Bailey has examined it with some expert Egyptologists and concluded that it is indeed a marker.

"What we don't know is what it's a marker for. King Alfred believes that there is a secret room in the Great Pyramid and that the raven/crow/ibis marker is a key to unlocking it."

Ali looked again carefully. "It's definitely an ibis," he said. "There are two images here, one superimposed over the other. The first one is most definitely the ibis. Look, you can see its long beak. The second has a different profile, a shorter, snappier-looking beak and its hunched body resembles that of a crow or a raven. Most definitely.

"Now, the ibis represented the god Thoth, the Egyptian god of wisdom, knowledge and writing. If you look carefully, you'll see the ibis is sitting on a perch. This means it is most definitely Thoth because that was the hieroglyph for him. An ibis sitting on a perch."

"What about the other image?" Branwen asked.

"Well, I'm no expert, but it looks to me like a Celtic representation rather than an Egyptian one. I get the ibis/Thoth symbolism but I know very little about the Celtic symbols."

"You're right about the ibis," Branwen said pleasantly.

Ali looked delighted with himself and stood a good inch taller before catching the amused look on Steve's face.

"And tomorrow, you can deliver a short seminar on those findings," Branwen said. "Who's coming tomorrow, Steve?" she enquired.

"Just the usual," Steve said, busying himself with the log basket.

Ali swallowed. At least she'd said a short seminar. That was something at least.

"Can we just grab a sandwich?" Ali asked, a note of distraction in his voice as he shuffled his yellow notes into a pile. "I'd really like to press on this evening, if I may."

"Of course, if that's what you want." Steve Waterman gave him his lop-sided grin and turned to Branwen.

She was still standing, unmoving, still as a statue, her long red dress falling in pre-Raphaelite folds from her petite shoulders. Her glossy brown curls tumbled down her back framing a face that like Helen's could have launched another thousand ships. It was as if she was listening to something or someone no one else could hear. Steve knew how to wait. To disturb her reverie would cause an awful torrent of abuse, hurled down without fear or favour.

Ali noticed how Steve handled matters and was impressed. It would not have entered his egotistical head to wait for her to emerge from wherever she was. If he wanted to talk, he talked. If he wanted answers, he demanded them. There were only two people in the world who could command Ali Alalladin's fear and respect: Commander Taft and Sir Rufus. With a slight shiver, he made a mental note to add the singular Branwen to that number.

Steve Waterman busied himself with laying the fire. Arranging a small pile of kindling in between torn up strips of newspaper then piling small logs on top before lighting it all with a phosphorous match. Ali watched, fascinated.

This was an art form in itself, he mused. How many years had people made fires? Millennia, of course. Fire making was the most primitive skill known to man.

As the sticks crackled and the logs glowed, a deep sense of peace settled on the room. Outside, snowfall was reaching the windowsill and covering the lower panes of glass. Inside, Branwen stood as still as a statue, her eyes closed. If you listened carefully you could hear a thin discordant note faintly whispering in the frantic wind outside.

Steve disappeared and then returned carrying a large tray loaded with covered platters of sandwiches and a Thermos of tea for Branwen, one of coffee for himself and Ali. A sideboard of cups, saucers, sugar, milk and spoons was soon laden with the evening's repast and, still, Branwen remained in her trance like state.

"Is she all right?" Ali whispered to Steve as they helped themselves to the platters.

"She's fine, Ali. Don't worry. It takes a bit of getting used to but you have to remember that Branwen is very special, very special indeed. She's not like other people. You either accept that and get along with her or you impose your own expectations and end up post traumatic." He offered another lop-sided grin, which Ali responded to half-heartedly, before adding, "And don't get any daft ideas, lad. She would make mincemeat of you."

Ali was beginning to see what he meant.

"Here, put on these cotton gloves." Steve Waterman produced two pairs of white, fine cotton gloves from his jacket pocket. "Branwen wants you to look at this." Steve ambled over to a locked box sitting on a pedestal in the corner of the large room and unlocked it with a small key on a long gold chain. Carefully, he lifted out a rolled scroll of parchment written in faded sepia brown ink. Ali was reminded of the documents he had studied at St Catherine's in the Sinai. His heart beat faster as he realised what he was looking at.

"Look, I have to write up my daily report and send it off to Commander Taft. Make some notes on this scroll ready for Branwen. Remember that you have no access to cell phone or Internet whilst here. We are on a lockdown with this level of documentation, Ali."

Ali nodded wordlessly. He understood. This was basic procedure in all containment scenarios he had been involved with over the last ten years. He sat back on his chair and tried hard not to look at the silently standing Branwen, her face as pale as the swirling snow outside.

Gently, he unrolled the scroll. Its fragments had been expertly re-aligned, he could see, which meant that this was an original artefact probably curated at some point in its recent history. The University at Manchester had a world-class reputation for this type of reconstruction he knew. Why weren't they here then? Why him? He made a mental note to ask Commander Taft about that. When he next saw him.

It was written in hieroglyphs. Neatly drawn columns filled each section of the scroll and each section contained beautifully drawn images of gods, lotus plants, profile depictions of robe-clad women and kilt-clad men wearing jewels, amulets, the heads of falcons, the heads of the ibis. The men with one foot forward, the women standing still, holding the lotus flower close to their noses. Although the colours were faded, the vibrancy remained. Ali found a magnifying glass in a drawer and scrutinised each image carefully before making rapid notes on his yellow legal pad.

He noticed a strange glyph he hadn't come across before. This wasn't the traditional depiction of Thoth as Ibis sitting on a perch. This was something else entirely. He recognised the raven/crow shape that Branwen had shown him in the collection of photographs taken in the Great Pyramid. It was the same glyph! There was no record in the entire canon of Egyptology of the raven/crow. It was not representative of any of the pantheon of gods known in either Upper or Lower Egypt.

Yet here it was.

He scratched his head and looked up. Branwen was curled up in a small ball on the leather chesterfield in front of the log fire. Silently, he walked over to her and gazed longingly at her sleeping face. Finding her fur-lined cloak on the floor by her chair, he carefully placed it over her, feeling a strong surge of protectiveness wash unexpectedly over him.

He re-read the entire scroll. He re-read the scribbled notes. He made some more. He sifted through the reams of yellow paper he had made notes on all afternoon.

Knowing that there was something important if he could just make sense of the strange set of images in the scroll. Knowing that, somewhere, there was a reference point that would make a connection … if he could find it.

He carefully extracted his notes on the Pelusiac branch of the Nile where in 2000 BC a canal had been dug to the Bitter Lakes. Yes, the link he was searching for referenced a built artefact, a built environment, not an esoteric representation.

If the crow/raven/ibis image discovered in all its faded glory on the roof of the King's Chamber meant anything, it had to connect with a similar image. There wasn't one to his knowledge. The Egyptian pantheon held the falcon and the ibis in high regard. Nowhere, that he could recall, was there any mention of the raven or crow. It was a Celtic symbol, not an Egyptian one.

Or was it? What about The Wall of the Crow – south of Heit el Ghurab? The gigantic wall built on the Giza Plateau at the same time as the Great Pyramid?

He had never paid it any attention. No one paid it any attention, but that was its name. The Wall of the Crow.

The wall was 33 feet high and 40 feet thick at its base. Built entirely in stone it served as both a bridge and an ancient gateway.

Why was it called the Wall of the Crow?

Because the wall defined a division of two hemispheres.

The Great Pyramid sat, literally, in the centre of the world. The wall defined the division of those two hemispheres along a circumference line across the earth. The name of the wall referenced the ancient knowledge of flight and distance in the expression 'as the crow flies'. It was a massive structure that no one really looked at; no one really noticed, set on a part of the plateau never flagged-up for tourists to explore. Yet in ancient times this wall and its bridge with its massive lintel, the largest stone recorded on the vast site, had played a significant role in the life of the complex.

It was said to be the original entrance gate to the Great Pyramid.

This was the connection! He punched the air in relief. There would be no sleep for him tonight he knew. His mind whirling with the possibilities, weighing up what, exactly, this connection really meant. He continued with his notes well into the early hours of the morning. Glancing up at the snowed-up window, he could just discern the faint glow of morning high in a gloomy sky.

Finally, exhausted, he put his head on his arms and fitfully dozed, not even stirring when Steve Waterman silently threw a blanket over his shoulders before carefully carrying the still sleeping Branwen gently to her room.

CHAPTER 27

Tapping co-ordinates into her specially adapted GPS watch, Ceris adjusted her night goggles, taking a moment to orientate herself as the dark tunnel resolved into a wash of pea green. She could hear a rush of water close by, so she must be close to the ancient sewers, she thought, running the length and breadth of the great city. She was close. The red beam on her specially adapted chronometer pointed to the left as she came to a crossroads with three tunnels to choose from. She frowned. This was taking her away from Vatican City, not towards it. It couldn't be right. She paused, tapping the speakerphone on her watch. A faint ping told her it had been picked up.

"Pendragon?" a familiar voice enquired. Ceris relaxed. "Sir Rufus?" she whispered. "I seem to be going the wrong way ... away from, not towards Vatican City."

"No, you're going the right way, Pendragon. The artefact was moved an hour ago. I've had the co-ordinates changed. You are going in the right direction. Do you need assistance?"

"No, sir. I'm good. Do I need a re-brief?"

"Just get to where the co-ordinates take you. I'll update you then."

"Right, sir. On my way."

Ceris shook her head. This was all a bit odd, she thought. Why move the artefact out of the Secret Archives? Someone knew they were after it. How had that leaked out?

It was inevitable, she thought. Once Lord Farndon had broken contact with the elusive Aristobulus, it didn't take a genius to work out he'd been rumbled.

The fact that she'd arrived at Leonardo Da Vinci late that morning hadn't gone unnoticed either, she assumed. She had to be careful. Commander Taft had warned her that she was in danger of becoming the 'Poster Girl' of the Interregnum. Stories of her courage and bravery had begun to leak out to the press. Even though it was being managed, some things just couldn't be controlled.

And society was looking for heroes, having lost its old models.

A jumble of thoughts passed through her mind as she followed the steady red beam for another mile through the damp, dank tunnels, marvelling at their construction, most of which had been built well over a thousand years ago. This truly was an artefact itself, she thought, as, relentlessly, she pressed on.

The stone tunnel merged into a handcrafted brick one with a lower roof, curved and carved in places with faded graffiti. Two inches of water, stagnant and still, sloshed around her army issue boots as she ploughed on. Three small doors appeared in the tunnel. They were made of thick oak reinforced with iron strips both vertically and horizontally. The red beam flashed frenetically. This was it. She had reached her destination.

She squatted on a worn ledge running the length of the brick-structured tunnel, taking a sip of water from her hip flask. Listening carefully with her ear to the door she could hear nothing, just a scattering of rats as her torch beam threw them for a second into sharp relief.

Her wrist phone pinged. As she pulled it to her mouth to speak, the door behind her swung open, creaking on its rusted hinges in a sinister fashion. A blast of warm, dry air hit her back and shoulders as a pair of strong muscular arms swept down on her in a vice-like grip.

She screamed, flailing with her arms, her legs, her elbow sinking into the soft flesh of his face as she head-butted her assailant who, for one timeless moment, appeared to sway and stagger while still keeping hold of her tight in his steely grip. She relaxed, letting each muscle uncoil ready to slip down from his massive arms but he realised what she was doing and tightened his hold until she could barely breathe.

Hauling her unceremoniously through the small narrow door he flung her roughly on the stone flags, bare, cold, hard. She winced with pain, looking up at her assailant. He stood impassively, coldly looking down at her. She turned her head slightly.

"Welcome to Rome, Miss Pendragon," accented tones announced in an amused voice from behind her. She was hauled backwards through another, unseen door by a mountain of a man who didn't speak a word.

Hands tied, feet secured with a thin rope, Ceris found herself sitting on a bare wooden chair in a basement room piled high with cardboard boxes, old carpets rolled into corners, gilt-framed paintings, their faces turned to the whitewashed walls. The room was small and square with a corbelled ceiling showing faint cracks, thin damp patches. The air was fetid, oppressive, hot, sticky, uncomfortable, and windowless. She looked around calmly, her expert eye seeking out any means of escape. Nothing. Not yet anyway.

She focused on the three men standing over her. One was huge, six foot six at least and built like a battleship. He glared at her, nursing his cheek, which was turning blue after the almighty head butt she had given him. His partner in crime was not as tall or wide, but he had small, nasty eyes and an expression that spoke of a deep thrill at the prospect of violence or worse. Both of them were wearing Janitor jumpsuits with that distinctive logo she had seen somewhere before. The papal hat and the crossed keys.

Then number three, of average height, immaculately dressed in a cream Hugo Boss suit and crisp white shirt open at the collar revealing a thin gold crucifix on an equally thin gold chain. He was the one with the accent she guessed. She was right.

Delicately, he unfastened her GPS tracker while mountain man held a portable body scanner over her head. Lifting her into a vertical position, the other thug took great pleasure in running the device all over her body, rubbing it suggestively on her breasts then on her inner thighs. She tensed her muscles. He let out a childish giggle. Armani man slapped him across the head. She felt grateful and immediately recognised that he knew what he was doing. What was the name for it? That was it – Stockholm Syndrome – where you create gratitude in the hostage who, in return, wants to please.

"Anything?" Hugo Boss man asked his number two.

"She is clean, master," he said, a note of disappointment in his heavily accented voice.

"Smash the GPS," he ordered. "I want her moved immediately. Get her in the elevator. The chopper's on the roof, waiting. Go, go now!"

Ceris felt herself lifted bodily over the shoulder of mountain man. She didn't scream, she didn't speak. She knew that to do so would give them permission to tape up her mouth and possibly bag her head. Best to stay quiet and calm. It worked. It meant that she could physically orientate herself and this she knew was essential to retaining some vestige of emotional control in any hostage situation.

Its blades rotating frenetically, Ceris was dumped heavily into the rear seat of the chopper, which immediately took off, its noisy engines deafening without ear protectors. She glanced down. She couldn't recognise the building she had been in, but she did recognise the two blacked out SUV's speeding away from a side street nearby. "Special Ops," she mouthed to herself and was rewarded with a slick of black tape across her mouth.

The pilot banked and turned, following the line of the River Tiber. They were heading south. The Tyrrhenian Sea was 22 kilometres away as the patchwork of buildings, farms, roads and cars faded away to be replaced with the azure blue of the deep waters below.

✝✝✝

"Signal's gone," Sir Rufus rasped, smoothing his hand through his thinning hair. "Where's the Rapid Response Team?"

"They're waiting outside. Shall I give them the order to go?"

"Outside the embassy?"

"Yes, sir. They're in an unmarked van. Two actually. Vans that is."

Sir Rufus glowered as he paced up and down the British Embassy office in the Italian capital. "We can't just blast in," he grimaced. "It would cause an international incident. Why didn't we see this coming, Taft?"

Commander Taft sighed. He had arrived at the embassy moments before, following a strident command from his boss to get the first plane out. "We did, sir," was all he said cryptically. "You said yourself that it was a possibility and if it did indeed play out, then it would prove, once and for all, that the Americans were playing Caesar."

"Hmmmm," Sir Felix acknowledged, throwing himself on an empty chair near the door. "Any ideas?"

"Several," Commander Taft grimaced at his boss. "Most you won't like, but maybe one of them you will."

"Give me the one you think I will like then, Taft. We have to make a decision soon, a unilateral decision. The buck, as the Americans so elegantly put it, very much stops here."

"We play it out," Commander Taft said carefully.

"Play it out?" Sir Rufus wore a puzzled expression on his pale face as he frowned at his subordinate.

"She's become a bargaining chip, sir. The Americans will want to do a deal. What do they want from us? We have to have something that they want. When we give them that something, we get Pendragon back."

"Well that's obvious, Taft. It doesn't take a Doctorate in Philosophy to work that one out. Explain yourself, man!"

Commander Taft shook his head. He could read his boss like a book. This Knight of the Realm was deeply upset. He had allowed one of his assets, one of his best assets, to fall victim as a hostage. It was a dangerous game, hostage-taking and hostage negotiation. Ceris' life was literally on the line here.

"Well, hear me out, sir, and tell me what you think," he said confidently.

Sir Rufus looked at him blankly. "How on earth did they know we were there?" he said sadly.

"Here," Commander Taft said quietly. "It has to be here, in this embassy. Let me check. I'll get the Rapid Response Team to do a sweep of the building. We'll get hold of all phone/fax/email records and track them down. It's impossible to be off the radar these days, sir. Impossible."

"Good man," Sir Rufus responded, brightening slightly. "And your brilliant idea, Taft?"

"Pendragon has a biological tracker made of the latest Nano technology. Not even the Americans have it yet, which means that they can sweep for embedded chips, but not find hers. Advantage.

"Secondly, she is very highly trained, including hostage situations. If there's a way to escape, she will. I expect she'll be held in level one containment. Possibly off shore to avoid upsetting the politicians. Her tracker will give us any co-ordinates.

"And three, we know the artefact was moved to the American Embassy ... but it wasn't the artefact we wanted. We laid a false trail, didn't we, sir? The Book of the Bishop is still in situ ... In the Vatican. I suggest we take it tonight."

"Good points. Do we know what we're looking for, though, Taft?"

"No, sir. But I know someone who does."

CHAPTER 28

"We know you work for the British Government. We know you were sent to get, to steal, a precious manuscript belonging to the Vatican Library. From the Secret Archives no less! Why? What does your ridiculous government want with it?"

Hugo Boss Man, or as she had just learned, Luca Del Rossa, look-alike Mafia boss and general smooth talker, sat opposite a tired, defeated Ceris, still shackled, still wearing the black strip of tape across her lower face.

In one swift movement he ripped it off, leaving her momentarily seeing stars. Her mouth felt dry, patchy with the awful glue that inadvertently she had licked off her lips, but she was grateful that she could at least breathe through her mouth. Her nose had begun to clog with the chemical smell of the industrial tape.

"No comment," she said, gagging as the filthy glue dispersed on her tongue.

"I see." He looked closely at her expressionless face. "I see you have experience in this type of situation?"

"No comment," she choked.

"Let me tell you what I think, then," he said, stretching his legs out so that they almost touched hers. She moved her tightly bound ankles and winced. The thin rope was contracting not expanding in the early evening warmth, cutting into her flesh.

"I think your government's looking for evidence. Proof. It wants to show your British people that your ... what is it you call it? Ah yes, your 'Interregnum', is it not? Your Interregnum is blessed by Holy Mother Church. You are a very, how you say, 'odd' society.

"In my society, if we need proof, we invent it. But no, you British have to do the right thing, don't you? Stiff upper lip, is it not?" Del Rossa beamed at her, his tanned face and white smile positively delighted with his choice of words.

Ceris smiled back at him. A friendly smile. She knew she had to establish a rapport with her abductor but that rapport had to be managed somehow.

"You know I can't tell you anything, Mr Del Rossa," she said sadly. "I have taken an oath. A sacred oath. And an important man like yourself, I'm sure, knows all about sacred oaths. I wish I could help you, I really do, but I can't. Please, let me go and I promise I won't talk of this to anyone."

Del Rossa laughed. A strong, deep, masculine laugh. He shook his head and snapped his fingers. "Very good, Miss Pendragon. Ah yes, I know your name. Surprised? Perhaps not. You and I are very similar, are we not? We both work for the good of our countries.

"Now tell me, this book, this manuscript that you wanted to steal. It is of no significance, I think. My people tell me that you have a similar manuscript in your Bodleian Library. Why would you want another one? It does not make sense. My people think perhaps you are playing games with us. These are dangerous times, Miss Pendragon. It is very dangerous to play games with Del Rossa, too. Perhaps we can help each other … you tell me what you really want and I will tell you what I really want. A fair exchange, no?"

Ceris looked blankly at him. "I have no idea what you're talking about," she said carefully. "I think there's been a terrible mistake, Mr Del Rossa. I'm really not very important, you know. And I honestly don't know how I can be helpful. I was just …" She tailed off as he jumped to his feet, pointing a furious finger right in her face.

He glared at her, his brown eyes firing with anger. "Ah yes, I see. You were just taking a stroll down the Coliseum tunnels. Of course you were. I am so stupid, Miss Pendragon. You must forgive me. Why didn't I think of that? A pleasant afternoon, what could be more refreshing than a brisk walk down an ancient tunnel. That happens to pass by several sewer pipes and a concealed entrance into the Italian Embassy.

"You think me stupid? You and your government are the stupid ones, I think. Who would want to go through a Reformation, a Counter Reformation, a 17th Century Interregnum and now another one? The British people are mad, Miss Pendragon. Quite mad, as your people are fond of saying.

"Let me tell you, my country has had its problems, but we solve those problems through maintaining a fragile status quo, not by turning it upside down. Have you heard the expression 'Nature abhors a vacuum'? No? What you are creating in your so-called 'Great Britain' is just that. A vacuum, a dangerous, very dangerous vacuum and, as in nature, something will come along to fill it, Miss Pendragon.

"You have a history of invasions, have you not? Well, it is common knowledge this side of the channel that the Americans are very interested in filling that vacuum. You are a perfect landing strip, my dear, for their expansionist policies into Russia. But you know this, I'm sure."

Del Rossa paced around the spacious lounge deck, throwing her dagger looks as he ranted on. She maintained a silent observation carefully noting that he was both unpredictable and passionate. The burbling about the Americans piqued her interest, however. Commander Taft had briefed her on recent intelligence from GCHQ. They were talking not just strategy but tactics now, which meant they were deadly serious.

Drones had been spotted crossing both the English Channel and the Irish Sea, taking aerial photographs of the new internment facilities nationwide. One had been spotted hovering over the College of the Druids being built on the island. A pair of drones had hovered for a good ten minutes over Glastonbury too, forcing the Protector to reluctantly arm all security there and deploy crack marksmen. Daily COBRA meetings were now the norm, he'd said. Something was most definitely brewing.

She tuned back in to what Del Rossa was saying.

"Take her below," he snarled as Mountain Man grabbed her under the arms and lifted her in one swift sweep, spitting at her to keep quiet if she knew what was good for her.

Plodding heavily down the metal staircase toward the lower deck, he put one hand over her mouth, pressing hard, laughing horribly when she gagged at the smell of diesel. Her face felt as if it had been smeared with a glutinous evil-smelling viscous film.

She could hear voices above her, coming from the lounge deck. Hugo Boss man's distinctive Italian-accented baritone, mixed with a clear, Boston-accented female voice. She strained her ears but couldn't make out the conversation. The American sounded aggressive she thought. Probably CIA.

Ceris took a deep breath. This was definitely getting dangerous. If they took her, she could end up in the female Guantanamo somewhere in the Philippines, and she'd be there for the next twenty years at the very least. She swallowed her nerves. Keep focused, she told herself sternly. And watch for the Optimum.

The Optimum was elite speak in Ceris' security circles for the one single moment in every hostage situation which could change the chessboard to the hostage's advantage.

It could come from a single moment of inattention when a key or a knife or a sharp object could be grabbed and hidden away. It could be a distraction manoeuvre whereby you take the guard by surprise through exhibiting unexpected behaviour thus wrong-footing him or her to gain an advantage. Or it could simply be taking an almighty risk such as throwing yourself out of a car or a window and praying that the gods would protect you.

Or it could be through cyanide.

Every senior operator had a cyanide pill hidden in a watch, in a pen, a ring, the waistband of a pair of panties or a pair of boxers. Standard issue. Sometimes, the Optimum could be achieved simply by biting down on the gel casing and letting the carefully calibrated poison stop the pain.

She kept calm as Mountain Man pushed her through the door of a small cabin, laid out with a double bed, a small dressing table and a single built in wardrobe all painted in white. Even the bed linen was white.

To her eyes it looked clinical, depersonalised. He pushed her onto the bed, grinning lasciviously through broken teeth, his breath stinking of garlic and gas. He prodded her suggestively, poking his finger into her breast, cupping the other with his oil-stained hand. She noticed that all his fingernails were bitten to the quick.

Mountain Man sliced through the rope binding her feet with an old-fashioned Swiss army knife. She was impressed. These particular knives were collectors' items and since her initial training, when the class had gone to an Arms Auction where one similar had sold for two thousand pounds, she had made a promise to herself that one day …

He pointed the thin blade in her face and made a stabbing movement from which she recoiled with a sharp intake of breath. He laughed, a sneer more than a laugh, she thought, as she closed her eyes and held out her wrists. He sliced through the restraint, deliberately cutting into the palm of her hand, drawing a thin trickle of thick red blood.

"What is this?" He took a step back, holding her hand out flat, pointing with the bloodied knife at a delicately executed marking on her inner wrist.

"A tattoo," she said sullenly.

"This a bird?" he said, squinting myopically, leaning heavily over her.

"It most certainly is," she said, grabbing his knife with one hand while the other twisted his testicles in a clockwise then an anti-clockwise motion. Before he could react, her knee flew into his surprised face, knocking him off balance, his hands flailing as they tried to gain purchase but there was nothing there. She kicked out twice: sharp jabs into his solar plexus. He straightened and she took a running jump off the double bed, her feet smashing into his twisted arm knocking him off balance as he tipped over, his heavy weight thundering into the dressing table behind him splintering its ornate triple mirror into large jagged fragments. He looked astonished. That was what she remembered when she looked back on it all. He looked astonished.

She grabbed one of the fragments, slicing through his jugular like a razor. His blood pumped frantically over the pristine white carpet, the white bed linen turning a patchwork of pink and red. He gagged and choked, clutching his neck, whimpering, the blood mixing with the oil on his hands, covering the badge on his jumpsuit, discolouring the papal hat and the crossed keys.

She wiped the blade on his jumpsuit before slipping it into her pocket.

She didn't look at him. It was a job. He was a job. She felt nothing.

She had to get out. There was no window in the airless space but the door wasn't locked. He hadn't locked it as they'd come in. She removed her army boots, took the key from the door and locked it behind her, the scarlet smell of iron deep in her nostrils.

Creeping stealthily back up the metal stairs, she could hear voices coming from the lounge cabin just below the boat's deck. Two voices. Armani Man and the same Boston-edged voice. They were talking quietly. No one else appeared to be about. She crept closer, crouching down behind a wide square pillar.

"I'll take it from here," the American said smoothly. "What did you get out of her?"

Del Rossa shuffled his feet. "She just said 'no comment', signora," he replied sorrowfully. She tutted in exasperation.

"Do you know what I think?" she said sharply. He shook his head. "I think we're being played Luca. That's what I think. She's a decoy. They don't want that bitch of a book or manuscript whatever. This is a flushing exercise. It's got Sir Rufus' hand all over it … Tell me, what exactly is so goddamn important about this manuscript?"

Del Rossa shrugged his immaculate shoulders. "The manuscript lays claim to America," he said.

"What?" she shouted. "You have got to be joking!"

He shrugged his shoulders and tutted. He did not appreciate women who were loud and brash in their speech and she was both. He felt very disappointed.

"Signora, you asked what was in the document. I am, in good faith, trying to tell you. Trying to answer your question. I do not appreciate being screamed at because the answer you wanted wasn't the one I could give you!"

Ceris had to admire his attitude. He'd get on with Branwen!

She reminded herself that he could also be difficult and unpredictable as she decided to wait for a few more minutes. The conversation might develop. Mountain Man wasn't going anywhere. She was fine for a little while. Another few minutes, then she'd make her way out.

"Here," he said, a note of disdain in his voice. "Here is the document. See for yourself, signora." He handed her a red leather-bound volume emblazoned with the Crown of Great Britain. Inside was a slim parchment folder containing five thin parchment pages the colour of old gold. "This is, as you can see ..." Ceris heard papers rustling as they looked at the delicate pages.

"This is the royal charter, a copy, of course, not the original, giving authority to the Virginia Company, dated 10th April, 1606. See, the date is there," he pointed, tapping the evidence for effect. "And here is the signature of the King. King James I."

"And?" The American agent was tapping her foot with impatience. Ceris strained her ears to hear as their voices lowered. She crouched in a squat, ready to jump and run should she need to, her eye on the five steps leading up to the deck of the cruiser and the wide blue water beyond.

"And. The original company was closed down a few years later, but the charter and its letters patent were never rescinded. It was law and that law was never repealed. Which leads to this." He handed her another sheet of old gold parchment on which had been hand copied the 1871 Act, passed by Congress, which created the District of Columbia as a separate entity from the rest of the States.

He pointed meaningfully at one of the articles. "See, signora, the District of Columbia is now designated as a separate entity. It is now a corporation. Just like the City of London. Just like Vatican City. So we have Washington, London and Vatican City as separate entities. I had not realised however, signora, that the Vatican was the first of these three countries within a country. I had thought it was Rome.

"I have learned something valuable, signora. Three states within three states. If you think that the British are playing games, perhaps this is a message?"

She extracted the parchment from the folder, looking quizzically at his face.

"This is the Act passed by Congress in 1933," he said. "Do you notice anything different?"

She frowned, scouring the document intently before sharply inhaling. "It's the Emergency Banking Act. It declares the United States of America bankrupt." She waved the document around, her face a picture of frustration and impatience. "Are you playing games here, Luca? I'd strongly advise against it!"

He smirked and shook his head. "I am not playing games, signora, why would I? To what end would it serve? I am, as you know, acting on behalf of my government, who have instructed me to give you every assistance in this matter. It is of little consequence, indeed no consequence to me or my country, if you should remain ignorant of your own history. Though I would advise against it.

"It would appear, signora, that the English are sending you a coded message. Your America belongs to the City of London. The Corporation of London, to be precise. And has done since 1933.

"Benedictus, signora. Rome wasn't built in a day."

Ceris froze and crouched lower. It was him! He was Aristobulus! She had to get out, get off the boat. She had to find Sir Rufus. She had to tell him!

It was time to move. Her sixth sense had kicked in and she could feel that familiar tingling sensation in the soles of her feet. Her muscles tensed as she calculated distance and how high she needed to spring jump to clear the four-foot chrome barrier ahead.

A panicked roar erupted below deck. A babble of choice Italian-laced expletives ranted up the spiral metal stairs. Someone had smashed the fire alarm in panic, releasing an eardrum-bursting cacophony that rattled the brain.

At the sound of heavy feet climbing metal stairs, Ceris knew it was time to go. She sprinted forward, crashing into Boston woman, sending her sprawling into the arms of Hugo Boss Man himself. He reached for his holster, but it wasn't there.

He picked up a heavy ornate paperweight, exquisite Murano glass, took aim and threw it with a cricketer's arm. It hit her on the back of her head, sending her spinning up the five steps to the deck as he ran after her, grabbing her leg as she fell.

The world began to swim as she struggled to get free of his grip but he wasn't as strong as he thought he was. No stamina. And Ceris knew that if she could just hang on she could wear him out in a few minutes.

Impractical. Boston woman had a gun and she was about to use it. Ceris lifted her one free leg, kneeing him in the side of his impeccably styled head. He groaned and let go of her. The American pointed the gun, waving it around, screaming at Ceris to lie on the floor, hands above her head.

"Take a running jump!" she said to them both as she staggered to the prow and flipped herself over the four-foot barrier, leaving trickles of blood on the chrome rail. She held her breath. A shot rang out and Ceris felt herself sinking, slowly sinking. The water wasn't a beautiful blue and she felt shocked at that. It was dark, murky, and difficult to see.

The last thing she remembered was clutching onto a long strand of seaweed, marvelling at its cool, spongy texture as she closed her eyes.

CHAPTER 29

"I don't understand ..." Sir Rufus looked blankly at his Commander as they stood over the massive battered leather tome, its gilt-edged pages thickened with damp, mould and age.

"I don't either, sir." Commander Taft bit his bottom lip as he re-read the thin gilt lettering, barely visible in the fading light of a Roman evening.

"Is there a note?" Sir Rufus asked, rubbing his balding pate and looking each one of his fifty-eight years.

Commander Taft passed him a neatly typed sliver of paper, the length and width of a bookmark. "Just this," he said sadly, handing it to him. 'Benedictus', it said. 'Rome wasn't built in a day'.

"How is she?" Sir Rufus asked.

"Touch and go, sir. Lucky we had the dive team on hand. Lucky we got to her before her bio tracker faded. She arrested twice, sir."

"I know, Taft. Dreadful business. Dreadful. We shouldn't have let her do it, you know. I feel very responsible, very responsible indeed."

"I know sir. I feel the same, but it's what she wanted. She volunteered and we did tell her that it could be extremely dangerous. She badly wanted to do it."

"Doesn't make me feel any better though. Does it you?"

"No, sir. It doesn't."

"Will you be visiting her this evening?"

"I will, sir, though the medics have put her in a temporary coma while they assess the damage."

"They do say that hearing's the last thing to go. Expect just talking to her could help."

"It's worth a try, sir."

"Indeed. Have you informed Robert Bailey?"

"No, not yet. But we'll have to get him here, or send this book to him for analysis. What do you suggest?"

"Take it to him, Taft. Don't say a word until we know for certain what her injuries are. Bailey has to be kept on task. And that's from Madam Protector, not me. They discussed it this morning in COBRA. Out of my hands. Can you make out the title of the thing, Taft?" Sir Rufus squinted at the lettering as he polished his reading glasses with his tie.

"The Book of the Bishop," he read the title, slowly enunciating every syllable.

They looked at each other. "Final bit of the jigsaw, Taft?"

The Commander nodded his head.

"And what do we do about our friend here?" Sir Rufus pointed at the cryptic sliver of paper.

"We talk to him, sir. When we discover who he really is. We won't know until Pendragon can give us information. All we do know is that he was on the boat. It's too much of a coincidence otherwise. Pendragon in a coma, CIA woman on a plane out of here and The Book of the Bishop landing in our collective laps like this. I suggest we try sending a text to that locked-down number again. The one Lord Farndon sent his photographs of the King's Chamber to and see if we get a response."

"I can see where you're going with this, Taft. Good man." Sir Rufus scratched his head. "And what about the CIA woman? She's gone underground since the shooting I understand," he said.

"Her embassy has repatriated her, sir. She's gone."

"Ah yes. Standard procedure, of course. What about the electronic sweep of the embassy? Any news?"

"Only that the order came out of our Egyptian embassy. Coded response, classic counter intelligence set up. It's going to take time to thoroughly decode, sir."

"I see. I take it you've organised counter intel in Cairo?"

"Already done. Waiting game now, sir."

"I see. Let me see that note again, Taft."

Taft handed it over.

"We've got to speak to Pendragon, Taft. This is the same marker old Farndon received when he sent his pictures of the King's Chamber. Who was she with on that boat?"

"Security only saw the American get on the boat. A smaller craft motored out after a helicopter drop-off but whoever was on it, including Pendragon, was kept below deck. No images, no pictures taken. I suspect they had blockers bouncing back any transmission from mobile units. Their boat circled the yacht, the passengers embarking from the opposite side to where our surveillance teams were. It was a botched job, sir."

Sir Rufus' face was pink with indignation as he paced the room. "So you're telling me we still don't know who this Aristobulus character is?"

"We don't. But if he's sending us an ancient tome that we were perfectly prepared to steal from the Secret Archives, then surely, that tells us something?"

"What's in the book, Taft?"

"I can't read it, sir ... it looks like a mixture of old Brythonic, quite a bit of Greek and a fair bit of Latin. It needs an expert. It needs Robert Bailey ... Or Ali Alalladin."

"He knows all those languages?" Sir Rufus was impressed.

"He does. He came to us as an academic expert initially, very bright and very loyal. He speaks twenty-two languages and reads twenty-three."

"Which is the one he reads but doesn't speak, Taft?"

"Ancient Brythonic."

"Get the book to him. And get Branwen out here. If anyone can save the girl it's her. Tell her she mustn't speak of Pendragon to Bailey. No one must speak of her to Bailey. If anyone asks, she's on special operations and incommunicado."

"Nice bit of Italian there, sir." Taft offered his boss a watery smile.

Sir Rufus reciprocated with one of his own.

CHAPTER 30

Luca Del Rossa held his head in his hands. He hadn't bargained for this. Impetuously, he had taken the Book of the Bishop from his boss' desk, angry with the Americans, angry with his own government, angry with the girl throwing herself off the boat like that. Angry that she had slipped away, leaving a trail of blood and gore that he had to account for to his superiors. He was tired of his life. Where was the beauty? Where the harmony? Why was his life so hard, so difficult, so unsatisfying?

When his superiors found out what he had done, when the Vatican found out what he had done, he could find himself hanging under a bridge in London, like that banker, the one who had messed with both.

His mother had told him, years ago, that he would come to a bad end. "You don't think!" she had screamed at him when he had emptied her purse containing a few euros, all they had for food that week, into the open sewer running parallel to the shanty apartment block they lived in on the edge of the great metropolis.

He had been angry with her. He had wanted a Calvin Klein shirt he had seen in a shop window downtown. Sixty euros. She had laughed and told him he was stupid. He would show her stupid!

"You and your red mist," she had said. "It will be the undoing of you!"

She had been right. He was royally undone.

He poured himself a large glass of Merlot and sat on his small balcony overlooking the piazza. He could see out but no one could see in, fringed as it was with palm plants, their feathery leaves creating the perfect barrier.

He would try to get the book. He would go back to the British Embassy and tell them there had been a terrible mistake. Yes, he would do it now. He would finish his wine and head out back to the embassy.

A phone rang. Not his usual mobile but the one he kept for special ops. The one that couldn't be traced. No one had that number. It must be a patched call he surmised. Untraceable.

"Good evening." A British voice spoke: calm, collected, used to being in control.

He said nothing.

"My name is Commander Taft. I want to thank you for letting us have the Book of the Bishop."

He remained silent.

"I'd also like to tell you, in person if I may, that if there is anything that I or my government can do to reward you personally … we are, I repeat, most grateful."

Luca Del Rossa gripped the old Nokia handset tight and took a deep breath. "I am in trouble," he said. "If they find out what I have done … Whitehall Bridge will beckon." His voice choked with fear, his hand shook, spilling the ruby red wine over the shabby brown carpet. It looked like blood. A terrified gasp escaped from his mouth.

"Who are they?" the Commander asked carefully.

"My boss," Luca stuttered with a heavy sigh.

"And who, may I ask, is your boss?"

Luca Del Rossa flung himself on the single chair in his tiny bedsit.

"I am a freelance, as you say in your country. I fix things. For the government, for the Mafia, for the Vatican. If there is a messy job to sort out then I help to do it. Mostly tributes these days. Sometimes a bit of intimidation, scaring people who don't pay their tributes on time … you know the sort of thing."

Commander Taft didn't. "Why the book? Why hand it over to us?"

"I was very angry with them. I had been told to wait in the basement room of the Italian Embassy with my two enforcers … thugs you would call them, but we call them enforcers because that's what they do. Enforce."

Commander Taft's face wore a look of incredulity as he motioned to Sir Rufus to listen in on speakerphone.

"So, your operator is sitting outside the secret door, sitting on the ledge of the old brick tunnel – I used to play there as a child – and we grab her, take her to the top of the building and a helicopter transfers us to a small yacht out in the bay. It belongs to the Cardinals.

"She is very calm. We restrained her, but she was very clever, she killed Mario. Terrible mess. I threw a paperweight, a heavy one. It hit her but she kept going. CIA shoots and she falls into the sea. I did not want her to be badly hurt, you must believe me. I think she must be dead. I am sorry.

"My boss is very angry with me and tells me I will pay. The Americans are very angry with him and he will pay. The Cardinals are furious with us both, he tells me. We will pay dearly.

"He has your book on his desk, the book about some Bishop. I know it is the one your people want. Your Lord Farndon told me. He has been here, talking to the Cardinal. I slip back into his office, take it and bring it to your embassy. This is everything. I have nothing to pay them with. Except my life."

"What did the American want?" Sir Rufus mouthed silently to his deputy, flapping his hand in a gesture of impatience.

"There was an American on board, I understand," the Commander stated evenly. "What was she there for? If you tell me everything I promise I can help you."

"She is CIA," he said quietly. "She knew you wanted the book, the other book, the one that was taken to the Italian Embassy from the Vatican, the one about how London owns America.

"A call was intercepted from your Embassy, saying they were planning to take it after the reception for the Americans. That book was very interesting. I read it and discovered it was to be handed over to the Americans. They did not want anyone to find out the truth about America. I found out that it is a copy, the only copy they said, the original remains in Oxford, in the Bodleian Library. I was told to hand the book over to the agent then I was to be sent to Oxford to take the original. That will not happen now."

"I said I can help you and I will. Can you get to the airport?" Commander Taft asked. "I have a charter plane on standby. Leaving for London in an hour."

"I have no money, no passport ... they will know what I have done and will come here and kill me. I am a dead man!"

"Tell me, Luca. Do you have a code name?"

"A code name? What is this? My name is Luca, Luca Del Rossa."

"What does 'Benedictus, Rome wasn't built in a day' mean, Luca?"

The silence was electrifying. "Luca? Talk to me! I know you're there," Commander Taft hissed, his pulse rate raised to fight or flight levels.

"I am here," the miserable voice of the young Italian whispered. "Benedictus is the senior Cardinal," he said. "And 'Rome wasn't built in a day' is a reference to ..."

"I think I know what it's a reference to ..." Sir Rufus said out loud.

"I think I know too, sir," Taft replied. Both looked hard at each other, their faces pale, their eyes full of concern. Taft shook himself. He ordered a blacked-out SUV and within minutes it was on its way to Del Rossa's studio apartment. Sir Rufus sat heavily in his leather desk chair and pressed his contacts button.

"Sir?" Commander Taft pointed to the door.

"Of course, Taft. I very much hope there's some improvement."

The door closed softly. Sir Rufus turned to his desk phone.

"Archbishop?"

"Rufus, old friend."

"What's happening, Odo? Been a tad busy over here the past few days, feel a bit out of the loop if you get my drift."

"Ah yes, time marches on, does it not? Developments, old sport. We have had some developments. Very interesting ones too, I might add. You should be here, Rufus, not gadding about indiscriminately in the Eternal City."

"Developments? What developments?"

"Are you all right, old chap?" the Archbishop asked, a note of concern in his voice. "You sound a bit, well, strung out. Is everything all right over there?"

"You know about Pendragon?" he asked.

"She is in my prayers constantly," the venerable old man replied. "We've sent Branwen. She should be with you in a few hours. And before you ask, no. Robert doesn't know. He's in Cairo for the next few weeks researching … though perhaps it would be best to let him know. I am not happy at all with the government decision on this, Rufus."

"I have to agree, but what can we do?" the security chief acknowledged, sympathising with the prelate. Robert had a right to know, for heaven's sake. He had once been the dearest person in her life and he in hers. If that didn't give him a right to know then he didn't know what did.

"Tell me," Sir Rufus said carefully. "Tell me what you know about Benedictus. We have problems with someone bearing this name and, despite Taft's best efforts, we can't get a handle on it. We did think it just meant blessings but I've concluded that it is most definitely a name. And the name of a very dangerous man.

"You know everyone in the old and new churches, Odo … or if you don't you can go fishing for us, I'm sure. At the moment, it's a puzzle and one we have to solve. It's become extremely urgent."

"Do you mean the Cardinal? If it's the one I'm thinking of, that's his nickname! It's Cardinal Sfozzi really, but he's called Benedictus because everywhere he goes he says 'Blessings', accompanied by a sort of royal wave. Quite amusing actually, though some would say it's more annoying than amusing. I try to be tolerant. It does sound as if he's your man, Rufus. No other by that name over there as far as I'm aware."

"In confidence, Odo, what more can you tell me? I have some sensitive intelligence regarding the man and I need your input."

"He's a first rate scholar, old chap. Highly intelligent, speaks four or five languages, meteoric rise through the ranks, about the same age as you. Heavily tipped as a front runner for the top job when the time comes."

"Yes, yes, but what about his … inclinations, Odo?"

"What do you mean?" The venerable Archbishop was mildly shocked.

"No, no, I don't mean that! I mean, what does he believe? Does he exhibit any odd ideas, different view of the world, anything on those lines I suppose?"

"Well, yes, now you mention it. He makes regular trips to Egypt. Oversees some of their church's archaeological digs. Buys up old bits of manuscript from some of the dealers at the Khan el Khalil. And, rumour has it, has a very frosty relationship with the Greek Orthodox brothers who can't – so I was told at an interfaith convention a few years ago – abide him. Very arrogant, evidently, and very dangerous. They all walk on eggshells when he's in town.

"This is just hearsay though, old boy. Second hand gossip I expect you could call it.

Dare I ask why you're so interested in him?"

"I think he's orchestrating the gathering storms, Odo. I think he's the main player behind the surveillance drones. I think he's convinced the Americans that if they don't get us first, we'll get them. They have might on their side and we ... well, we have right I suppose."

"I don't follow, old chap." Archbishop Odo sounded bemused.

"I'm not sure I do either," the Head of National Security confided. "Connections, Odo, connections. Why on earth would a high-ranking Cardinal, tipped for the top job, involve himself in terrorist activities? Because that's what these drone events are, make no mistake! They transmit data in real time, Odo, so you can shoot the buggers down all right but they've already transmitted sensitive information over the pond."

"I think there's more to it, old friend," the Archbishop said carefully. "Think about the seminar we had in Glastonbury when Robert, Steve Waterman and myself gave a little talk each, an update on events ... When was it? ... Two years ago? Something like that. My memory's not so good these days. Regardless, can you remember what we discussed afterwards, in the Scriptorium? You and I had a discussion about power vacuums? We talked about how a modern-day Aristobulus could act as a Trojan horse? Now, who do you think that could be? ... Could history be repeating itself?"

The Head of National Security paused for a moment. Something clicked into place.

"Good God, Odo! You're right. Why didn't I see it before? We need to make a move. And we need to make it quickly."

CHAPTER 31

"What do you mean she's under arrest?" Angela Astley was incandescent with rage. "She's my Foreign Secretary, for heaven's sake, Rufus! You can't arrest the Foreign Secretary."

"She's Aristobulus, Angela," Sir Rufus said sadly. "We have all the evidence we need. She's been working all along with Cardinal Sfozzi in Rome and Endegard in the White House. She's been passing on everything to the Americans via the Vatican. It's all here." He handed her a thick buff folder tagged with the red Top Secret logo.

"Where is she now?" the Protector asked, aghast.

"Where all traitors should be," Sir Rufus said menacingly. "In The Tower."

"Talk me through it," she said, her face a picture of ashen disbelief. "I can't believe it, you know. Not only was she a wonderful Culture Secretary, but she really seemed to relish her promotion last year to the Foreign Office and I know her civil servants hold her in high regard."

"Yes, we're looking into that, too," the security chief said with an arch expression.

"And do you know what, Rufus?" she sniffed.

He shook his head.

"I thought she was my friend. How clever is that?"

"You were not to know, Protector," he said sadly. "The set up was masterful. Here, let me walk you through it all."

"Yes," she said bleakly. "We can't afford to let anything like this happen again. How compromised are we?"

Sir Rufus sucked in his breath and held her troubled gaze steadily with one of his own. "Truth?" he groaned. "Totally. We're totally compromised. They know everything. They have a complete set of data regarding timescales, building programmes, training schedules, intelligence gathering, and military manoeuvres. You name it, they've got it."

"But why, Rufus? Why would she sell us out? I don't understand … I can't believe I misjudged her or that I misjudged myself in appointing her to such a sensitive position … it's unprecedented. And it's on my watch too."

"It happens. It's a terrible shock when it does, of course, but with all due respect, we don't have the luxury of time to agonise about it now. We have to make some serious decisions."

"Yes, of course, yes. You're right, Rufus. I think I'm in a state of shock and I don't have time to indulge myself right now … but still … how could she?"

"She was bought, plain and simple, Angela. It's all there," he said, pointing to the buff folder on the coffee table between them.

"She was promised your job, basically. But first, she had to push for the disestablishment of the church, implement a co-ordinated campaign of 'Hearts and Minds', I think you'd call it. Once that happened, the Vatican would move in to re-establish the church with American backing. Remember that tag line? 'Rome wasn't built in a day'? Well, it seems Rome has never got over their first Bishop of Britain, Aristobulus, being martyred here. It's a case of historical revenge really.

"You see, we are their first born, Angela. The British Church was the first Christianised community in the world. What Aristobulus lost, they hoped Queen Mary I would recover. When Elizabeth I reversed it all, they arranged for the country to be invaded and the Queen to be excommunicated. This is, hopefully, the last chapter in a very long story of the subjugation of these islands by Rome. Spiritually, economically, politically and militarily.

"What did America get out of it? Well, in a way you can't blame them. When we found proof that those Letters Patent of James I had never been revoked; when we found proof that the creation of the District of Columbia created *America* as a corporation and not a country; and when we found proof that the Declaration of Independence was a philosophical document not a legal one, well, like anyone else, they'd fight for what they believed to be theirs.

"And they took a leaf out of our history books, Protector. Same as Henry VIII. Loot the archives, rip up the charters and letters patent proving that America is still owned by Britain."

Angela Astley turned aside and reflected. Her shoulders tense, her face a picture of furious passion and outright dismay. "Do you feel the hand of destiny on your shoulder, Rufus? I'm beginning to feel it on mine," the Protector said, as she stood with her back to him, looking out at the grey afternoon from the white-netted window. She pushed her shoulders back and lifted her chin, a gleam of purpose in her tired eyes as she turned to face her Head of Security.

"To business, then. Do you suggest a change of plan?" she said briskly.

"No, I don't think that's necessary," Sir Rufus replied.

She arched an eyebrow. "And why not?" she queried, slightly perturbed.

He clasped his hands together earnestly and began. "If we change anything too quickly we tell them we're rattled by all of this. I mean, what can they actually do? We have secured all air space. Naval vessels and coastguards monitor all of our shipping lanes. Cctv cameras monitor the coastline twenty-four hours a day. And we have an army of shift workers monitoring those cameras.

"The curfew has worked far better than expected and you mentioned in COBRA that there was a surplus of cash that could be distributed without compromising economic forecasts.

"I suggest that we use that surplus to buy a little goodwill. Give the people something to be happy about. Organise a Day of Truth, for example, where we beam the full story of these momentous events to the nation and give it all a positive spin. We could have street parties, special exhibitions, specially commissioned television programmes telling the story of it all.

"Tell them the truth, Protector. Then when the negative propaganda campaign begins – as it will – we have the potential for a positively programmed result."

She looked at him disbelievingly. "Are you suggesting bread and circuses?"

He shifted uncomfortably in his chair, not looking at her directly, before he replied, "Yes, Protector, that's exactly what I'm suggesting."

"And what do you think it will achieve?" she calmly asked, a note of disappointment in her voice.

"Have a look at this," he said as he pointed the remote to the wall screen.

A panoramic view of the pyramids appeared on the screen to the background sound of a pipe band playing a haunting lament. The camera panned downwards, toward the timeless face of the sphinx and across the plateau, framing a massive lintel stone in the centre of what looked like a bridge.

"This is The Wall of the Crow, Protector. The lintel stone you can see in the centre there is the largest dressed stone recorded on the plateau. We know that this once was the processional route, the original entrance route to the Great Pyramid."

The view changed, showing the interior of the King's Chamber in the Great Pyramid. Panning up into a corner of the massive granite ceiling an object could faintly be seen, a yellow chalk marker outlined the image.

"What is that?" she asked, intrigued.

"It's a symbol, an outline of an ibis merged with the silhouette of a crow or raven – they belong to the same family I understand – crows and ravens, that is," Sir Rufus replied.

As the King's Chamber faded, a panoramic sweep of green hills, green fields, birds nesting, birds flying and a mighty river tumbling over glistening rocks came into view, sweeping majestically upwards until it stopped, focusing on an old ruined castle set against a background of moody sky and scudding clouds.

"Castle Dinas Bran!" she said, recognising its bleak outline from the painting. A bare leaved tree leaned at a forty-five degree angle on the edge of the mound. A murder of crows sat silently in the tree, watching carefully the team of archaeologists busily digging trenches below. The scene faded to be replaced by a still shot of the sarcophagus back in the King's Chamber. Sir Rufus switched the remote to standby and turned to face his boss.

The Head of National Security wore an expression of serenity as he gazed longingly at the still image of the empty sarcophagus.

Angela Astley looked at him in wonder. "Is this what I think it is?" she asked tentatively, overawed, uncertain.

"Yes. Yes it is, Protector,' he smiled. "The original, pre-Christian, 4500 year old empty tomb. Proof that the 33 AD empty tomb was a natural progression from its earlier antecedent. Proof that *The Other Exodus* really happened. And proof that its belief system was transplanted to these shores.

"We now know that the empty sarcophagus was the first, the empty tomb of Jesus the second and somewhere, here on this island, there is the third. The Sacred Book of Bran reveals these truths. When we find Whiting's Archive, the third truth will be made clear. We are the inheritors of the three truths, Protector, and nothing can take that away from us. Once the people have the full story, do you honestly think they will want to go back to how we were before?"

"But I don't understand," she said. "Why the Book of the Bishop? What relevance does that have?"

Sir Rufus looked at her. "It's a book of incantations, Protector," he said seriously. "According to Robert Bailey, they are dressed up as narrative poems, praise poems in the main, I suppose you could call them, that would have been sung or spoken at ancient gatherings.

"The old kings would have had their own bards, poets really, who were responsible for both remembering all the history and stories of the tribes and sharing them as a form of entertainment in the mead halls during peace time, bellowing them out loud to the enemy during the wars and battles when they were under siege.

"The words have power and, when spoken in the right way, at the right time of year, in harmony with the movement of the seasons, the movement of the stars, a terrible harmonic would be unleashed. Victory or defeat would be in the hands of the Druids orchestrating that harmonic perfectly.

"Ali Alalladin tells me that these poetic incantations follow the exact same structure as those found on Egyptian obelisks. Many of these obelisks have spell chants and praise chants engraved upon them.

"In summary then, Protector, the Book of the Bishop is a collection of hymns, spells, chants and invocations that, for reasons of security, the Vatican decided to hide away in the Secret Archives.

"Aristobulus himself, in the 1st Century AD, collected these poems, hymns and chants into this book as he travelled through Prydain and he compiled a narrative record of his experiences, seeing these rituals performed in various sacred places.

"It was his setting it all down in writing, in this book, that inflamed Bran and his Druids. For over the millennia these words were committed to memory in the Druidic Colleges for a very special reason and never written down for fear of their potency ending up in the wrong hands. You see, events in Egypt threw up a cohort of priests who used the ancient magic for their own selfish ends. And that resulted in a terrible chaos. A mass migration took place, two migrations in fact, one to the Promised Land in the east, Canaan, and one to the Promised Land in the west, Prydain.

"That was the reason for Aristobulus' execution, ordered by the great Royal Arch Druid himself, Bran the Blessed. As we know, the Roman Catholic Church made Aristobulus a saint and his feast day is still celebrated as one of the Holy Martyrs.

"Robert Bailey found a reference to it in both the Sacred Book of Bran and in the Windsor Archive. Ali Alalladin found the connection to Egypt and is convinced that once the Brythonic is translated and the tonality experimented with, we will find ourselves with a very powerful sonic style weapon!"

"So, you still think a period of bread and circuses will work Rufus?" the Protector queried. "Even after these findings?"

"Yes, I do. I think it's imperative that we keep the population on side through a carefully orchestrated media campaign. Give them something to feel proud about."

Angela Astley's head was reeling. She understood Sir Rufus' logic; indeed she too believed that what they were creating in 21st Century Britain was the fulfilment of a slowly evolving destiny. But it was too soon. The population had only recently come out of the mass servitude of debt, depression, game shows, reality television, football shirts. Small steps, as Odo would say. Patience! As he would also say.

"No, Rufus. I understand completely what you're saying and I have every sympathy. Indeed, I strongly agree with your basic premise. But no, it is too soon to make all of this public. The people remain programmed and the deprogramming will take years, not months. No, we will deploy Red Alert across all agencies. See to it that the American Ambassador is called to present himself to me. I want him and his acolytes out of the country on the first plane to Washington. And while you're about it, serve notice on the Italian Embassy too!"

Sir Rufus blanched. "Is that wise? It could cause pre-emptive action."

"Do you know, Rufus, I don't really care if it does! This started with a hostage situation, did it not? With Bran trying to get his son Caradoc released from Rome after he was captured in a battle on these lands. After an army tried to invade and destroy its ancient culture. After Aristobulus was sent here by the enemy on a 'hearts and minds' exercise. After the people rose up against the atrocities committed in the Menai Massacre and the Iceni Genocide.

"No, let this history play out, Rufus, let fate meet destiny. I will not play diplomatic games with either Rome or America. This land is our land and we are sovereign here!

"Serve notice also that I am sending auditors to the District of Columbia and the State of Virginia. Tell them that if they dare to try anything on I will immediately seize all assets and sell them off to the highest bidder. And if that bidder includes Russia or China, or even North Korea ... then so be it!"

Sir Rufus groaned. This was not what he had planned. He could only hope that she would have a change of heart once the anger had subsided. He carefully looked up at her through his hands spread mournfully over his face.

"Oh stop it, Rufus! I can't bear melodrama." She laughed and threw a cushion at him then walked briskly out of the door to her inner office humming a familiar, discordant tune.

Sir Rufus sat still on the overstuffed armchair and looked morosely out of the net curtained window into the silent Downing Street outside. He made a phone call on his mobile then sat down again, staring unseeing at the fast disappearing light outside.

Street lamps came on, startling him for a moment as he settled back into his deep reverie. He made another call. There, it was done. Two ambassadors, two exits, two new enemies made. He sighed and pondered his next move, frozen in a self-imposed cocoon of semi-conscious detachment.

The door silently opened as two people entered. Framed in the wide aperture they looked at each other and then at him.

"Sir?" A familiar voice echoed in the large, sparsely furnished space. "Sir?"

Sir Rufus, startled, began to rise from the armchair, then fell back. "What on earth are you doing here?" he said, in a not unfriendly tone as Commander Taft settled himself on a chair opposite. Sir Rufus turned to his companion. "Pendragon," he smiled, delighted and overcome in equal measures.

"Good to see you, too, sir," she said, smiling back, her face thin from the stay in hospital, her head shaved, a stubble of new growth just coming through.

"It's Red Alert," he told them both quietly.

They looked at each other and then back at him, their faces impassive yet pale with the news.

"How much time before they attack?" Taft asked.

"They'll try diplomacy first, of course. If Protector decides to carry matters forward, however, we're looking at a lead time of roughly a month."

"So, Red Alert," Taft repeated, looking at a space above his boss' head.

"I know, I know, Taft. She's made up her mind. Says it's the end game of something started in the 1st Century AD. We've got to play it out. I think she might be right. It's a drama, all right."

"We can do this, sir," Ceris said, her face animated, her eyes clear and fearless.

"Do you know how much airpower, firepower, man and machine power the Americans have? Do you know how many people would side with the Vatican, raise money, more men and machines? It's impossible, Pendragon. If we make enemies of America and Europe, we're doomed."

"Can I join in this little soiree?" They all stood up as Angela Astley swung into the room and beamed at them. "Now, no fighting talk, young Ceris," she said. "And as for you, Sir Rufus. Why so morose? I am reliably informed that both ambassadors are very willing to discuss matters, so we begin from a position of strength, do we not?"

No one said anything. No one dared to say anything. For one flashing second, the thought of a palace coup shot like a bolt of lightning through Sir Rufus' mind and he blew his cheeks out to disperse the awful thought, much to the amusement of the Protector.

Could she read his mind? He turned an even whiter shade of pale as he buried the thought.

"Come with me, Sir Rufus," the Protector said, beckoning him to follow her to the open door. "There's someone I want you to see."

The Head of National Security followed her into the Green Room. Its huge conference table with the green upholstered chairs neatly tucked underneath held an air of anticipation, as if something was about to happen and that something would be momentous. This was the iconic space where all national and international decisions were made; where for centuries now, history had been written, wars declared, cease-fires decided upon, abdications agreed.

Sir Rufus followed her in, stopping in surprise as the familiar profile of King Alfred presented itself. He was sitting quietly at the head of the vast table, his head in a leather-bound tome that looked to be very worn and very old. Sir Rufus felt strangely sad as he looked at his monarch. The King had recovered but the right hand side of his face still drooped noticeably and he had obvious difficulty using his right hand and arm. He stood up unsteadily in an old-fashioned attempt at simple courtesy, greeting them both warmly. Angela Astley sat next to him, pointing to Sir Rufus to take the opposite chair.

"We have it," the King said simply. "We've found the archive! Though why he had it secreted away in Dinas Bran Castle we don't yet know.

"Richard Whiting, the last Abbot of Glastonbury's archive. I can't tell you what this means, Sir Rufus ... except to say that it was for these precious documents that the saintly priest paid the ultimate price.

"He was hung, drawn and quartered on Glastonbury Tor by Henry VIII's Cromwell and his henchmen all those years ago ... The year 1539 to be precise. We thought it was just a myth, a story, that a great cache of precious manuscripts had been hidden away. A contemporary of Whiting, by the name of Leland, on visiting the library there called it the greatest library since Alexandria. And we've found it!"

Sir Rufus offered his congratulations, yet weighted down with the morning's events he couldn't seem to summon up sufficient enthusiasm to sound at least tolerably pleased with the news. Ever sensitive to matters, Angela Astley frowned.

"What is it, Rufus?" she asked.

He shook his head miserably. "Forgive me, Protector, and Your Majesty, but wonderful as the news of the archive is, of course, I don't see how it helps our present situation. We have America on one side about to dissolve the so-called special relationship before they very likely declare war on us, and Rome on the other rightly outraged that we've stolen their Book of the Bishop. It's a mess."

Angela Astley looked at him with a mixture of both contempt and understanding.

"Do we want a war?" she asked him, holding his eyes coolly, calmly.

"Of course not," he said angrily. "Why on earth would we want a war when we have spent the past eighty years trying desperately hard to maintain some sort of peace! I'm sorry, Protector, but pushing both America and Rome, as we seem to be doing, is playing with fire. I want nothing to do with it. Nothing!"

"You appear to think that everything we've achieved so far counts for nothing, Rufus. You appear to think that my tactics and strategy are faulty. You appear to think that might will always overcome right – it is on this specific point that we differ, I see.

"If I told you that America has known about this, shall we say … problem, with their legal status for some weeks now and that they, like us, want to find a solution, what would you say to that?"

"I'd say it was a cause for celebration, Protector."

"If I told you that it's not the Americans but Rome that has pushed matters to the brink these past few days, what would you say to that?"

Sir Rufus shook his head and kept his silence.

"I am working with the President, Rufus, not against him and the American people. We share our heritage with them just as much as we share our heritage with each other.

"There are Brythonic descendants all over the United States of America and they, like us, want to find out if some of them have the ancient gifts. This is a flushing exercise, pure and simple. And between us, Britain and America that is, we have flushed out some very interesting intelligence. Intelligence, Sir Rufus, that you, if you had been doing your job properly, should have discovered yourself!"

"I see you have lost confidence in me, Protector," he said.

"Is this a resignation, Rufus?" she said icily.

"If that is what you want, Protector, then yes."

She held the door open for him to leave and popped her head around the door of the study room next door.

"Commander Taft?" she beckoned. "I have a proposition for you. And, Ceris, come in too. This affects you both."

CHAPTER 32

"Are you ready for this?" Ali Alalladin banged the side of the sarcophagus with a wooden mallet, setting off the mighty sound of F sharp reverberating up and around the King's Chamber until they could feel its vibrations in their feet, their hands, their whole bodies pulsing in harmony with the primeval noise.

He set the disc on play as the sound of a thousand voices chanting the ancient hymns and praise songs soared throughout the bleak grey room and up into the roof space beyond.

"Bang it again, Ali," Robert Bailey instructed. "We need to increase resonance and depth."

Ali did as instructed, stealing a glance at the composed Branwen, her gaze fixed on the jagged edged corner of the great granite box.

"Stop!" she demanded, holding up her hand in an imperious command. They paused, frozen for a moment as she pushed with all her weight at the jagged corner. A grating sound could be heard coming from the depths beneath.

Robert leaped forward, grabbing the corner, helped by Ali who pushed with all his might. Inch by inch, as if in slow motion, the strange sarcophagus began to shift to the right. Robert glanced up at the barely visible outline on the corner of the ceiling. The ibis/raven/crow profile had shifted too, protruding from the ceiling, framed in a small cartouche.

"It's Thoth," Robert whispered. "A Celtic Thoth. Look, Ali!" And he pointed to the definite profile of a jet-black crow set parallel to the ibis on a perch, the hieroglyph for Thoth.

"It's extinct in Egypt," Ali offered, sweating, every muscle straining under the weight of the mighty box. "The ibis. It's extinct. Some say that when the ibis died out, the true knowledge, the ancient knowledge or Thoth's knowledge, went with it."

"And the original first letter of the Greek alphabet comes from hb or ibis … they do say the Greeks inherited their culture from ancient Egypt," Robert offered, puffing with the exertion.

Ali said, a note of awe and wonder in his voice, "Who was it … that's it, Horace, the great Horace, the Roman poet. He said, and Virgil agreed with him, that the crow is a prophet. Its presence can predict war and calamity, peace and prosperity. Interesting, they were sitting on a large perch on that blasted tree when Whiting's archive was found at the castle."

"And to the Druids, the crow was considered sacred because it carried the soul from one life to the next," Branwen announced reverently.

The grating noise abated though the tonal reverberations still echoed through the great monolith as the three of them stared down. A small, square shaft had appeared beneath the sarcophagus. It looked steep, vertical even, no light just a matt blackness, which reflected back on itself when Robert shone his torch into its interior.

"We need lights, ropes, ladders," Robert announced unhappily.

Ali looked him up and down. "You'll never fit in," he said with a grin, pointing at Robert's protruding stomach.

It was true. He had let himself go. Little exercise, too much comfort eating and a raised status second only to Archbishop Odo himself had fostered a comfortable existence. All he had to do was focus on the translations, organising the teams of experts under his control. It had been a wonderful two years but they were right, he had let himself go and he felt embarrassment at Ali pointing it out. Especially in front of Branwen, who never seemed to put on weight, never seemed to age and always wore that dreadful long red dress. He scowled at her.

"Ha," she laughed at him.

"To worship the gods

To do no evil

To exercise courage,"

she said playfully. "The ancient triad of the Druid's role in society. May you find courage my friend … and exercise!"

Robert said nothing. Ali said nothing. There was something in this place that gave Branwen power. She could feel it, they could feel it.

"Go, go and get the equipment we need to explore the shaft," she said as they stood there looking at her, a trace of fear mixed with admiration on both of their faces. "I will stay here until you return. Go. Go now!"

Ali looked at her longingly. She returned his gaze with a stare as hard as the granite walls.

"Come on," Robert grunted. "The sooner we go, the sooner we return. Don't go exploring anything until we get back," he shouted. She said nothing, sinking elegantly to the floor. She sat cross-legged with her eyes closed, waiting.

"God, she's hard work," Robert Bailey muttered to Ali Alalladin as they exited the grand gallery and made their way to the watchman's hut.

"I think she's rather wonderful," Ali said easily. "She's very attractive, Robert."

"You think?" He arched an eyebrow. "Can't say I've ever noticed. She's too ... superior for my tastes," he grumbled.

Ali smiled to himself as he led the way up the spiral pathway and into the shabby hut.

"Over there." He pointed at a canvas bag containing ropes, gloves, and hard hats with battery lights attached to their fronts. He unclipped a series of hard aluminium ladders from a rack on the back of the door then rummaged about in a dusty cupboard for some supplies.

"Boiled sweets, a large bottle of water and two packets of biscuits." He shrugged.

"It will have to do," Robert sniffed, unimpressed. "What's this?" Robert pointed to a set of black full-face masks.

"Oh, they're fully oxygenating breathing masks. The dust can be deadly further down in the deepest shafts on the plateau. Clever design, it means you can see and breathe when the sandstorms arrive too. Wore one when I was playing security guard here some time ago and we had an almighty sandstorm come in from the western desert. Very effective."

Robert pushed the set of masks into the canvas bag.

✝ ⚥✝ ✝

Branwen opened her eyes. She could feel it even more strongly now as she waited for the presence to make itself whole. She held out both of her hands, the delicate tattoos appearing to pulsate in the fading rhythm of that tonal F sharp. She stood up, edging forward toward the gaping shaft in the dusty floor. Kneeling down, she felt along each narrow edge. There! A steep flight of stone stairs, cold and hard to the touch, the dust of ages swirling up from her scrabbling fingers, rising in thick clouds, stinging her eyes, making her choke. Her head swam as she coughed, drawing in yet more of that heavy, thick sand mixed with dust mixed with four thousand years of whatever it was buried beneath the strange sarcophagus.

Her head felt thick, dizzy, as she desperately tried to hang on to some sense of what was upright and what was not. She sank to her knees, grimly holding onto the jagged edge of the sarcophagus. She felt the room swimming, spinning, going faster and faster until she couldn't see or feel or think. She grabbed the jagged edge with both hands, managing to swing her body in one heavy lurch of a movement, thudding heavily into the granite box. Its cool interior calmed her, the racking coughing abating as she laid her forehead on its cold surface. The massive tonal sound began again, only this time it was much, much louder.

"What on earth?" Ali Alalladin shouted as he ran down the spiral pathway, coming to a skidding halt as the exterior of the Great Pyramid began to shimmer in the overhead sun. The plateau had been cordoned off by the security services at the express request of Britain's Protector. A battalion of soldiers surrounded the perimeter and Ali could see from his panoramic spot close to the mighty pyramid, that some wore expressions of fear, others expressions of delight. All frozen in a static stillness before someone shouted an order and a contingent of soldiers, in full body armour, ran like the wind toward the Great Pyramid. Ali turned, to see Robert Bailey scrabbling heavily down the steep incline towards him.

"No!" he screamed, mopping his brow with a grey handkerchief. "What the hell has she done?" he shouted, the booming sound emanating from the mighty pyramid still echoing across the vast plateau.

Ali lifted his hands in a gesture of total incomprehension as he threw down the set of folding ladders onto the hard rock. The metal clanged in protest.

Robert dragged the canvas bag over, sat on it and wrung his hands in despair. "She's done something, Ali. I know her, she's trying to put one over on us. It's typical of her. She wants me to fail ... always has done."

Ali looked at him incredulously. "What is it with you, Robert?" he asked. "Why do you always think she's out to get you? Haven't you learned yet that she doesn't think like that? It's just not her style to play mind games, petty politics or anything so ... so ordinary! She is the most extraordinary person, Robert. Surely, even you can see that."

"Oh you all love Branwen," Robert said, sneering nastily at his companion. "Do you know what she's done, Ali? Do you? No, of course not. She's only messed up our one and only chance to get into the secret room, that's what. Look, the military are all over the place. They'll be up there now. In the King's Chamber. We've lost it, Ali ... we've lost it." He put his head in his hands, moaning something that Ali couldn't quite hear.

Ali squatted down next to him. "What have we lost, Robert?" he asked carefully. "Tell me. What have we lost?"

"Everything," Robert said, a catch in his voice as he spoke. "Everything."

Ali left him, the canvas bag and the folded aluminium ladders and walked briskly toward the entrance to the pyramid. He heard the sound of a siren wailing in the distance as he flashed his identity card to the soldier standing guard. The guard looked frightened.

"What is it?" Ali asked.

"The noise, sir. This big booming noise inside. We have an old story about this. It means the end of the ages."

"The end of the ages?" Ali looked at him straight in the eye. "I've never heard of this story and I am an expert in Egyptian History," he said, his brows furrowing intently.

"It is a story passed down the generations, sir," the soldier said. "Never written down. Told by father to son, mother to daughter. It goes back to the first time. When Egypt was the land of Khem."

"One moment," Ali said, his blood racing. "Wait here. I will be back in a short while. I have to first see if my friend is all right. Will you wait and tell me your story when I return?"

The soldier nodded. He wasn't going anywhere. Knowing his commanding officer, he'd probably be on duty here all night.

†✝†

At last, the F sharp sonic booms were fading. Branwen opened her eyes to find six fully armed soldiers staring intently at her through their upturned visors. She sat up, mentally noting that the length of the coffer was exactly the right length for one as small and dainty as she. A tall, handsome Egyptian offered her his hand as he delicately lifted her out, holding onto her elbow as, unsteadily, she wobbled. Her heart was still racing though her mind was crystal clear.

Another soldier was on his knees, looking intently down the small square shaft, careful not to disturb any more swirls of ancient dust. Two other soldiers entered the chamber carrying a series of rope ladders and breathing equipment. Ali smiled at her, relieved that she was all right, and then took the senior officer to one side to ask if he could go down.

"No," was the terse reply. "I have orders," the officer said sternly. "You will leave. Escort them out, Fahad."

There was nothing he could do. Four burly soldiers, two in front and two behind, moved them toward the small entrance door. Ali was surprised to see that Branwen didn't argue with them but meekly followed their instructions with a heartfelt sigh.

"Robert's sitting outside," he said quietly to her. "And he's not very happy with you."

"Ha. He wants to control me. I can see through him and he knows this."

"No, I don't think it's that at all, Branwen. He genuinely believes that you want to undermine him ... that you have no respect for him. He really does believe that and it saddens me that you, with all your gifts and powers, can't see it. Can't get beyond that. The man is in pain and you – you are a Healer."

She paused and looked at him. "You are wise. For a man," she laughed. "And you are right. I have spent too much time trying to prove that I am better than he ... but it is insecurity, Ali. My own insecurity that he has all the academic knowledge. His insecurity because I have the esoteric. We are as bad as each other, are we not?"

"Yes. Yes you are," he laughed. "But what are you going to do about it? What is it the Protector said? ... The old ways have to go. Where bread, circuses, egos and pettiness live, humanity dies a little every day. Go. Go talk to him. He wants to know, as do I, what happened to you in the chamber ... I think I know, but first, I have to speak to someone. Will you tell me what happened later?"

She nodded silently as she made her way over to a dejected Robert Bailey, still sitting in the sand, looking morosely out to the vast desert in the distance.

"You," he mumbled without looking at her.

"Yes, it is I," she replied, sitting down near the large canvas bag. She scrabbled about inside and found an unopened bottle of water, warm to the touch, flat and tasteless. She drank a quarter of it in one long gulp, wiping her mouth with a delicate hand.

"You were right Robert," she said simply. "You knew it would be there. And it was. I have been unfair to you. I see that now and I will tell you what I told Ali. I have been jealous of you. Yes, that is the word, jealous." She shifted herself into a more comfortable position. "You see, I wanted what they gave you. I wanted to be the next Arch Druid. But because I was never allowed the education that you received, of course, it was never to be.

"Instead of being satisfied with what I had, which was bountiful, I went out of my way to make life difficult for you. Yes, I believe that you have flaws and faults. Like me, I also have similar flaws and faults. I am not perfect. You are not perfect. Yet I expected you to be another incarnation of the Blessed Bran himself.

"I begin to see the errors of my ways and for that, I offer you a sincere apology. I will not behave so disrespectfully again." She looked at her feet as she finished, her long brown curls and long red dress covered in a light film of white sand and dust making her look older than her years.

Robert put his hand out to hers. She clasped it tight and turned to him.

"You don't know what that means to me, Branwen," he smiled, his voice thick with emotion. "I have also been unfair. I too have been jealous, oh so very jealous of you and your amazing insight, your phenomenal powers ... I have felt, in comparison with you ... a fraud at times. I too am sorry. I want us to have a good relationship, Branwen. I always have but I'm too pig-headed to do anything about it. Another of my many flaws. I walk away from people instead of walking towards them ... and I take things far too personally. I have become unforgiving."

"No, I see now that there is no place for forgiveness in this life," she said seriously. "For the bigger things. If a man hits you, do you turn the other cheek or hit him back? If a legal document is stolen stating that your country belongs to you, do you give that country to another? No, the time for that type of forgiveness is behind us. In the future, we must state our case and fight for our rights to live as we wish to. To take back the heritage that once was ours. That was stolen from us in the 1st Century AD.

"I am a Healer, Robert, but even I know that sometimes it is best to cauterise or amputate rather than to continue administering the medicine. We have to have faith. We have to be bold."

They smiled at each other. A smile born of a new understanding and an easy affinity, each content to view the other as an opposite part of a very powerful whole. They sat there in an easy companionable silence for a moment or two until Robert, taking a deep breath asked, "What happened in there? Did you see it?"

"Yes," she said calmly. "But it's not there, Robert. I felt something. I saw something cloudy, vapourish, strong and strange. I received an impression of understanding, compassion, all-knowing somehow, tinged with a deep, strange sadness.

"They will explore the shaft, I know. It will lead to a small room deep beneath the Queen's Chamber. I am sure of that, but whatever was hidden is gone. I am certain that it has gone. Indeed, I was told gently that it has been removed to its new home, taken many thousands of years ago when Osiris ruled this land."

They both turned at the same time to see Ali walking towards them, his pace energetic, his face anxious, alert.

"Are you actually talking to each other?" he grinned, slapping his thigh in merriment before hunkering down next to Robert and giving him a friendly punch on the arm.

Robert shrugged his shoulders, "I think we've reached a new understanding," he said. "A better understanding, we hope." He smiled at Branwen and Ali was struck at the beauty of the smile she responded with.

"Do you know, Branwen, I don't think I've ever seen you smile before. It's a first! Here, let me propose a toast." He picked up the warm bottle of stale water and held it up in tribute.

"To the west, to the mansions of Osiris, to the west thou art going.

Thou who were best among men, who did hate the untrue."

"Hymn to Osiris?" Robert asked.

Ali nodded and took a thirsty swig from the bottle.

They looked in disbelief at each other as Robert croaked, "To the west."

"It's not here," Ali shouted. "It's never been here. At least, not since *The Other Exodus*. Oh what a fool I am." He hit his head with his hands as Branwen looked at them both and sighed.

CHAPTER 33

"So, what was in the shaft in the end, Commander?" the Head of National Security, Sir David Taft, enquired, wincing as his deputy power-walked ahead, leaving him annoyed with himself and the creaking knee that always played up in damp weather. She slowed down and looked a little embarrassed, pretending to adjust the strap on her briefcase as she waited for him to catch up.

"It was empty, sir," she said, shrugging her muscular shoulders. She had the air of a super soldier with her finely toned physique, her short blonde hair swept back off her oval tanned face, her light blue eyes clear, resolute, determined.

"The soldiers climbed down into the shaft. It was very narrow, very steep, I'm told. The rope ladder ended after thirty feet and so another longer one was sent for and attached to it. Down, down they went, they couldn't see a thing because every movement stirred up clouds of dust, sand, debris until even their breathing masks completely clogged.

"Up they came. They were hauled up, I was told, by a mechanical winch. A doctor at the scene ordered an ambulance and off they went. Next day, they tried again with a new team, with oxygen packs and more specialist equipment borrowed off the American Embassy. Anyway, eventually, after a very slow descent that took four hours, so I'm told. They said the dust was horrific, sir. Eventually, they found the room, the secret room.

"It was empty. Nothing in it except, in the middle, there was a shape on the floor that was less dusty than the rest." She scrabbled about in her briefcase. "Here, look at the photos."

She handed over a selection of black and white photographs showing thick dressed stone walls on all four sides, a small narrow floor no wider than the shaft itself. The centre of the floor was strangely free of debris, lighter than the surrounding floor stones as if something had once rested there and had been removed. Another photograph showed carved indentations in the walls: falcon, ibis and the raven/crow.

Sir David frowned, "What are those, Pendragon?" he asked, intrigued.

"Representations I'm told, sir. The falcon represents Osiris who is deemed the founder of the world. The ibis represents Thoth, who gave the world writing, knowledge and understanding. The raven/crow represents the messenger who takes the soul to its new home. It's considered a Celtic representation, I'm told. The crow that is … yet the only known reference to a crow in Egyptian iconography is the Wall of the Crow on the Giza Plateau. And the Egyptologists never mention it. How strange is that?

"Anyway, nothing like this has ever been found in Egypt. It's completely flummoxed the academics who are avoiding it by ignoring it according to Robert. He seems to find it all rather amusing."

"Ah, so you two are communicating again?" He raised an eyebrow quizzically and was pleased to see his deputy's complexion turn a fetching shade of pink. "I'm told he's become more approachable?" He deliberately changed the subject to spare her further blushes.

"Yes, Steve Waterman's heaving massive sighs of relief. Spoke to him yesterday. He says Robert is treating Branwen with deep courtesy and total respect. She's reciprocating too. Big surprises all round, sir. I doubt it will last."

"Why not?"

"Human nature," she said enigmatically and grinned at her boss.

He raised a sardonic eyebrow. "Oh to be as gifted as those two, Pendragon."

"If it's all the same to you, sir, I'd rather put my faith in these." She flexed her biceps and triceps, making them both laugh out loud.

"So, what do they make of it all?" Sir David narrowed his eyes as he looked up from the set of photographs.

"Something about a Hymn to Osiris. Couldn't get any proper sense out of them, sir. It looks as if they've found a clue and just want to check things out. Protector is set to make an announcement you said?"

"Yes, after the ceremony at Glastonbury. Archbishop Odo will take the service there, with King Alfred setting into place the final stone. It's all being televised of course, beamed around the world, with the Archbishop of the District of Columbia assisting him. We'll pan to Dinas Bran Castle for the second part of the ceremony where Robert and Branwen will present Whitley's archive to the world and then ..."

As they entered the bunker designated for the latest COBRA meeting, Ceris was steered toward a small meeting room by Taft.

"I'm anticipating something going horribly wrong, Pendragon," he said quietly, closing the door behind them silently. "Just had some intelligence in from Strike Command who have been assiduously monitoring traffic off the east coast of Ireland all day. Something's brewing. Not sure what exactly, but I need you to get over to the island. Liaise with Waterman, give me hourly updates. Something's not quite right and I've a horrible suspicion it's coming out of Glastonbury. There's a chopper waiting for you at London Airport. Get over there now. And keep your phone open."

The bunker was buzzing. Chiefs of Staff, Permanent Secretaries and the Protector herself, sat around a dark wood oval table, their eyes firmly fixed on the set of wide screens on the wall opposite.

"The Reserves are ready," the Chief of Staff announced. "Dover's cordoned off. We can't use firepower from the air, ma'am. Too much risk of hitting civilians."

"Send the RAF to Valley on Anglesey," the Protector said. "I want full protection across the island and easterly, toward Dinas Bran. They must not get hold of the archives. Or the cauldron."

Taft looked at her in amazement. "You've found the cauldron?" he said.

"We found it some time ago. Hidden away in a secret space off the Jewel Room in Windsor Castle. King Alfred didn't want it found. Two reasons: one, it was dangerous and two, he couldn't bear to let it go ... Historical value, only material link to the druids. He both fears and reveres it, Taft."

"They're heading west, ma'am. Nothing heading in the other direction. Looks like they plan to leave London and Canterbury out of it," her Permanent Secretary burbled excitedly.

"Yes, it's the archives, the Book of the Bishop and the Sacred Cauldron they're after. I knew it," she said. "Get as many personnel as you can to the island. Where's Odo?" She looked around at the vacant chair to her left. "Where is he?"

"Ma'am," the Chief of Staff interrupted. "We're blockading the port with small vessels. We've pulled in the Ninth Division off Salisbury Plain. The Port Authority's switched on the Great Barrier but it will take another half hour before it's fully operational."

"Get me camera data on the whole of the south east coast. Where are the leakages likely to be?" she demanded.

"Distraction tactics." The Head of Security shook his head, frowning intently at the multiple screens on the wall opposite, two showing the slowly rising Great Barrier at the mouth of the ancient port.

"Explain," the Protector fired, her focus on the age-old series of beacons now being lit across the southern coast. That ancient signal, a coded message so deeply buried in the nation's blood that the firing of the beacons meant imminent, deadly, invasion.

She caught her breath. How many of the people in this small, emotionally charged room could trace back their ancestors to a similar time of invasion: whether Romans, Normans, Saxon Hordes, Scandinavian gangs looking for land, hope and glory and their descendants. Those who had forbears who had fought in two of the bloodiest wars ever seen.

Always sensitive to her role as leader, she stood straight and proud, her eyes calm, her chin resolute, her very presence emanating courage, control and command as she looked Taft straight in the eye.

He held her gaze fearlessly. "They're heading for Wales, Protector. They'll not enter via Dover. They're playing distraction tactics, just as the invading hordes did thousands of years ago. They're heading for Anglesey."

"He's right, Protector." Her Chief of Staff pointed to number three screen. "Look, they're making a sweeping manoeuvre to the left. They'll run around the Lizard, up through the Severn Estuary or maybe carry on north and enter the Celtic Sea.

"Yes, I think that makes more sense, Protector, the Celtic Sea. It's an easy drive once they make landfall, down the A5 to the castle. We need a blockade at Holyhead Port, not Dover. We need to deploy further north, ma'am."

They silently watched the scene unfold as a hundred or more powered longboats turned in synchronised movement, heading away from the straits of Dover and out into the English Channel, sailing west, toward the Celtic Sea.

"Are the new Nimrods armed?" she asked her Chief of Staff.

"Yes, ma'am. On standby. They can be over the Celtic Sea within fifteen minutes."

"Predicted civilian casualties if we laser bomb?" she asked him.

"At a conservative estimate, we could end up taking out some of the oil rigs so it could be in the range of six to eight hundred souls, ma'am."

"What if we let them head towards the island and take them before they enter the port?"

"Probably a better option, ma'am." He snatched a note from his desk sergeant. "Be advised that there are two Irish Sea ferries, a cruise ship and a container facility in situ."

"What is it, Taft?" Protector asked, noticing him slowly close off his mobile.

"It's the Archbishop, Protector," he said seriously. "They've got him. Cardinal Sfozzi wants a meeting with you. He says that if you meet him half way, literally and figuratively, he'll return Archbishop Odo unharmed."

"Half way?" she repeated, her face a picture of concern, her eyes tinged with anxiety.

"In the middle of the Celtic Sea, half way between the coast of Wales and the coast of Ireland. If you agree to his terms and conditions, the Archbishop will be released ... and King Alfred."

"King Alfred!"

"Yes, Protector. They have them both. Taken from Glastonbury an hour ago. Facilitated, I understand, by Lord Crispin Farndon himself."

She looked carefully at her Chief of Staff, his hand clasped around one of the many telephones on the desk. She looked at her Head of National Security, his face drawn yet resolute. He shook his head from side to side. She looked at her Permanent Secretary, practically dancing on the spot with eager anticipation, waiting for her command. The bunker room was silent, save for the background hum of computer terminals and low voices monitoring a myriad of cameras and screens.

"Tell him no, Taft. Tell him we don't negotiate with terrorists. Where's Air Marshall Faraday?"

"Here, ma'am." He stood up from his seat at the far end of the conference table.

"Deploy Nimrod," she said crisply. "Wait until they're off the coast of the island. Then do it."

"We have a problem, ma'am," the Chief of Staff announced, wiping the sweat off his brow with the back of his hand.

She turned to look at him, her face calm, her demeanour cool and controlled. "What is it, General?" she asked.

"Submarines, ma'am. Just surfaced off Puffin Island. Heading for the mainland now in powerboats. They must have towed a cargo submergible behind them. There are a hundred powerboats, each boat with ten mercenaries heading for the port – that's a thousand soldiers, ma'am. Armed and very dangerous!"

"Why weren't we warned of this?" she asked, her voice icy, her face furious. No one said a word. "Well?" she roared.

Sir David cleared his throat. "I think you'll find your answer over there," he said, pointing straight at the Permanent Secretary who froze as she squared up to him.

"He's colluded with Sfozzi, Protector. They don't want to see you succeed. Bev Jenkins and Sir Rufus have used him as a go-between in an effort to return to the previous status quo. He assured me that he was simply following orders and I believed him. This event just proves how very wrong I was, Protector."

"Arrest him!" she shouted, her voice venomous, her anger palpable.

"So. First my Foreign Secretary – how I regret promoting that woman. Then my Head of National Security. And now my Civil Service. What were you thinking of, Taft?"

Taft looked at her with sadness in his eyes. "I don't see how we can survive this."

"Oh, we'll survive it all right," she spat, the fury evident in her flashing eyes. "I need people around me I can trust, Taft. Can I trust you? Why didn't you inform me of your doubts before this happened?"

"I thought we had the main players, ma'am, I really did. I had no idea there were other players in the game. Apart from Lord Farndon that is. I offer my resignation, of course."

"Accepted," she said abruptly. "Get me, Pendragon. What? I don't care if she's on her way to the island. I want her here. Tell her she's just been promoted and I want her here now."

CHAPTER 34

As night morphed into early morning, dark clouds scudded menacingly overhead as they stood on the narrow banks of the straits. Below, gunmetal grey waters swirled angrily toward Beaumaris and its massive castle. The scent of winter, sharp, frosty, clean, timeless was in the wind blowing easterly, its strength gathering as ripples in the water grew into waves, high-foamed liquid barriers, pushing the speedboats back toward the open sea.

Against the mighty wind could be heard the growing swell of voices, singing, chanting, a hundred or more ovates, clad in the grey robes of the apprentice novice. They stood on the very spot where their ancestors had stood in 60 AD, shaking their wands of office at the murky greyness below, whipping up the foamy waters into whirlpools on which the light vessels spun and spun around in a never ending vortex. The foreign mercenaries threw themselves into the raging waters, some disappearing from view, some making it onto the banks of the straits, hacking with their knives at the ovates standing too close to the water's edge until their screams filled the surrounding air, carried on the wind to the edges of the island, terrifying the inhabitants who shuddered, locking their doors, hiding behind drawn curtains, praying for the danger to pass.

Overhead, three Nimrods, their sleek black outlines, their yellow hooked noses, flashed like lightning toward the north of the island, blue laser beams slicing through the remaining boats struggling in the vortex below.

Ceris shouted the command, "Regroup! Everyone back, away from the edge, get back into the field. We're done here."

One boat, caught on the edges of the swirling pools, tried desperately to power into the calmer waters beyond. To no avail. It up-ended amidst the terrified screams of its occupants as it too sank without trace into the grey murky depths below.

On the northern end of the island, half of the boats had made landfall. Five hundred mercenaries headed for the Druidic College in the centre of the island, armed, mobile, dangerously close to the newly consecrated circular set of stone buildings.

Inside was the Sacred Cauldron. Inside was the Book of the Bishop. Inside was the greatest collection of ancient scrolls and manuscripts ever collected, greater even than the mighty collections held at the Bodleian. Here was the other history of the world. *The Other Exodus*, writ large, made real, challenging the old order, the Roman Order, with every brush stroke, with every illuminated word.

"Give the order, Faraday," the Protector said with a sigh.

"Ma'am." Air Marshall Faraday spoke quietly into his headset. "Deploy."

All eyes swivelled simultaneously to the row of screens displaying real time footage from the Celtic Sea. One of the Nimrods flashed across the sky and held a static position directly over a large vessel below. It was surrounded by smaller boats bouncing up and down in the growing swell of frothy six-foot waves.

Taft couldn't look. His face creased in misery as he averted his eyes for a moment then forced himself to look again, just as a mighty blue laser beam hovered over the vessel directing the incendiary to its mark.

The explosion was ear shattering. Everyone in the room gasped as the ship disintegrated into a thousand pieces, sending a waterspout fifty feet up into the grey wintry sky. A flotilla of smaller boats that had surrounded the larger vessel spun about in the water, dipping dangerously, slowly sinking as the swell of water crashed back, submerging them in moments. A grey swirling sea met a grey overcast sky. There was nothing to be seen except a vast horizon of empty space.

Taft picked up his cell phone, buzzing relentlessly as he stared at it, uncomprehendingly. He tentatively felt for a chair, grabbing its seat, desperate to hold onto something solid as he shakily settled himself.

"They're trying to breach the outer walls," she said, adrenalin pumping. "Robert is doing something to stop them," she finished.

"What do you mean, doing something?" Taft responded.

"He's reading from one of those old parchments. He says it's an ancient spell."

"What on earth are you on about, Pendragon? I've never heard of anything so stupid in my life. How many are 'they', exactly?"

"Quick estimate, around four to five hundred. All well equipped, all wearing body armour, all determined by the look of it. There was a massive explosion a few minutes ago, sir. Do you know what happened?"

"Don't worry about that, Pendragon. There's none of them left, you only have to worry about your four to five hundred for the moment. Protector wants you here. You should've had a call by now. She wants you to get back to London and she wants you to take over."

"Take over what?" Ceris sounded puzzled as Taft swallowed his pride and told her about what had happened. She said nothing for a moment. He felt unaccountably ashamed. He felt profoundly depressed.

"I can't," she said finally.

"You have to," he gasped, his eyes meeting the still furious look of the Protector standing opposite, arms folded in a stern gesture of uncompromising authority.

"I've only just got here. It's all going down here, sir," she spluttered. "We have Robert, Steve and Branwen holed up in the Druidic College. Ali on his way down the A5 to a secret rendezvous and I'm here trying to hold off five hundred mercenaries who want to strip the island of its treasures. It's not going to happen," she said with an ironic laugh. "How long before the army gets here, sir?" she asked.

"Not long, they're in the air as we speak. Give it another forty minutes and they'll be with you."

"I don't know if we can hold the buggers off that long, sir. There's a detachment five miles away according to Steve. He's monitoring traffic cameras and he estimates there are at least a hundred of them in stolen vehicles heading this way. Oh my God! They're here! Tell the General they're breaching the outer wall as I speak. They're throwing everything at the building, sir. I have to go."

Taft slowly closed down his cell phone and looked blankly into space. "They're attacking the College of the Druids," he said calmly. "Pendragon is on the perimeter with a handful of soldiers. She's waiting for the army to arrive. General, it's over to you now."

"Patch me into satellite surveillance," the Chief of Staff said briskly. "I want 360 degree coverage of the site and I want it now."

"Sir," four desk corporals chimed in unison as the top four screens in the command centre flickered from scenes on the Celtic Sea to a panoramic sweep of the magnificent College of Druids.

"Get in closer," Faraday commanded tersely. "I want to see the field behind the college. Make sure it's suitable for choppers landing."

As the satellite swung closer, Taft could see a pair of magnificent bronze doors opening, their swirling embellishments glinting and flashing in the weak winter sun. Out stepped Robert, clad in a long white robe, a black wool cloak thrown over one shoulder. His head, covered in a flowing white headdress with a gold swirl design at its centre, his dark hair, uncut for over a year now, flowing over his shoulders, contrasting with the thick golden torque, like a miniature breastplate, that sat on his upper chest.

He looked magnificent. He looked terrifying.

Robert stood on the wide marble steps holding his wand of office in his right hand. At his feet, the magnificent Sacred Cauldron of Bran stood on its wooden plinth, strange misty vapours gently blowing out of its intricately wrought rim. As he began to chant, the vapours increased in size and density until he couldn't be seen behind the thick mist covering both him and the College of Druids.

A flash of red on the domed roof. Taft drew in his breath as Branwen appeared, her long red dress and white wool cloak blowing in the southerly wind, her long brown curls held off her face with a golden headband across her alabaster forehead. She looked magnificent, standing straight and fearless on the thatched dome. Her wand of office pointed up ahead, straight at the scudding clouds. The pale sun climbing higher in the grey sky overhead looked as if it wanted to escape from her determined focus.

Ceris watched in silence, crouched down behind a stone wall separating the College from the road outside. She heard the roar of engines, smelled the diesel of motorbikes flashing past and into the college grounds. She heard the sound of gunfire and the screams as Branwen let loose her torrent of verbal abuse on the mercenaries gathered below. She peeked her head above the wall, ready to attack, ready to take down the invading horde. She flapped her hand downward, in a gesture of 'keep still, don't move', as her small army of soldiers crept further forward to see what was happening. The roar of helicopters in the distance reassured them.

The mercenaries heard it too, but they had also set their sights on the College of Druids and the priceless treasures it contained. A mighty roar went up as twenty mercenaries breached the marble steps, kicking over the Sacred Cauldron. Robert watched as it span around, bouncing down the marble steps, the vapours coming from its interior thickening around the immediate vicinity until everything was submerged in the thickest, greyest, choking fog. Like a vast wall, the fog rose around the circular building, trapping everyone inside its strange dense vapour.

"Robert!" Ceris screamed as the mist momentarily thinned. He was lying on the bottom step, still clutching his wand of office, the other hand frantically trying to find the up-ended cauldron. A smear of ruby red blood stained his white robe. She could see his head, the headdress blown away on the rising wind, his face a mass of bloody gore.

She knew it was almost too late as one of her soldiers grabbed her by her trouser belt to hold her back. "No, ma'am," he said in a low voice. "You mustn't look."

Furiously, she ripped his hand away and ran, ran as fast as the wind overhead, now blowing itself into an almighty gale, fast as her frantic heartbeat, pounding, leaping over the inner perimeter wall, long jumping it onto the marble steps where he lay. She held his face in her hands and moaned, "No, Robert. No. Don't leave me. Please, Robert. Stay with me. Don't go. Please, please don't go."

He gently squeezed her hand, his eyes bloodied, the head wound pumping puddles of blood all over her. "I love you," he said simply. "So very much."

She didn't remember anything else afterwards. She was told that the helicopters had landed in the field behind; a detachment had taken her and Robert's body inside the College. Branwen had refused to come down and was still swinging her wand of office at the scudding clouds until six burly soldiers had manhandled her between them to remove her from the roof.

The invasion had been thwarted. Rome hadn't won but the casualties, nevertheless, were severe. Two hundred soldiers, four hundred mercenaries, Archbishop Odo, King Alfred and, of course, Robert, Robert Bailey. All perished. All dead.

Steve Waterman surveyed the scene outside and sighed deeply. It was time. He checked his watch against the stone sundial next to the College's fountain and squeezed his eyes shut for a moment to stop a tear escaping. He looked around, at the vast open landscape dotted with ancient trees, well-kept hedges, roads freshly tarmacked, black snakes slithering toward a destination that always led south. "All roads lead to Rome," he thought to himself. "Even this one," as he headed off in his MG toward the A5, the same ancient Roman road trodden by those terrifying Roman soldiers almost two thousand years ago.

CHAPTER 35

As the world's television cameras panned in on the windswept summit of Dinas Bran Castle, Angela Astley, Protector of Britain, stood on a central dais in the square courtyard behind the castle's brooding archway. On her left stood Ali Alalladin, his Armani suit crisp and smart in the cool summer's evening. On her right stood Ceris Pendragon, wearing the black uniform of the Special Services. Gold-braided, immaculate, lean and strong she drew gasps of admiration wherever she went these days. Everyone called her 'The Pendragon'. She now outranked even the Chiefs of Staff.

Next to Ceris stood Branwen, attired beautifully in a long red dress, her cream wool cape folded over her arm, her long brown curls held back by a thick golden band. At her neck, the torque last worn by Robert, covering her body in delicate golden Celtic swirls. She held his blue and gold striped wand of office in her left hand. The Sacred Cauldron of Bran, now empty, stood at her feet, denoting her newly consecrated status as Arch Druid of Prydain. She sighed to herself as she contemplated the years of study ahead of her assisted by 'that boy', as she called Alalladin.

As the President of Egypt stepped forward, a fanfare of Arabic music swelled into the vast space and beyond, down into the small town, across its Roman bridge, up into the Berwyn Mountains surrounding the green pastures, mighty river and tinkling streams below.

Ali Alalladin stepped off the dais to greet the President. Shaking his hand respectfully, he pointed to the cord dangling from a blue velvet curtain set against the ancient castle stones. He paused, before, looking directly into one of the cameras, he recited the famous lines.

"To the west, to the mansions of Osiris to the west thou art going,

Thou who were best among men, who did hate the untrue."

The Egyptian President beamed into the camera, politely bowing to The Protector as he took the end of the cord offered by Ali. He turned, still holding the cord, his eyes misting with the emotion of it all and kissed Ali first on his right cheek and then on his left. Ali nodded dumbly, overcome with the significance of the moment.

Hastily arranged microphones stood in a jumble in front of them both as Angela Astley joined them in front of the blue velvet curtain. They stood respectfully to one side as she cleared her throat, as the television cameras jostled for pole position. Silence fell over the gathering as she spoke.

"Four thousand, five hundred years ago, give or take a century or two," she smiled, "the original founders of our country listened carefully to their wisest men and women, the high priests and priestesses of that ancient land we know today as Egypt. They built a monolith designed to educate their finest students in the meaning of life and the transcendence of death.

"They believed in Truth. They believed in Courage. They believed in Life and they believed in Knowledge. Sacred Knowledge, the knowledge of the stars, the knowledge of other worlds, the knowledge of living life based upon truth, knowledge, courage and social cohesion. The monolith they built represented a star, symbolic of who we are, where we belong. For is it not true that we are all of us made of stardust?

"Its measurements coded a prophecy, a prophecy that could only be fulfilled once their greatest minds, their greatest people, had migrated in what has become known as *The Other Exodus*. A people saddened by their leaders, their Pharaohs who wanted more and more mighty monuments built to house not only their gods, but also their ever expanding egos.

"And here, to The West, they came, bringing with them an artefact so precious, so important, that it had to be secreted away high on a western hill in a place that could only be found by following a series of sacred and very tantalising clues.

"Today, we are proud to return this important, unique part of our world heritage to its rightful home, safe in the knowledge that when it is returned it will herald the prophetic change so dearly hoped for all those thousands of years ago. A return to a society deeply committed to Truth, to Courage, to the Way of the True Warrior, the Way of Peace.

"A new age is dawning my friends. And right, as well as might, is on our side. For it is written, in the words of Manetheo, in the inscriptions found in Amarna and in our own sacred archive, Archbishop Whiting's Archive, compiled by the man who was, as you know, the last Archbishop of Glastonbury, destroyed and dismembered because of his refusal to hand over the secret knowledge to Henry VIII and his henchman, Cromwell.

"Recently, the brutal symbolic circumstances of his tragic death were explained to me. Crucifixions and empty tombs have played a symbolic part in our shared history. We will honour their memory.

"This treasure, this amazing symbol of unity, of right triumphing over might, that the President of Egypt has kindly agreed to unveil, will also act as a memorial once it is placed where it belongs. A memorial to our shared ancestors, a memorial to King Alfred, Archbishop Odo and to our first Arch Druid of the modern age, the late Robert Bailey.

"His successor is here today and, once her training is complete, she will lead this land in its esoteric life."

She paused and looked around her. For one heart-stopping moment she thought she saw her old friend, Odo, in the crowd to the side of her. She squinted her eyes. No, she was mistaken, but it left her a little shaken. Tremulously, she continued.

"My friends, in the words of the ancient ones, *Ikhet!* Or glorious light! Together, we will herald the dawn of not just a new day, but a new age."

As the velvet curtain swished back, a gasp came from the crowd, then an almighty cheer. Flash bulbs popped, white lights dazzling those close to them as the choir of Glastonbury Abbey joined in with the choir of Canterbury Cathedral to sing the ancient *Hymn to Osiris*.

But all eyes were not on the choristers, or on Mr President. They weren't even looking admiringly at Ceris' gold-braided uniform or Branwen's amazingly detailed torque.

The Protector stood silently as she too gasped in awe at what was behind the velvet curtain. There it was, unseen for almost five thousand years, the elusive final piece of the jigsaw. The Capstone of the Great Pyramid. Taken from Egypt when the pyramid was completed thousands of years ago. Brought here, to be protected by the first, the original 'Wall of the Crow' in what became, over time, Crow Castle, Bran's Castle, Castle Dinas Bran.

Branwen heard the song of the wind. She stepped forward, all eyes turned toward her. Excited conversations melted into the surrounding stones. As the wind dropped and clouds overhead dispersed, revealing a tranquil blue sky above, they could hear the chattering of birds in the multitude of trees surrounding the ancient mound. Sleek, black, knowing birds – Ravens and Crows. One flew directly over Branwen's head then lazily settled on top of her wand of office.

"They came here to protect it," she said simply. "They knew that an invasion was imminent and so they left The Tower and flew here." She smiled, a rare, rather thoughtful smile.

"Except this one." She looked over to the dais where Ceris was still standing, her broad shoulders covered in golden braid, the mighty dragon on the standard behind her glowing gold and red against the darkened castle stones.

"You can go home, blessed one," she said, talking to the bird directly. "The danger is finally over, Robert … For now."

†††